Claims Upon My Heart

D0068498

Claims Upon My Heart

Will Chloe listen to her heart, or will stubborn devotion to her dream jeopardize her chance for love?

Kay Rizzo

Pacific Press Publishing Association
Boise, Idaho
Oshawa, Ontario, Canada

Edited by Bonnie Widicker
Designed by Tim Larson
Cover photograph by Sinclair Studios
Typeset in 11/13 New Century Schoolbook

Library of Congress Cataloging-in-Publication Data:

Rizzo, Kay D., 1943–
    Claims upon my heart / Kay D. Rizzo.
        p.   cm.
    ISBN 0-8163-1133-1 Paper
    ISBN 0-8163-1156-0 Hardcover
    I. Title.
    PS3568. I836C57 1993
    813'.54—dc20   92-43931
                                    CIP

94 95 96 97 ● 5 4 3 2

Contents

Flying Sparks and Smoldering Embers

"A party, a party! We're going to a party!" six-year-old Jamie chanted as all five of us crowded into the sleigh. Drucilla and Ian sat in the rear seat, while James, Jamie, and I squeezed together in the front. Catching Jamie's enthusiasm, the team harnessed to the sleigh began to prance in place, jangling the sleigh bells and adding to the evening's festive mood. Sam and the men waited on their horses behind the sleigh.

It would be the event of the season for the farm families southeast of Hays. Each year Zerelda and her husband David invited ranch families and their farmhands to her November taffy pull. The seasonal event provided the community with lots of good food, music, and dancing— along with opportunities to court and to gossip. "My favorite is the courtin'," Zerelda had confessed one day in the McCall kitchen. "Come June there will be a flurry of weddings, you'll see. So, would you like to pull taffy with Bo? Darcy? James?" Zerelda ignored my glare. "Or maybe one of the Russell boys?"

"Dear friend, if you wish me to attend your shindig, you must promise not to matchmake for me!" When she opened her mouth to object, I lifted one eyebrow threateningly. "I mean it, Zerelda. No matchmaking!"

Solemnly she'd vowed not to, yet I felt uneasy. It hadn't

taken many conversations with Zerelda to discover she loved being married and believed everyone else should be married too.

For the entire ride to the Pagets' place, Jamie bounced on the seat and talked seemingly without pausing to take a breath. "Daddy, can't the horses go faster?"

James chuckled. "Son, calm down. You'll wear yourself out getting to the party and have no energy left to enjoy yourself once you get there." Glancing over at me, James winked. "And we were worried he'd never talk?"

"Dad!" Jamie folded his arms across his chest and groaned. "I won't say another word." I poked the boy in the ribs. He giggled and resumed his excited chatter.

The sounds of guitar plucking and laughter greeted us as we entered the Pagets' yard. David greeted James from the wide barn door. "Have your men unhitch the horses and bring them in here. We've got plenty of room."

We tumbled out of the sleigh, eager to have a good time. James and the farmhands took care of the horses while Ian escorted Drucilla and me to the house. Jamie ran on ahead. On the back porch, we stomped the snow off our boots and opened the kitchen door to the aroma of hot apple cider heating and candy syrup boiling on the stove. Most of our neighbors were already there. The kitchen table groaned with an abundance of good food. Molasses cookies, carrot cake, potato cake, Indian pound cake, pioneer plum pudding, and doughnuts galore.

Zerelda called to me from the other side of the room. "Chloe, you and Drucilla haven't met most of the people here, have you? Ian, you haven't either." She nabbed a young man leaning against the hearth and dragged him over to Ian. "Horace, meet Ian McCall, James's brother. James, meet Horace Tate. He and his wife Prudence own a spread south of here." She released the man's sleeve and brushed it apologetically. "Horace, would you please introduce Mr. McCall to the others? Thanks, you're a peach.

"Now, ladies, let me introduce the two of you to the rest of my guests." Whirling about, she marched both Drucilla and me into the parlor, which had been cleared of most of the furniture and rugs. She hurried from cluster to cluster, introducing Drucilla as "dear Mary's sister" and me as the "miracle midwife" who delivered Jenny Evans's twins.

Somewhere along the way, I lost Drucilla, but never my hostess. I struggled to keep the names straight. Meta Archer I remembered. Amy Simons; Beth Zuell, the sixteen-year-old bride three months pregnant with her first baby; Widow Kline, who came to the Kansas frontier from Russia in 1876 with her husband and five young sons. The short, plump Russian lady's blue eyes sparkled with laughter, and she shook my hand and welcomed me.

"Our property sits back to back. You can see Minna's barn from my kitchen window," Zerelda explained as she led me toward the next group of guests. "We bought the land from her brother-in-law, who decided to return to Russia. Minna farms the place alone. Her husband Karl and youngest son Sterling died in a hunting accident three years ago."

By the time James and Ian entered the parlor, Drucilla and I had been absorbed into the circles of friendly conversation. I noticed that Sam and our farmhands congregated in one corner of the large room with a group of hired men from other farms. Jamie had disappeared to parts unknown.

I laughed to myself. *People are the same everywhere.* The divisions in the room matched every grange social I'd ever attended. The one distinct difference here was the few single women and the high number of eligible men. *Reality of life on the prairie,* I thought.

Little by little, the women gravitated to the kitchen, where the taffy was now on a baking sheet, cooling enough to be handled. The conversation flowed from favorite recipes to over-the-back-fence gossip to the horrific tales of childbirth. One glance at Beth Zuell's ashen face, and I knew I had to interrupt. "Ladies, you're going to scare us single gals into spinsterhood."

Meta grunted. "Not likely. Single gals in these parts are snapped up long before they reach their twenties." I heard an embarrassed cough behind me and recognized it as Drucilla's.

Minna Kline's announcement that the taffy was ready to pull came just at the right time. One glance at the glint in the woman's eyes assured me that it had been no accident. Zerelda bustled from the room and returned seconds later with the men in tow. Someone else called the children in from outside, where they'd been playing Fox and Geese in the snow. Taking advantage of the confusion, a number of the farmhands—including Sam, Shorty, and Jake—slipped out the side door.

Our hostess clapped her hands to silence us. "All right, ladies, Meta will give each of you a pat of butter." She nodded toward Meta. "Butter your hands; then choose a male partner and butter his. Widow Kline will give you the taffy. Have fun."

As the females scurried across the room for their butter, I grabbed Zerelda's arm and pulled her aside. "I thought you vowed there'd be no matchmaking."

She looked at me amazed. "Honey, you can't pull taffy alone, can you?"

I uttered an exasperated sigh and looked up in time to catch James's eye. He looked away, and I felt a twinge of pain for him. He had preferred not to attend the party, but Ian insisted it would be good for him. Now I wondered about Ian's assumption.

With the married women leading the way, the gender-imposed Mason-Dixon line melted. Mrs. Kline placed a greasy yellow glob in the palms of my hands as Drucilla sashayed over to Ian. Nervous, I glanced about the diminishing cluster of men and boys. James and Darcy eyed me from opposite ends of the group. It wasn't until after I smiled at James and started toward him that I realized Bo was standing directly behind James. Both men had claimed my smile. My dismay must have shown on my face, for James turned toward the grinning farmhand, then back to me, his face darkening. Abruptly he turned on his heel and strode out the front door.

I groaned, adjusted my smile, and approached Bo. "Bo? Would you like to pull taffy with me?"

His grin stretched wider. "I'd be honored, Miss Chloe."

"Here." I plopped the melting butter into his hands. By the time we received our lump of hot candy, the fun had begun. Long strings of gooey candy, accompanied by squeals and laughter, passed back and forth between the couples. I attempted to carry on a conversation with the shy farmhand, but my mind kept wandering to James and his strange behavior.

Our taffy thickened, turning first pale yellow, then white. I divided the finished product with Bo and bit off a chunk. I couldn't help giggling—the party guests looked like a herd of cattle, patiently chewing their cuds.

My musings were interrupted when James burst into the kitchen shouting, "The Kline house is on fire!"

Widow Kline gasped and ran to the window. "Oh, no. Please, God, no." While we women crowded around Minna, watching the yellow flames dance against the evening sky, the men bounded from the house toward the barn. For an instant, we stood motionless, fascinated by the deadly sight. Then Mrs. Kline broke free and rushed out of the house.

As the door slammed behind her, someone whispered the thought everyone else in the room was thinking. "Thank

God there's snow on the ground." If it had been late summer or early autumn, the dry grass would have fed a raging fire capable of destroying thousands of acres before it reached either a river or man-made firebreak.

"I'm going over there to give the men a hand." Zerelda pushed to the sink and pumped water into the metal basin, then washed her hands. "Anyone who wants to come with me, grab a pail off the back porch. Amy, since you and Beth are pregnant, stay here and take care of the children. I'll send home any who manage to sneak over that way."

Zerelda grabbed her coat, dashed out of the house, and hurried across the snow-covered field. The rest of us scrubbed the grease from our hands, then followed our hostess's example. I slipped, struggled to my feet, then fell again as I tried to run through the snow. I heard my dress rip, but kept running. As I stumbled into the yard, some-one grabbed my wrist and hauled me into the line they were forming between the well and the disintegrating farmhouse. An ominous message passed down the line, "Green firewood."

Behind me, men shouted to one another as they led the farm animals away from the wooden structures. I could see James's outline at the front of the bucket brigade, tossing pails of water onto the ravenous fire. Tiny sparks flew high in the air, then cascaded down on us like fireflies in summer. I passed heavy buckets of water until I thought my arms would stretch to my ankles. My throat felt raw from the smoke; my eyes smarted. When it was obvious the house couldn't be saved, we shifted the bucket brigade toward the barn. The constant wind out of the west car-ried the burning cinders toward the wooden structure. We fought until the barn's charred skeleton was silhouetted against the dawn sky.

I looked around the circle of soot-covered, exhausted

men and women staring at the smoldering embers of Widow Kline's once-prosperous farm, pain of defeat distorting their faces. Everyone knew that their homes, their investments, their lives could also turn on the spark from a piece of green firewood. I spotted James over by a fence post, squatting in the ashes and mud, his head buried in his hands. Starting toward him, I felt a sharp pain snake up my right leg. Somehow I'd hurt my ankle and hadn't realized it. I limped over to James, bent down, and touched his shoulder.

"Are you all right? Can I help?"

He lifted his head, shaking it slowly. "It will be a sea of buffalo grass come spring. Is it worth it? Is it worth it to put your lifeblood into something, only to have it snatched from you by a capricious God?"

I knelt down beside him. Ignoring the sudden pain in my knee, I reached out to him as I would to his son. I wrapped one arm about his shoulders. "I'm so sorry. What can I say?"

At my touch, his wall of reserve collapsed, and he wept with ragged sobs. I didn't have answers to his questions. Yet somehow, I knew the questions he'd asked had more to do with the loss of his wife and his infant daughter than they did the smoldering ruins.

As I continued to kneel with my arm around James's shoulder, exhaustion, the tragedy of the night, and the emptiness of snow-covered prairie overwhelmed me. I lifted my eyes to the overcast November sky. *Is this all there is to life? Endless sorrow? Loneliness? Defeat?*

How can I help this man find the answers, Lord, when I can't find them myself? I don't know how long we knelt there, but by the time James cleared his throat and backed away from me, everyone else had left. His embarrassment showed through the layer of soot covering his face. He stared down at his hands. "I am so sorry. I was out of line.

Please accept my apology."

"For what? For reaching out to another human being when you're hurting?"

"I had no ri—"

"Look, at that moment, you needed the strength of a friend, and I was there for you. Sometime someone will need your strength, and you will comfort him." I sat back on my heels and winced at the sharp pain in my ankle.

James noticed me wince and asked, "Are you all right?" Before I could answer, he chuckled, then threw his head back and laughed.

"What is so funny?" Irked, I pinched my lips together. His laughter increased as he removed a glove, reached into his pocket, pulled out a white handkerchief, and dabbed at my nose.

I pulled away from his touch. "If you don't mind!"

"You should see yourself. Your eyes and the tip of your nose are the only parts of your face not blackened by soot. Even your hair is charcoal black."

"Hmmph! What audacity! You think I look humorous." I couldn't believe this man's gall. I jerked the handkerchief from his hand and rubbed a circle of soot from his forehead. "There! Find a mirror and have a laugh at your own expense."

He stood up and held out his hands to me. "We'd better go pick up Jamie and the others. Sam and the men left earlier to do the chores."

I winced again as he helped me to my feet. "You are hurt," he stated. "Why didn't you say something? Is it your leg? Or your foot?" He reached down to check my injury. "I'm afraid your dress is ruined."

"I think it's my ankle. I fell while running over here."

"It looks swollen." He knelt down and squeezed my foot gently. I grimaced. Without a word, he straightened, lifted me into his arms, and strode toward the field.

"What are you doing? Put me down." Squirming, I pushed against his chest.

Instead of loosening his grip, his hold tightened. "Not until I can examine your ankle. You might have broken it. Do you want to be crippled for life, woman?"

I continued to struggle. "It's not broken. I know about these things. And I know it's not broken."

"Fine!" he growled, plopping me into a snowdrift. Towering over me, his arms folded across his chest, James stated, "We can do this one of two ways. I can carry you, gentlemanly, in my arms as I was doing, or I can throw you over my shoulder like a sack of grain. It's your choice."

I tried to struggle to my feet. He nudged my shoulder, causing me to topple back into the drift. "Uh-uh! That wasn't one of the choices. Try again."

I don't know why I felt so angry at James. I was being unreasonable—and I knew it.

I was still trying to come up with a graceful way out of my dilemma when he started chuckling. "You're quite a gal, Chloe Mae Spencer. A few minutes ago, you wanted me to accept your help when I needed it. Why can't you do the same?"

I answered by holding my hands out to him. Once again he helped me to my feet and scooped me into his arms. I placed my arms about his shoulders. As he trudged across the field, I studied the distant horizon to avoid making eye contact. When we reached Zerelda's house, we found Ian leaning against the buggy, grinning like a coyote in a chickenyard. "I wondered when you two were coming home. I was about ready to send out the trackers."

"Chloe hurt her ankle. It may be broken." James strode up to the carriage and set me on the back seat. "Go get the others. I want to get her home before it swells more."

"Oh." Ian's face grew sober. "Just climb aboard. I'll tell Zerelda we're leaving. She's with Mrs. Kline."

Seeing one of Zerelda's sons poke his head out of the barn, I remembered my charge. "What about Jamie?" I groaned.

"I took Drucilla and Jamie home earlier and came back with the buggy," Ian replied as he started for the house. "After last night's traffic, most of the snow melted off the road."

The jarring of the carriage when James climbed onto the front seat sent waves of pain the length of my leg. I moaned and gritted my teeth.

"I'm sorry. Here, let me . . ." He lifted my legs and swung them onto the seat. "Now just lean back against the upholstery and relax. We'll be home before you know it."

Too exhausted to argue, I obeyed. My foot did feel better once it was elevated. Soon Ian returned with Zerelda in tow.

"Are you going to be all right, honey?" my friend asked. I lifted my head to reply. "Are you sure you don't want to check the injury before making the trip home?"

James shook his head. "No, if it's broken, the boot will act as a cast. And besides, once we remove it, we won't be able to get the boot back on. Chloe's leg is already swelling above her boot top."

Zerelda lifted my skirt to my knee and inspected my swollen leg. "Tsk! Well, if you're sure she'll be all right."

"Besides," James added, "you have your hands full caring for Minna."

"She's sleeping now." Zerelda glanced anxiously over her shoulder toward the house. "The woman's been through a lot, but she'll make it. She's one tough lady."

"We'd better be going." Ian shook the reins.

I waved to Zerelda, then leaned my head back against the armrest and closed my eyes. Ian turned the horses around, and we headed for home. I felt each jounce and rut along the way, but finally the carriage stopped beside the white picket gate. Jamie came running out of the house. "Daddy, Daddy, Miss Chloe, you're home."

I struggled to sit up. "Wait a minute, Chloe." James turned and steadied me in the seat. "Let me climb down first; then I'll carry you into the house."

Ian hopped down and circled the buggy. "Here, let me help."

I raised my hand to protest. "I-I-I can do—"

The corner of James's mouth lifted ever so slightly. "In my arms or over my shoulder?" he hissed. Not waiting for my answer, he lifted me into his arms. "I've got her. Just clear the way for us." James edged his brother aside. Jamie darted around us like a worried guard dog.

"I'll take her straight to her room. Ian, have Drucilla bring up a pitcher of hot water, soap, and clean bath linen. And I'll probably need a couple of splints and some cotton strips."

Bath linen? I stiffened in his arms. He glanced down at me and chuckled. "Relax." He climbed the front steps, and Jamie held the front door open for us. "Run ahead, son, and open Miss Chloe's bedroom door for me."

He carried me up the stairs and into my room and set me in the middle of my bed. "First, we'll see about your ankle. Then Drucilla will help you bathe and get comfortable."

I winced as he unlaced my boot and slid it off my injured foot. My woolen stocking had a gaping hole in the knee. Without warning James grasped the tear with his two hands and split the stocking down to the foot.

"Hey, I could have repaired that."

"Probably so," he mumbled while gently touching my injured ankle in several places. I winced as his fingers encircled the injury. He studied my face as he pressed the swollen tissue. "Does this hurt? Does that hurt? Does this hurt?"

"Of course it hurts," I snapped, the tears brimming in my eyes.

"I'm quite sure it's broken. I can't do much until the swelling goes down. You did walk on it, so it could need adjustment."

Remembering the time my father had adjusted Jesse's leg after the child fell from an apple tree, I groaned. James drew back in surprise. "Did I hurt you?"

"No," I wailed. "I'm sorry. I guess I'm a better nurse than I am a patient."

He grinned. "I hope so, for your patients' sake. Now you stay put while I try to hurry Drucilla along."

"No one needs to hurry Drucilla anywhere. I sent Ian to Hays for a doctor." The woman bustled into the room with the hot water. Jamie followed, carrying clean towels and soap. "Just set all that on the washstand, Jamie," she ordered. "Then both of you scat while I help this poor girl get cleaned up. Come to think of it, James," she lifted her nose and sniffed the air, "you could use a little cleaning yourself."

James saluted the determined lady. "Yes, ma'am, one hot bath for me. Be careful not to disturb the ankle before I have a chance to put a splint on it and wrap it."

"Out! Out!" She shooed them from the room, then looked at the injury. "Men! Before we try to remove those filthy garments, let's brace the foot." She reached into her apron pocket and pulled out two wooden spoons and a roll of clean bandages. "These should do the trick temporarily."

In record time and with the minimum of fuss and bother, Drucilla had me bathed and changed into my flannel nightdress. She didn't try to shampoo my entire head, only the dirtiest section, around my face, plus the strands that had escaped my braids. She whipped about the room, collecting my soiled clothing. "I'll place your Bible here on the night stand, in case you want to read."

She picked up the copy of *Moby Dick* beneath it. "Maybe you'd like this close by too. Now, stay on the bed, do you understand? On the bed! If you need anything . . ." She slipped a free hand into her skirt pocket and pulled out a small bell. "I found this on one of the shelves in the library. Ring the bell, and someone will come to help you."

I knew Drucilla was right. I'd learned from Hattie's experience what can happen if a bone doesn't heal properly. Leaning back against the freshly plumped pillows, I stared unbelieving at the complex woman bustling about my room. *Is this the same woman who tried to run me out of town on the next train west?*

She scooped up my clothing, wrinkling her nose at my destroyed stocking. "Ooh, he really mutilated this one, didn't he? I'm not sure if the soot will come out of any of our clothes, but I'll do the best I can. A little army soap and a lot of muscle might save the undergarments at least." She paused by the door and smiled. For the first time since we'd met, I saw a hint of Mary in her. "I'll leave the door partly open so we can hear you better." She shook one finger at me and in mock severity warned, "Now, be good, you hear?"

I'd barely closed my eyes when I heard a gentle knock. Two heads popped around the edge of the door. "Feeling better?" Jamie tiptoed to the night stand. "You sure look better."

"Thank you. I feel better."

James entered the room carrying a pail of clean snow, a stack of fresh towels, and a piece of heavy canvas. "I thought it might be a good idea to try to get the swelling down before the doctor arrives. Jamie is here to help me."

After folding the quilts back from the foot of my bed, they placed the canvas and two turkish towels under my swollen leg, the canvas to protect the dry bedding and the towels to hold the snow in place. Carefully, James removed Drucilla's bandage and splint. "Now, son, I'll lift Miss Chloe's ankle while you spread a thick layer of snow underneath. Good." I squealed when he eased my foot down onto the frigid surface. Jamie glanced nervously at me. James continued his instructing. "Now take large handfuls of snow and pack it around the ankle. That's right. That's enough. We need to be able to wrap the towel around it to hold the snow in place while it melts. Then we'll do it again."

Jamie's brow furrowed with concentration as he adjusted the towel around my foot. "Son," James continued, "roll this towel and put it under the edge of the canvas so the water can run down into the pail instead of all over the bed. I'll do the same on this side. Good, that should do it."

James's treatment worked. By the time Ian returned with Doc Madox, the swelling on my ankle and leg had gone down enough to allow him to set the broken bone. Once the doctor finished and left his instructions for my care, Drucilla appeared at the door.

"Now a surprise for you, Chloe." She waved an envelope. "This should keep you busy and out of trouble for a while. I'll be up with lunch in a half-hour or so."

I thanked her and tore open the envelope bearing a San Francisco postmark.

Dearest Chloe,

How many times have you wired that you were coming to California, then changed your mind? I'll believe it when I finally see you step off the Union Pacific and not a moment sooner. I could understand if you decided to head back to Pennsylvania, but stay in Kansas? I don't understand. However, I am a patient man, so the invitation remains.

I've more free time now that Cy has become a part of Nob Hill's society. He spends most of his evenings escorting San Francisco's most eligible debutante, Miss Pamela Vandersmith, to parties and to the theatre.

I felt a twinge of regret knowing Cy was courting this high-society woman. *If I had gone on to California . . .* I laughed aloud. If I had gone on to California, I'd still be reading about Miss Pamela Vandersmith. The only difference would be my location—China, instead of Kansas. I read on. "Last Sunday, I boarded a ferryboat and rented a mount from the stables on the other side of the bay. I was eager to see the colossal trees Californians call redwoods."

Chloe Mae, I've never seen trees so majestic in my life. It wouldn't be an exaggeration to say the smallest tree there trims the giant oak across the road from our house in Pennsylvania down to the size of a fence post.

He went on to tell about the other wonders of California. "Wait until you see the city of San Francisco. It has to be the busiest city in the world. People from all lands live here, speaking all different languages. It's like the whole world merged together in one city."

I had time to reread the letter before Jamie appeared at my door, carrying a tray of food. "Aunt Drucilla said I could eat my lunch up here with you." He rounded the bed to the other side and spread out a square tablecloth on the quilt. "She suggested we have a picnic together." He hopped up on the vacant side of the bed and lowered his voice. "Ya know what? I kinda like Aunt Drucilla better than I did."

"Ya know what?" I whispered back. "I kinda do too."

He chose half of an egg-salad sandwich and took a bite. "It's too bad she's going away, huh?"

I blinked in surprise. "Going away? Where did you hear that?"

He finished chewing his mouthful and gulped down a swig of apple juice. "I heard the grown-ups talking in the kitchen just now. Uncle Ian is going with her, back to Boston."

I nibbled on my half of the sandwich. "Why?"

"She got a letter today too." Jamie sighed. A dark look swept across his face. "My Grandmother Bradley is sick and needs Aunt Drucilla to take care of her. Poor Aunt Drucilla doesn't want to go. I can tell."

I glanced down at my wrapped ankle. *What a time to break an ankle! I can't stay in this bed for six weeks or so. Who'll take care of Jamie? Who'll keep the house running smoothly?*

Jamie took a second bite and lowered his eyes. "Daddy says you're not to know. So don't tell him I told you, all right?"

Stifling a smile, I solemnly agreed to the conspiracy. The child continued. "He says you wouldn't have the sense of a horsefly to stay in bed if you knew."

"The sense of a horsefly?" I arched by eyebrows and cleared my throat. "What else did your daddy say?"

Jamie thought for a moment. "Well, he told Aunt Drucilla and Uncle Ian not to worry about anything, that he could keep you under control."

"Hmmph! Under control?" I glowered above my sandwich. "Hmmph! Did they say how soon they'll be leaving?"

"Probably in a day or so."

Obviously I need to have a word with this man. I'm not a child and refuse to be treated like one. "Jamie, where is your father right now?"

"He just left for the Paget place to see if Mrs. Paget will help us out after Aunt Drucilla leaves."

That I too would have immediately turned to Zerelda for help didn't improve my attitude toward the man. *The sense of a horsefly?*

Holiday Blessings

Fire licked at my feet and ankles, forcing me back against a gray stone wall. Acrid smoke and the odor of singed hair filled my nostrils. I opened my mouth to cry for help, but no sound came out. A spark fell onto my clothing, and I clawed at my blouse, trying to put out the flames. *No! No!* I tossed from side to side. A sharp pain in my ankle started me awake. *A dream. I was just dreaming.*

I stared at the plaster ceiling over my head. There was no fire, no smoke—just a throbbing ankle. I wasn't used to napping in the afternoon and felt so helpless just lying there. A cup of chamomile tea sat on the night stand beside my bed. Propping myself up on my elbow, I drank the lukewarm brew, then returned the cup to its saucer.

I heard a knock, and Zerelda's face appeared around the edge of the door. "Yoo-hoo, are you finally awake?"

I shook my head, trying to brush away the ashes of my frightening dream.

"Now, young lady, what do you expect to do, sleep all afternoon?" Zerelda waltzed into the room and sat in the chair beside the bed. "This is the third time I've peeked in on you in the last two hours. I brought you something to do." She emptied a flour sack filled with holey stockings, then dropped the wooden darning egg on top of them. "I'd intended to darn socks today but came here to take care of

23

you instead. If you thought that little ankle would allow you to laze around, think again. My husband needs a pair to wear in the morning."

I held up one stocking, then another. "Zerelda, what are you doing here today? You aren't scheduled to clean until tomorrow. And how is Widow Kline?"

She removed a darning needle and spool of thread from a brocade sewing case. "Minna was resting when I left. When we talked at lunchtime, she said she's thinking of going back to her family in Russia come spring." Zerelda measured a length of thread, then broke it off with her teeth and threaded the needle. "But what about you? James said you will have to stay off that foot until Christmas." She handed me the threaded needle and folded her hands across her stomach. "There! That should get you started."

"Thanks." I stuffed the darning egg in the heel of the first stocking and set to work. "I can't believe this has happened. And there's no way I'll stay in bed for six weeks!"

"Stay in bed? Who said anything about staying in bed? The doctor said to stay off the foot." The woman clicked her tongue in mock disgust. "By Thanksgiving Day you should be able to hop around with crutches. Sam is making you a pair even as we speak. The farmhands are worried about you, you know."

"What about Drucilla and Ian? Jamie said they're leaving for Boston as soon as tomorrow."

Zerelda smiled. "That's why I'm here—to care for you while Drucilla packs."

After weaving the needle into the stocking so I wouldn't lose it, I shifted in the bed. "Zerelda, I love you dearly, but you have a home and a family to care for. You can't—"

"Now don't worry. James and I have that all figured out." She stood and plumped my pillows, then gathered the stockings into a neat pile on the far side of the bed. My eyes widened in horror. *James? I can't have James caring for my personal needs.*

"Relax." She patted my arm. "We have it all worked out. Minna needs a place to stay until she leaves for Russia. In exchange, she will care for you and Jamie, as well as the house."

What could I say? It was a carefully thought-out plan, leaving me no recourse but to cooperate. I knew I should be grateful, and I was—as much as I hated admitting it. But a small part of me wanted to be angry at James, and I didn't know why. That irked me the most, not knowing why I felt upset with him.

I darned stockings the rest of the afternoon. When the room grew too dark for me to sew by natural light, I lighted the lamp on the stand next to my bed and continued darning. Only three toes were left to darn when James brought a supper tray to my room. I placed the stocking I was darning on the night stand and adjusted the covers.

"Well, how's it going? Zerelda said the swelling in your ankle has gone down. That's good." I balanced the tray on my lap while he poured me a cup of hot chocolate. Hmm, it smelled so good. I stared hungrily at the plate of fluffy scrambled eggs and hot buttered toast, then at the bowl of canned applesauce with blueberries. "Oh, everything looks delicious. Zerelda shouldn't have gone to so much trouble."

James strolled over to the window and adjusted the shade, his face hidden in the shadows. Striking a match, he lighted the kerosene lamp on the desk and replaced the chimney before answering. "She didn't. Zerelda left hours ago."

I bowed my head and whispered a short blessing, made shorter by the mouthwatering aroma of the scrambled eggs. Removing the carefully folded pink-linen napkin from the tray, I placed it on the bodice of my nightgown. After the first forkful of the eggs, I groaned with pleasure. "Mmm, these are delicious. Be sure to tell Drucilla that her supper is even more appreciated since I know she's busy packing."

I heard a chuckle and looked up, only to find his face still engulfed in the shadows. "After you finish eating, she'll be in to help you settle for the night. You can thank her then."

"Everything tastes so good. I guess I wasn't too hungry at lunchtime. Oh, by the way, when is Mrs. Kline coming to stay? It was very nice of her to agree to come and nice of you, James, to offer. Thank you."

He stepped into the circle of light around my bed. "Minna was a logical solution to the problem. Besides, as Zerelda put it, Minna needs someone to care for right now, and you need caring."

"I am sorry about all the inconvenience I've caused."

James smiled and jabbed his hands into his back pockets. "Life is like that. You take the good with the bad. We'll manage, don't worry." He tipped his head toward the Bible on the night stand. "Isn't there a passage in that Book about rain falling on everyone?"

I shrugged. "I feel so useless."

He laughed and pointed to the pile of darned stockings. "Oh, don't worry. Zerelda has plans for you. She'll see that you earn your keep one way or another."

I looked up into the face of the man, half stranger, half friend. "James." I held my hand out to him. He folded his browned and calloused fingers around mine and moved closer to my side. "I know I haven't been the most coopera- tive person today, but I do want to thank you for every- thing. You and Zerelda are terrific friends."

He stared at the invisible circles he was making with his thumb on the back of my hand. "This morning, at the

Kline place, when you comforted me . . ." His voice grew husky. "Thanks."

At the sound of clicking heels approaching, he released my hand and cleared his throat. "Now, if you'll just finish your applesauce, I'll return the tray to the kitchen. By the way, Sam and Bo and the other men send greetings. They'll come visiting once I transfer you to the library."

"The library?"

"Hi, there." Drucilla walked through the doorway. "How are you feeling? I'm just about packed. I sure hate leaving you like this, Chloe."

"Oh, I understand. Your mother needs you." I handed the food tray to James. "Oh, yes, thank you so much for the delicious meal."

A surprised look crossed her face. She glanced at James, then back at me. "I didn't prepare your supper. James did."

My mouth dropped open. "James?" I whispered as he disappeared into the hallway. I heard the sound of his boots clomping down the stairs. "James?"

She nodded. "James."

Early the next morning, Drucilla brought my breakfast to the room. While I ate, we chatted about our first impressions of one another. She also confided her true feelings about returning to Boston. "I don't want to go, Chloe. I'm not the same person I was when I first came west, and I'm not sure my parents are going to appreciate the changes."

Remembering her formerly selfish, manipulating behavior, I arched an eyebrow. "You might be surprised."

Her face softened. "And then there's Ian. He plans to return to his Colorado mines before winter. If he asks me to go with him . . ." Her words drifted off in a delicate blush.

Our conversation halted when Zerelda arrived with the smiling Minna Kline and her new wardrobe, supplied by the women of Hays. Drucilla excused herself and helped settle Minna in the room she herself was vacating. By noon, Sam had loaded Drucilla's and Ian's luggage in the wagon, and Drucilla and Ian came to say goodbye. After Ian wished me well, Drucilla kissed my cheek. "Get well. Do what the doctor says, you hear?" She paused. "And thanks, Chloe, for giving me a chance. I know it wasn't always easy."

I reached up and hugged her. "I'll miss you."

Tears sprang into her eyes. She turned and walked to the doorway, then paused. "I'll miss you too."

She gave a tiny wave and disappeared from my view. I rested my head against the pillow and listened to the click of her high-heeled boots as she descended the stairs.

Life for me settled into a predictable routine as we anticipated the holidays. Minna entertained me with stories of the early days on the Kansas frontier. Jamie loved her stories as much as I. We shivered when she told of pioneers battling wolves. I choked back tears when she told of a pioneer woman who was stranded in her wagon during a blizzard and of others who went insane during the long winter months and had to be transported, in chains, back east to their families.

Jamie spent part of each day learning to read from the children's books Minna found on the library shelves. Together we read *Robinson Crusoe*, *Gulliver's Travels*, and Robert Louis Stevenson's *A Child's Garden of Verses*. However, no matter what else we read, Jamie insisted we recite "The Night Before Christmas," which he'd decided to memorize as a surprise for his father.

The day before Thanksgiving Doc Madox declared it safe for me to use the crutches Sam made for me. I hobbled

about until my armpits ached from the unaccustomed
pressure. On Thanksgiving Day James and Sam carried
me downstairs to enjoy the family dinner, which Aunt Bea
had driven out to enjoy with us. After the meal James
announced that he had a surprise for me in the library.

He'd moved his desk across the room and set up a small
bed, bureau, and night stand in its place. "Now that you
can get around safely, Minna and I figured you'd enjoy
being nearer the center of the goings-on around here."

Tears glistened in my eyes. It had been lonely upstairs
alone, listening to the happy sounds coming from other
parts of the house. Now I would be able to take my meals
at the table with the family. And with the library next
door to the first-floor bathroom, I could take care of my
personal needs without assistance. Additional advantages
became apparent that evening when Sam and the farmhands came to pay their respects and continued throughout the holiday season with visits from the neighbor
ladies. I had little time to myself anymore.

One evening during the week after Thanksgiving, I
decided, once again, to return the gold coin to my father.
Sitting at James's desk, I penned a letter home to my
parents. As I reread the letter before inserting it into the
envelope, I realized how different this letter was from the
earlier ones. I could detect a maturity that hadn't been
there previously. For the first time, I realized that while I
ached for Pa's forgiveness, I was confident in my heavenly
Father's forgiveness. I sealed the letter with a prayer.

In the days that followed, I became more mobile. I traded
the crutches for a cane. The day before Christmas, a gentle
snow fell, creating a perfect Currier and Ives painting
outside the library window. Aunt Bea arrived just before
lunch, her sleigh loaded with packages. Among them were
the catalog orders I had placed weeks earlier. I tore into the
packages with the eagerness of a five-year-old. Everything

was perfect, right down to the metal Revolutionary War frigate for Jamie. I wondered if the gifts I had ordered to be sent to Pennsylvania would make it there before Christmas morning.

That evening I watched while Jamie, Minna, Aunt Bea, James, and the farmhands decorated a small evergreen tree James had ordered from Denver. Jamie's face glowed with happiness when his father suggested that the child be the one to place the homemade tin star on the top. Carefully, Aunt Bea lighted the stubby white candles perched on the branches. Relaxing in the candlelight, we listened first to Minna's description of Christmases in the "old country" and then to Aunt Bea reading the Christmas story from Luke 2. As we gathered around the living-room fireplace to sing Christmas carols, my emotions flip-flopped between contentment and homesickness.

When the last strains of "Silent Night" faded, Aunt Bea yawned and stretched. "I'd better get some sleep if I'm going to help Minna in the kitchen tomorrow morning." She rose to her feet, wished each of us a good night, then went upstairs to her room.

Following her example, Sam and the farmhands wished us all a Merry Christmas and returned to the bunkhouse. James gathered his sleepy son into his arms and carried him upstairs, and Minna began to blow out the candles on the tree.

I grabbed my cane and rose to my feet. "Don't worry about the lamps, Minna, I'll turn them off before I go to bed." I turned off the lights one by one. When the room was totally dark, except for a candle on the mantle, I hobbled over to the window to watch the falling snow. Unable to resist, I limped to the front door and stepped out onto the porch. Snow had drifted across the outer edge of the porch, but by the door, the wooden floor was dry. Walking over to the porch post, I hoisted myself onto the railing.

To my right, I could see the bunkhouse lights go out one by one. The reflection on the snow from the light in Minna's room faded, leaving only the smoky glow of the moon behind the clouds and the whitened landscape to supply light. I ached to run in the snow, to feel the tingle of snowflakes melting in my eyelashes.

I heard the door behind me open, and James stepped out onto the porch. "It's beautiful, isn't it?"

I nodded and breathed in the crisp, clean air. "A year ago, I never imagined I'd celebrate my next Christmas in Kansas, of all places."

Ambling over to where I sat, James placed his hand on the porch post. "A year ago, Mary and I were dreaming of spending our next Christmas in our very own place in western Kansas." He tapped the post firmly with the side of his fist. "So much for dreams, huh?"

For the next few minutes, we watched the falling snow in silence. Finally I spoke. "I wonder where I will be this time next year. Maybe I'll be basking in the California sun or eating exotic rice dishes in Canton."

"If it works out that way, you'll be missed."

"I know. And I'll miss Jamie too." I smiled and hugged myself.

"Not only Jamie . . ." Without further comment, James turned and disappeared inside the house.

What was that all about? A shiver skittered up my spine. The December cold had finally penetrated my heavy wool dress. There was nothing left to do but hobble into the library and prepare for bed.

Christmas Day dawned clear and sunny. We gathered in the parlor immediately after breakfast. Jamie recited his poem perfectly. Then we opened the presents.

I smiled to myself as each person opened the gifts I'd purchased. Jamie loved his metal battleship. Aunt Bea appreciated the compilation of O. Henry's short stories. I gave Minna the imported lace handkerchief that I'd purchased for Drucilla. Sam paraded about the library with his bright red muffler wrapped around his neck. I smiled as James opened his gift from me—a pair of leather gloves. I'd ordered them before I realized how appropriate they would be, considering all the times I'd borrowed his.

As for my gifts, Jamie gave me a picture he'd painted of me on my crutches. He said I could hang it on the wall in my room. Aunt Bea's gift, a pale-pink cashmere wool shawl, took my breath away. I caressed the whisper-soft fabric against my face. "Thank you, Aunt Bea, it's beautiful."

Her eyes reflected my pleasure. "I ordered it from Denver."

I opened James's present for me, a first edition of *Poems* by Emily Dickinson. Opposite the title page, he'd penned, "December 25, 1898. To Chloe Mae Spencer, the only woman I know who can see poetry in a Kansas blizzard. Yours, James Edward McCall."

"Oh," I sniffed back my tears, "that's so nice. Thank you."

He blushed and looked away. After the last present had been opened, Minna announced that her gifts to everyone were in the dining room—freshly made eggnog and Christmas stollen.

After Christmas dinner, James bundled Jamie and us ladies into the sleigh and took us to Zerelda's for an afternoon of cookies, cocoa, and conversation. Neighbors came and went throughout the afternoon. As usual, the children headed upstairs, the men drifted into the parlor, and the women clustered in the kitchen. Since the women refused to let me help, I relaxed in a rocking chair and listened to the holiday chatter. It felt good to be out around other people once again.

The year 1899 blew in with a fury of white. A blizzard

began before dawn on December 31 and continued throughout the day and into the night. The men followed the rope lines from the house to the barn and from the barn to the bunkhouse.

On New Year's Eve, Minna, Jamie, and I heated only the kitchen to conserve firewood. James had left the house after supper to care for Honey, his favorite saddle horse. The horse had foundered after breaking out of his stall and into the grain room. James and Sam were trying to pull the horse through the crisis.

After we did the evening dishes, Minna and I wrapped ourselves in quilts and sat around the hearth, Minna knitting and I, embroidering. Jamie sat on the floor in front of the fire wrapped in his favorite red-plaid wool blanket.

Minna's stories were endless. Some were her own; others she had heard from early settlers. She told of the great buffalo herds that had roamed the prairie in the early days. "When the government began laying railroad track across the state, hunters like Buffalo Bill Cody and others signed on to provide meat for the construction crew. They slaughtered the animals by the thousands, leaving much of the animals' carcasses to rot in the sun. As the herds dwindled, the Cheyenne and the Sioux tribes retaliated."

Jamie's eyes widened as Minna continued her story. "One morning, a renegade band of young Sioux braves raided Jedediah Fletcher's place. They stole his wife and his horses, scalped Jedediah, and left him for dead." She paused and bent down toward the captivated child. "But he didn't die. Old Jedediah lived to be eighty-seven. But he couldn't grow any hair worth beans."

Minna sat back and poked her knitting needles into a ball of blue yarn. When she remained silent, I couldn't contain my curiosity. "What about his wife? Did he ever find his wife?"

"Hillary? Nope. Never did see her again. Every few years some trapper would drift into town and claim he'd seen a woman answering to Hillary's description with first one tribe, then another."

"What? Didn't the government help him look for her?" I knotted the embroidery thread and pushed the needle into the back of the fabric.

"Oh, yes, by the mid-1870s, the U.S. Army had relocated most of the tribes onto reservations. They returned many white women to their families, but not Hillary."

Losing interest in the fate of Hillary Fletcher, Jamie turned and gazed into the flames. Within minutes he'd curled up and fallen asleep. When I noticed, I started to speak, but the older woman put her finger to her lips. "He wanted to welcome in the new year so badly. Why don't you keep the water boiling for the men while I put him to bed?"

I nodded. As she carried the child from the room, I pinched the bridge of my nose, then rubbed the back of my neck. My burning eyes told me that I'd embroidered enough bachelor buttons and daisies for one evening. The clock in the hallway struck eleven as James stomped up the back stairs and into the kitchen. Behind him came Sam and Jake. Darcy and Bo were catching a few hours of sleep while Shorty stayed with Honey. Lines of worry and exhaustion etched their faces as they shed their hats, gloves, and coats.

I poured hot prairie coffee, a drink made with sundried, finely ground peas, into three mugs. Handing a cup to James, I said, "Here, this should warm you up a bit. How's Honey?"

"It's still touch and go." He shook his head and sat down while I handed the two other mugs to Jake and Sam. "We're going to take turns staying with him throughout the night."

I sat down at the end of the table and placed my chin in my hands. "Hmm, he's not any better?"

Sam shook his head. I thought for a moment. "If Honey were human, I'd fill him with either dandelion or comfrey tea. But how do you get a horse to drink hot tea?"

James eyed me curiously. "Does it have to be hot?"

"I imagine the heat helps soothe the digestive system, but the herb itself is what does the job."

James leapt up from the chair and slammed his mug on the table. The hot liquid splattered on the tabletop. "Can you make up a large batch, say, two gallons worth?"

My mind raced up the stairs to the attic, where I stored my dried herbs. I nodded slowly. "But how are you going to get the horse to—"

He leaned across the table. "You brew the tea, and I'll get him to drink it. Can I find the herbs without your help?"

"Sure. The canisters are clearly marked."

"Great!" James grabbed a lamp and headed for the stairs. I'd barely drawn the water and placed it on the stove when he returned with the herbs. Sam and Jake returned to the barn while James waited for the tea to steep. I watched from the doorway as James and the bucket of steaming hot tea disappeared into the totally white world.

After straightening the kitchen, I sat down by the fireplace, waiting for the clock to strike midnight. I picked up my embroidery hoop, then let it drop onto my lap. I considered reading my Bible, but it was in the library, and my ankle was throbbing. So instead, I closed my eyes and wondered what Bible text would be appropriate for celebrating the arrival of 1899. The only verse I could remember was Psalm 37:5. "Commit thy way unto the Lord; trust also in him; and he shall bring it to pass."

Suspended in the hazy world between consciousness

and sleep, I jolted awake at the sound of a heavy tread on the back steps. The back door flew open, and James bounded across the room to where I sat. Grabbing my shoulders, he hauled me to my feet, my embroidery hoop clattering onto the floor.

"It worked! It worked, Chloe. It worked." His eyes danced with excitement. "I could just kiss you!"

My surprise must have shown on my face, for he instantly let go of my arms and stepped back, confusion and embarrassment filling his eyes. "Oh, I, uh, I'm sorry. I just had to tell you Honey's going to make it, thanks to you."

I glanced over at an equally surprised Jake standing in the open doorway. The farmhand coughed. "Um, excuse me, boss. I think I'll turn in for the night. I'll waken Darcy for the next shift."

James picked up the poker and jabbed at the burning logs. "That will be fine, Jake. See you later in the morning. Thanks for your help."

James removed his cap and jacket. "Guess I'll turn in too."

I untied my apron and lifted it over my head. "That's a good idea."

He mumbled a good night, then hurried from the room. After banking the fires in the fireplace and in the cookstove, I turned off the lights and went up the stairs to my room. My ankle had been declared healed enough for me to move back upstairs a couple days before.

During the weeks that followed, I saw very little of James. His son, however, was my constant companion. We'd added arithmetic to his lessons, and the child caught on quickly.

One morning Jamie sat at the kitchen table making flashcards to drill the multiplication tables. I sat across from him composing a letter to Hattie. Minna was on the back porch hanging freshly washed clothes on the line, when a horseman rode into the yard.

"Miss Chloe Spencer," the stranger yelled. "I'm looking for Miss Chloe Spencer." From inside the house I could see that his clothes were shabby and worn.

Minna eyed him suspiciously. "Why do you want to see her?"

The man leapt from his horse and ran up the steps. "My wife's havin' a baby. One of our neighbors told me Miss Spencer knows something about deliverin' young-uns. Is she here or not?"

Minna pinned a stocking to the line and reached for the next garment. "Why don't you get a doctor from town?"

"No time. Is Miss Spencer here?"

I stepped out onto the porch and introduced myself. The stranger identified himself as Chester Meade and his wife as Sarah. After hearing his request, I agreed to go with him.

Minna whispered to me, "You can't go riding off with a perfect stranger. Where's your sense, girl?" Then turning to the man, she said, "While Miss Spencer collects her medical supplies, you go out to the barn and get Mr. McCall. He'll want to drive her to your place in the sleigh."

The man nodded his head in agreement, then ran toward the barn.

"Minna." I slid my arm into hers and led her into the house. "I can't ask James to take me to this man's place."

She shook her arm free. "Well, I'm not letting you go alone, that's for sure."

Recognizing the woman's wisdom, I hurried upstairs for my medicine bag. After replenishing my supply of chamomile tea, I changed into my heaviest clothing. As I approached the kitchen door, I could hear Minna's voice. "I couldn't let her go off with a total stranger."

James's response followed. "You did the right thing. I

sent Darcy to hitch the team to the sleigh."

I pushed open the door. "I think I'm ready. James, I'm sorry for this inconvenience. If you're too busy, one of the other men could take me."

"No, I don't mind," he paused, "unless you'd rather have one of the farmhands drive."

"Of course not." I whipped my cape about my shoulders and tied my muffler around my neck.

James shook his head and strode to the hallway. "That cape won't do. It's colder out there than you realize." He returned with his extra jacket and gloves. "Use these."

I'd buttoned the last button on the jacket when the sleigh pulled up at the back door, and Darcy leapt to the ground. James extended his arm toward me. "Shall we go?"

We climbed into the sleigh and covered our legs with a sheepskin robe.

The brilliant blue sky lifted my spirits. It felt good to be riding in the crisp winter air. The long stretch of winter storms and my broken ankle had kept me snowbound. And as big as the McCall farmhouse might be, I suffered from cabin fever.

James flicked the reins over the horses' backs. "I'm sending Bo and Shorty to town tomorrow morning for supplies. Is there anything you want them to pick up? Minna gave me her list yesterday."

I thought for a moment. "I have two letters to post, and Jamie could use some drawing paper for maps. We're going to begin studying geography next week."

We rode in silence for a time. The terrain grew hilly, and the road wound between the snow-covered hills. Up ahead, Mr. Meade left the main road and turned toward the side of the hill.

I glanced about for a house or a structure of any kind. As we rounded a small knoll, I saw it, a door in the side of the knoll. I raised my eyebrows in surprise. "They live in a dugout?"

James nodded. "Looks that way. Look over to your right, and you'll see the door to a second dugout." At his command, the team stopped in front of the first door. "Many of the first pioneers in the area chose to live in dugouts instead of soddys. I just didn't realize people were still living that way."

Mr. Meade slid from his horse and charged the leather-hinged door. We followed in his tracks.

"Sarah! Sarah! I brought the midwife."

I stepped inside the dark, musty cave. A wobbly, hand-made table with two equally unsteady chairs occupied the center of the room. A layer of dust covered the rag rug beneath the table and chairs.

The thick earthen walls kept in the heat supplied by a rusty, two-burner cookstove. Next to the door a small hole, now covered with oiled paper, had been dug as a window. Mr. Meade pulled aside a brightly colored Mexican blanket that hung on the back wall. "She's in here."

The doorway was supported by thick wooden beams. James had to duck to follow me into the tiny bedroom. The stench from sweat and fear pinched my nostrils, and I swallowed hard, trying not to gag.

On the bed, a girl of fourteen or fifteen stared up at me through terror-filled eyes. Her hair lay in greasy tangles on a flour sack–covered pillow. At the sight of me, her face dissolved into relief. "Oh, thank you for coming, Miss Spencer," she sobbed. "I was afraid I would die out here before Chester could get back with help. I've never had a baby before; I don't know what to do."

"No one's going to die around here, Mrs. Meade." I'd never before seen such poverty, filth, and grime. Fighting the urge to flee the unventilated room, I removed my heavy jacket and handed it to James. *Focus, Chloe, focus!*

"Chester, I need your help." I gave the nervous husband the usual list of things to do while we waited for the baby's arrival. When I finished my instructions, he dashed from the room to fulfill my requests. Calling James aside, I whispered, "Do whatever you have to do to keep Mr. Meade occupied. The first things I need are clean sheets, hot water, and soap. I could use another kerosene lamp also."

"You got it." He saluted and hurried from the room.

I smiled at my patient and turned back the grimy bedcovers. "Now, how about you, Sarah? When did your labor start?"

A Season of Surprises

Chester and Sarah's son arrived at midnight. Following the difficult birth, the exhausted mother's face blossomed into a grin when she presented the child to her nervous husband. The proud father held the boy-child tenderly in his arms and looked over at me.

"Thank you, Miss Spencer. Thank you."

I chuckled as James helped me into the heavy jacket I'd worn. "Thank your wife; she did the hard work. You'll need to take this soiled linen outside and wash it. As for us, we'll be on our way home."

A look of concern flashed across the young father's eyes. "Shouldn't you stay? Will Sarah and the baby be all right without you?"

"They'll be fine. Just make sure Sarah gets a lot of rest and the baby is kept clean." I'd never spoken so directly to anyone about their hygiene before. James sent me a warning glance, which I ignored. "Your wife really needs your help during this next week."

Chester frowned. "I think you should stay."

"Nonsense, Mr. Meade. You are a strong and resourceful man. You'll do just fine." I turned toward James. "Are you ready to leave?"

James grunted and opened the door for me. Before Chester could raise another objection, I hurried from the dugout and breathed in the fresh night air.

Earlier, when I'd suggested that James leave and return for me later, he insisted on staying with me. It wasn't until the land flattened out once again that James spoke. "Have you read the quotation, 'Fools rush in where angels fear to tread'?"

I burrowed down under the sheepskin robe. "Yes, of course. But why?"

"After we got to the Meades' place, I remembered where I'd heard the name before. It was on a poster at the train station. Chester and his gang are wanted for holding up a train on the Santa Fe line and making off with a Wells Fargo shipment."

"Robbers?" I gulped and looked over at James.

"When I walked to the outhouse, I saw a group of men, all wearing holsters and standing in front of two other dugouts. The way they looked at me made me wish I'd brought along my rifle."

I didn't know what to say. An involuntary shudder passed through me. I recalled the gang of thugs that had stopped at the ranch while James was back east. I knew it wasn't anything I'd done that kept those criminals under control, any more than James's presence at the Meade place had kept this gang under control. It had to be a higher power than either of us. James must have been thinking the same thing.

"You know, maybe there's more to Mary's religion than I thought. Someone up there likes us, that's for sure."

"Are you going to turn Chester and his gang in?"

James took a deep breath and exhaled slowly. "I don't know what else I can do. Meade must have known the risk he was taking by leading us to their hideout."

"What about Sarah and the baby?"

"Maybe it will be a blessing for both of them to escape that hovel."

James rode into town the next morning to report the encounter. A few days later, the sheriff stopped by to tell us that he and his posse had apprehended the gang and sent them to Dodge City for trial. However, he and his men didn't find a woman or a newborn in the place. Where Sarah and her son might have gone, no one knew.

Spring came overnight. One day there were mountains of snow and bitter winds, the next, warm sunshine and melting ice. Big Creek swelled, leaving the roads axle deep in mud. The warmer weather made up for the isolation the mud imposed. I could feel my spirits revive as the patches of brown outnumbered the patches of white. In a few weeks green grass would cover the prairie, birds would return from the South, and wildflowers would burst forth in a riot of color.

The roads were still impassable for wagons when Aunt Bea sent Walter on horseback to the ranch with a packet of letters and a telegram. Minna insisted on preparing the young man a bowl of hot soup and a slice of homemade bread before he began the ride back to Hays.

While Walter washed up, Minna heated the soup. Finding a letter from Hattie, I sat down at the table and opened it. First she thanked me for the Christmas gifts, then told me about the birth of my newest sister, Maude. Engrossed in the letter when James sauntered in from the barn and asked about the mail, I merely pointed to the stack of mail in the middle of the table.

At his sudden gasp, I looked up. James gaped at the piece of yellow paper in his hands. "I don't believe it. I honestly don't believe it."

"What? What has happened?"

He handed me the telegram. I read it aloud. "March 28, 1899. James E. McCall, Hays, Kansas. Surprise! Drucilla and I got married today. Stop. Folks delighted. Stop.

Moving to Colorado. Details will follow. Stop. See you soon. Stop. Love, Ian. Stop."

The image of the despondent man lamenting his love for Drucilla flashed into my mind. "Hooray for Ian!"

"Do you know what you are saying? Can you imagine what his life will be like married to a woman like her? It wasn't an accident I chose to marry her gentle and docile sister."

"Gentle? Docile?" I felt the Irish rising on the back of my neck. Narrowing my eyes, I shook the telegram in his face. "You sound like you're describing your saddle horse or a pack mule instead of a human being, no disrespect meant toward Mary."

"I've known Drucilla since we were kids. She has opinions on everything."

Glaring, I spat out, "Believe it or not, most women do."

"What are we talking about here?" He ran his fingers through his hair and exhaled sharply. "I thought we were discussing Ian and Drucilla's marriage."

"We were until you . . . oh, forget it." My face flamed. "Excuse me, I need to check on Jamie." I stormed out of the kitchen. As the door swung shut behind me, I heard James shout, "Hey, what'd I say wrong?"

I brushed past a startled Walter and hurried into the library, where Jamie was trying to locate India on the globe. Earlier we'd been reading Kipling's *Jungle Book*.

As the child pointed to his find on the globe, I berated myself. *What is wrong with me? What am I so angry about? There's no excuse for blowing up like that. Pa always said my dumb temper would embarrass me someday. Now I'm going to have to apologize.*

"Isn't that right, Miss Chloe?"

I looked into Jamie's questioning eyes. "Uh, I'm sorry, Jamie. I didn't hear what you said."

"I said that China is right next to India. See?"

The boy pointed to the two countries on the globe.

"Almost, though I think there are some smaller countries in between. See? Here's Nepal and . . ." I looked up to see James standing in the doorway. I reddened and took a deep breath. "Jamie, will you excuse us? I need to talk with your father for a minute."

Jamie hopped to his feet. "All right. I wanna go see Walter anyway. He promised to bring me an old 'Monkey Ward' catalog so I can cut out the pictures."

I stood up and swallowed hard. Apologizing had never been easy for me. "James, I'm sorry. I don't know what came over me out there."

"No," he interrupted, "I'm the one who's sorry. I had no right to talk against Drucilla that way. If Ian loves her, it's none of my business."

"No, you were right. Drucilla can be a real pill. And who knows better than you, the man she was determined to marry. I had no right—"

"There are no hard feelings—between you and me?"

"No, of course not. I just feel so foolish for getting riled over such a little thing."

"Then we're still friends?"

I held out my hand. He clasped it in his.

"Still friends." I placed my free hand on top of his to seal the pact.

We spent a few minutes talking about Jamie's progress in arithmetic and geography, then about the kitchen garden Jamie and I wanted to plant behind the house. "He'll be ready to start school next fall," I reminded, fighting back the sadness I felt over the changes that would take place. I wandered over to an armchair and sat down.

James sat down at his rolltop desk. "With Hays such a long ride, I've been inquiring about the school in Herzog. It's smaller—one teacher for all grades. What do you think?"

"I'm sure it's fine."

My gloom must have shown on my face, for quickly James stood and rubbed his hands together. "Well, it's back to work for me. See you at suppertime."

I waited until I heard the back door swing closed behind James, then went to find Jamie. That evening Minna reminded us of her plans to return to her Russia. My mind refused to think about her leaving. I liked things the way they were. We'd become like a family.

When I wrote to Hattie about my feelings, she wrote back, "Your and Joe's leaving taught me a very important lesson, Chloe. Life is change. And change is necessary for growth. Look at the plants in your garden or at those goats of yours; they don't stay the same. You talk about your Jamie, growing up so fast. Believe it or not, even Worley is becoming a charming young man."

My Jamie? The thought disturbed me.

With spring came other arrivals on the ranch. Baby chicks, calves, and a colt. Faith, the littlest doe, gave birth to a buck Jake called Humble. From the glint in Humble's eye, I could tell he was misnamed. Old Satan frisked about the pen like a yearling. And one night, Sam asked me to help deliver a breech-born calf.

The warm sunshine and mild breezes lured me out of the house more each day. Flocks of birds, especially geese, honked their way north, and the finches returned.

When Aunt Bea sent out an assortment of vegetable and flower seeds, Jamie and I weeded and cultivated the plot of land behind the house. There we planted lettuce, tomatoes, carrots, radishes, bush beans, onions, squash, and corn, lots of corn. Minna helped me plant hollyhocks, portulaca, and petunias around the side and front of the house. The sunflower seeds, Jamie planted beside the carriage house.

In the evening after supper, when the breezes fluctuated between balmy and chilly, I would throw my cape over my shoulders, grab my Bible, and stroll down to the creek. Then before the sun set, I would wander back to the front porch, where I'd sit on the steps and read the Psalms until it became too dark to see the words.

On evenings when the sunset was more spectacular than usual, Jamie would come out and sit next to me. I'd wrap one side of my cape about his shoulders and draw him close. James, and Minna too, would wander out as the colors of red and lavender intensified. The three of us would listen to the older woman recite Psalm 23.

Many evenings after I put Jamie to bed for the night, I would look out my bedroom window and see James sitting on the steps by himself. If he saw me at the window, he'd beckon me to join him. I don't know how many hours we spent talking with each other about our families and about the silly things we did as kids. Other nights we'd argue world politics, especially about the President and the recent Spanish-American conflict. I loved it. It was the part of my relationship with Pa I'd missed the most.

There were evenings after James had been to town or after Zerelda visited when we'd share local gossip. When I shared my dream to care for the Chinese people, he listened, I mean really listened. One night he revealed his feelings about losing Mary. His cynicism regarding death and a future life rankled me enough to send me to my Bible for answers. As I produced biblical answers to his doubts, we began to study the Scriptures together. This search opened up other spiritual truths about which I'd never even wondered. His curious mind constantly amazed me.

One evening in the first week of June, I sat with my arms wrapped around my knees listening to James tell about his day. One of his mares had brushed up against a barb in the fence. As he told about the way he cleansed and treated the animal's wound, I glanced over at the man's profile and smiled to myself. James paused and eyed me curiously. "What are you smiling at?"

"You."

"Me? Did I say something humorous?"

"Not really." I blushed, uncertain how to proceed. "I was just thinking of how much you remind me of my brother Joe. You show the same tender concern for your horses as he does." I turned my face toward the horizon. "Sometimes you sound just like my brother, and other times, you resemble my father."

"Your brother? Your father? Hmmph!"

"Hey, that's a compliment." I straightened at the negative tone in his voice. "They're the only men, outside of Cy and Phillip Chamberlain, who have ever listened to me and taken what I had to say seriously."

He cocked his head to one side and lifted an eyebrow. "Cy and Phillip Chamberlain? Who are they?"

"I told you about Cy and Phillip, remember?"

He emitted a low growl, but said nothing.

Trying not to be detected, I glanced over at James. *Brother, father, friend—how do I describe my feelings for this man?* The thought unsettled me, and I tried to brush it from my mind. Taking a deep breath, I inhaled the sweet aroma of springtime.

"Umm! Tonight you can almost smell the very essence of new life in the air, can't you?"

Impulsively I leapt to my feet and skipped down the steps. "Look at those stars!" Flinging my arms into the air, I twirled once. "They are so close, I feel like I can just reach out and grab one. When you were a kid, did you ever make a wish on the brightest star in the heavens? Come on and wish on a star with me." Whirling about, I extended my hands to him in time to see him disappear into the house without a word. I stared at the door. "What did I say? What did I do?"

I hesitated going back into the house until I was certain he'd gone upstairs to his room. Sometime later, I stole into the house through the back door and found Minna asleep in the rocker by the fireplace. Her ball of yarn had rolled off her lap and across the floor. After picking up the yarn and rewinding it, I awakened her, and the two of us headed upstairs to our rooms for the night.

Just when I thought springtime on the Kansas prairie was the most beautiful time of the year, summer burst upon us in a flurry of color. By the third week of June, the ribbon of road leading from the house was lined with buttercups, brown-eyed susans, bluebonnets, and Queen Anne's lace. When Sam announced at breakfast one morning that he'd found a patch of ripe wild strawberries, Minna volunteered to make the shortcake if Jamie and I would pick the berries.

Sam asked Jake to hitch Saturn, a gray-and-white spotted horse, to the two-passenger buggy before the men left for the field. While Jamie got into his old clothes, I helped Minna clean up the breakfast dishes, then ran up the stairs to change into one of my older dresses. I slipped into a blue calico my mother had made for me for my fourteenth birthday. The use of heavy brown wash soap had muted the blue background as well as the clusters of posies scattered throughout. I undid the coil of braid around my head and let the braid fall down my back.

Jamie pounded on the door to my room. "Come on, Miss Chloe. Let's go."

"Coming." Grabbing a light blue sunbonnet and shawl from the shelf in the wardrobe, I bounded from the room and down the stairs two steps behind the child. "Grab a couple of buckets from the back porch. And don't forget your hat."

As I raced through the kitchen, Minna handed me a basket. "Here, I packed you a couple of sandwiches and a few molasses cookies."

Without losing a step, I took the basket from her hands and continued running. "Oh, thank you, Minna. You're a dear." I skipped down the back stairs and untied the reins from the hitching post. Jamie scrambled up into the seat and stashed the buckets by his feet. I hopped aboard. Tucking my skirts about me, I flicked the reins. Catching our spirit, Saturn pranced down the farm road like a young colt.

Jamie held onto his hat and started to sing, "Old McDonald had a farm . . ." We'd sung the song through three times before Jamie spotted where the men were working. We waved and shouted to announce our arrival. Their saddle horses were grazing in the field farther up the line.

When Jamie saw his father walking toward us, he alighted from the buggy and ran to meet him. I stopped the horse and stood up. "So where is that fabulous strawberry patch?"

James hoisted his son into his arms and carried him to where I stood. "It's down there near the creek about five hundred yards. You might want to leave the carriage here."

"Sounds good." As I reached down to get the buckets, Saturn reared and whinnied. I slammed back against the seat, my feet flying out from under me and the two pails sailing high into the air. The horse reared a second time, then broke into a run. As I bounced like a rag doll on the seat, I could hear the men shouting and running after me. One end of my shawl plastered itself across my eyes. I clawed at the fabric and prayed, "The reins, Lord. Where are the reins?"

Blindly I groped about for the reins. When my right hand encircled a piece of the leather strap, I whispered a prayer of gratitude and with my other hand yanked the shawl from my shoulders and face. The shawl and sunbonnet flew from the wagon. *Hang on! Whatever you do, hang on!*

The rig jolted over the ruts and ridges of the old farm road, each bounce loosening my braid and sending a little more hair whipping across my face. Behind me, I could hear frantic shouts and the sound of horses' hooves, bringing the horror of my situation clearly into mind. *If a wheel breaks loose or if the buggy overturns . . .*

Determined not to wait for the worst to happen, I stood on the brake and pulled on the reins. My muscles strained, my shoulders ached—but I held on, all the while shouting for the frightened animal to stop.

After what seemed like an eternity of panic, the exhausted horse slowed, then stopped. The terrified men galloped up and surrounded the rig. James pried the reins from my fists and handed them to Sam. Knowing my nightmare was over, I fell against the seat and buried my face in my hands.

"Are you all right, Chloe? Did you break anything?" James gently caressed my shoulder. "Are you all right?"

"I-I-I think so."

He held his arms out to me and lifted me from the carriage. "You're as pale as ghost. Are you sure you're all right?" he asked repeatedly.

When my feet touched the ground, my legs trembled like jelly, refusing to support my weight, and I crumbled into his arms. Brushing wisps of hair from my face, he whispered into my ear, "You're safe now. Everything's all right. You're safe now."

Sam and the other men crowded around us. Suddenly, I realized I was standing in the middle of a field in a man's arms. I drew back, but James continued to hold onto my shoulders.

"What happened?" I asked. "Why did Saturn spook?"

"A rattler," Jake volunteered.

My eyes darted around the circle. "Where's Jamie?"

"He's with Shorty," Darcy drawled. "By the way, here's your shawl and bonnet. Bo has the two buckets."

Sam chuckled. "You sure did make those buckets fly! One almost konked me on the noggin."

I tried to laugh, but my laughter sounded more like a whimper. "Do you feel up to getting back in the buggy?" James asked. "I can drive you and Jamie home."

I closed my eyes and nodded slightly. The last thing I wanted to do was get back into the carriage. "James, if it's all right with you, I'd like to drive. I don't want to spend the rest of my life afraid."

His eyes misted. "You are one nervy lady, Chloe Mae Spencer. What would I have done if I'd lost you?" Helping me back onto the carriage seat, he rounded the buggy and climbed in beside me. "Sam, hitch my horse to the back of the buggy. I'll ride along with Miss Spencer."

"Why don't you two head on back to the ranch?" Sam volunteered. "I'll give Jamie a lift back. He's always begging to ride with me anyway."

James thanked him, then handed me the reins. He placed his left arm behind me on the back of the seat and touched his right hand to the brim of his hat. "I'm ready when you are."

Trembling, I shook the reins. "Giddyap!" The skittish horse inched forward. A second flick of the reins, and Saturn cantered toward home. As the breeze started to blow my long hair across James's face, and he brushed the strands away with his hand, I felt a touch of blush creeping up my neck into my face. Then my heart pounded as he lifted the mass of tangled curls from my neck and smoothed them down my back. Suddenly, as if stung by a wasp, James withdrew his hand and his arm resting on the back of the seat. He cleared his throat and folded his arms across his chest.

We rode in silence, avoiding each other's glances. When we reached home, I climbed down from the buggy before James could help me. Minna emerged from the house. "You're back early. So where are the strawberries?"

I laughed. "That's a long story. We never did get to eat the lunch you packed either." I turned to pull the basket from under the front seat. It was missing. "Oh, well, I guess we contributed to some bird's lunch today, basket and all."

While James told Minna about my adventure, I headed upstairs. All I wanted was to soak in a warm bath. Much later, while rinsing the soap from my hair, I heard the rest of the men gallop into the yard. By the time I dressed, brushed the snarls from my wet hair, and went down stairs, only Minna remained in the house—Minna and two buckets of freshly picked wild strawberries. Jamie had insisted they pick the strawberries before coming back to the house.

During the rest of that week, James seemed to have a lot on his mind. He spent more time in the barn than usual, and I missed our evening chats. On Saturday evening, while Jamie went with his father to do chores, I invited Minna to take a walk with me to the creek.

We grabbed our shawls and headed out into the gathering shadows. When we arrived at the creek, I sat down on my favorite boulder. Minna chose to sit beside me.

With my finger I traced patterns on the rock's mottled surface. "Are you getting eager to leave for Russia?"

"In some ways, I guess."

"You don't have to leave," I reminded.

"I know. For so many years, I've been somebody's daughter, somebody's wife, somebody's mother. Now that I've been independent, running the ranch alone, I'm not sure who I am or where I belong." Minna gazed at the moon rising in the east. In the moonlight, the lines of time faded; her eyes looked less tired, less grieved. She turned to look at me.

"How about you? Have you decided what you will do when Jamie begins school this fall?"

I shrugged my shoulders. "Probably go on to California. I don't like to think about it."

She smiled. "You really love them, don't you?"

"Yeah, I guess I do. Uh, er, Jamie, that is. Not that I don't care for his father. I do, but as a, a, a friend." The more I tried to explain, the more I fumbled for words.

Minna chuckled and rose to her feet. "That's all right, Chloe. I understand more than you might think."

Blushing, I turned toward her. "Why? What do you mean?"

Wrapping her arm about my shoulder, she urged me toward home. "Nothing to worry about, child. Leave it all in God's hands, and you'll be fine." She paused and chuckled to herself once more. "Though I do question whether you'll be seeing California in the near future."

The rumble of wagons and the voices of laughing people drew our attention toward the rise beyond the house. "What's happening?" Thinking it might be an emergency, I broke into a run. The wagons stopped beside the house, and people of all ages spilled out.

Zerelda spotted us running toward them. "Surprise!" she shouted, swinging a large picnic basket. "We're here for a surprise party."

"A surprise party?" I looked at Minna. "Did you know anything about a party?"

Minna laughed. "No, but that's the fun of it, dropping in on someone unaware. They did it once at our house about an hour after we retired for the night."

By the time I reached the house, the men had come up

from the barn, and the kitchen was overrun with the neighbor ladies and picnic baskets filled with freshly baked goodies. In the parlor, Will Taylor was tuning his fiddle. Minna insisted on overseeing the kitchen detail while I acted as hostess. I sensed rather than saw James watching me circulate about the parlor accompanied by the strains of "Annie Laurie" and "Silver Threads Among the Gold."

After a while I stepped outside onto the front porch for a breath of fresh air. The children had initiated a moonlit game of hide-and-seek. Memories of playing games on the lawn with my brothers and sisters made me wish I could join them. *You're an adult now,* I reminded myself. *Behave.*

The screen door swung behind me, and Zerelda's low alto voice broke into my reverie. "So why don't you do it?"

"I beg your pardon? Do what?"

She didn't answer. Instead, she disappeared back inside the house only to return seconds later dragging the guests behind her. Tapping James on the shoulder, Zerelda bolted across the lawn. "Come on, James, you're it. The elm tree is home base."

For a second, everyone looked at each other. Then James took the stairs two at a time and dashed across the lawn toward the elm tree. "Last one home is it. One-two-three . . ."

We clattered down the stairs and skittered like beetles into the shadows. I ran around the corner of the house and hid behind a rambling rosebush. I heard a rustle behind me, and Jamie squeezed in next to me.

"This is fun," he whispered. "I like surprise parties."

I put my finger to my lips and whispered, "Me too."

We stood still while other players shouted and ran for the elm tree. Suddenly a shadow appeared from behind us. I heard James's voice. "One-two-three, I see you!"

Leaping from behind the bush, Jamie darted ahead of me. With James in hot pursuit, I found myself tripping over other players dashing toward the same goal. I slammed my hands against the tree and shouted, "Home free."

Zerelda wasn't quite so lucky. James called her out, and so began the next game. The older folks who didn't feel surefooted in the darkness stood on the porch, cheering us on while Zerelda counted aloud, "One-two-three-four . . ."

I glanced about, trying to decide which way to run. Remembering the cubbyhole under the back steps, I lifted my skirts and scooted around the corner of the house. Hearing someone running behind me, I turned—and plowed into James. As we crashed against the house with a thud, he grabbed my shoulders to keep me from falling.

When he didn't let go immediately, and I looked up, our eyes met and held. Then James bent down and brushed his lips against mine. I staggered back, stunned by new and strange emotions. At the sound of approaching footsteps, he turned and disappeared into the shadows, leaving me leaning against the side of the house to steady myself.

The footsteps turned out to be Zerelda's. She peeked around the corner, squealed, and ran for home base. Halfheartedly, I chased after her, making me "it" for the next game. James chose to sit out that game and the rest of the games that followed.

For the rest of the evening, James and I avoided each other. When Minna announced that refreshments were ready, I hurried into the kitchen with the rest of the crowd. Accepting a glass of punch from Bo, I glanced across the room in time to catch a short but definite frown on James's face.

We carried the refreshments out onto the porch, and Will took out his violin and started to play "Red River

Valley." Someone started to sing along; another followed. Soon we all were singing about a Texas cowboy's lost love.

As my first surprise party drew to a close, I smiled to myself. The party had been more of a surprise than any of the guests could have imagined. Zerelda gave me a hug as she and her family prepared to leave. "Thanks for being such a good sport tonight. How about we picnic together next week at the July Fourth celebrations in Hays?"

"Sure—if we go." I hadn't heard anyone mention the upcoming holiday.

She waved away my doubts. "Oh, you'll go. Everyone does. The town fathers will fire the cannon at dawn."

"At dawn?"

"Every town in Kansas salutes the day with a bang. If they don't have a cannon, they explode gunpowder on an anvil. You'll hear the explosions from miles around." She patted my hand and turned to leave. "We'll see you there. Don't make a dessert; I'm going to bring my mother's apple crisp."

"Umm, sounds good."

Waving and shouting goodnight, our guests piled into the wagons and drove way. I listened as their voices faded into the night, leaving only the crickets and the tree frogs to break the silence. As I sat down on the steps, James disappeared into the house. Minna took Jamie up to his room. A few minutes later, the light shining from the upstairs window blinked off.

Thoughts tumbled through my mind in frenzied confusion. I'd always imagined what my first real kiss would be like—and it hadn't been while playing children's games on the lawn. *You're acting like a silly schoolgirl, Chloe Mae!*

The more I tried to convince myself that nothing had changed between James and me, the more I knew everything had changed. I forced myself to remember each of the boys I'd had crushes on through the years, beginning with Tommy Edwards and ending with Cy Chamberlain. This time there were no giggles, no palpitations, no lovesick sighs, just a growing fear that reining in my runaway emotions for this man would prove to be much more difficult than reining in a runaway horse. I leaned back against the porch post and watched a wispy cloud float past the face of the moon.

Dear Father, where do we go from here? What other surprises do You have in store for me? The clock in the hallway gonged three before I stumbled up the stairs to my room, and the sounds of morning chores drifted in through my bedroom window before I finally drifted off to sleep.

A Friend From the Past

The next day brought two surprises into our lives. Minna was weeding the garden while I helped Jamie with arithmetic. I was making little progress teaching him how to add double-digit numbers—I don't know whose mind wandered more, the boy's or mine.

At the clatter of approaching carriage wheels, Jamie escaped onto the back porch. "Someone's coming!" he shouted. A second later, he popped his head around the corner, his eyes dancing with excitement. "It's Uncle Ian and Aunt Drucilla with Aunt Bea! And there's a stranger with them." Then he dashed down the steps to meet them.

I got up from the table and hurried outside, and Minna came around the corner of the house to join us. As the two buggies pulled to a stop beside the carriage house, Jake stepped out of the tack room, where he'd been mending a harness, and shielded his eyes from the sun. Ian alighted from the first one to help Aunt Bea and Drucilla down.

"Jake," Ian called, "could you water Mrs. McCall's horses and unharness the second team, please?"

Though I was curious as to who might be riding in the second carriage, I walked up to Aunt Bea and welcomed her with a hug. Ian kissed my cheek and asked for James. I pointed vaguely south, where, he had told Minna, they'd be riding fences.

Drucilla swept me into her arms, her face glowing with happiness. "It's so good to see you, Chloe." She stripped off a delicate lace glove and tossed it into the air. "It feels so good to be out west again." Glancing over her shoulder, I watched the stranger with the full beard climb down from the other buggy. The silver buckles on his boots glistened in the sunlight.

Drucilla followed my gaze, then broke into a smile. "Oh, I almost forgot. We met your friend on the train out of Kansas City."

"My friend?" I took a second look at the man dressed in black. He waved at me, but his wide-brimmed hat shaded his face.

She took my arm and steered me toward him, bubbling with excitement. "I couldn't believe my ears when he told Ian he was stopping in Hays on his way to California to see an old girlfriend. When he told us your name, I squealed, right there in the parlor car, in front of everyone."

It wasn't until he swept off his hat that I recognized the eyes. If I'd been a woman who swooned, it would have happened right there and then. Instead, I gasped, "Phillip Chamberlain! Whatever are you doing here in Kansas?" He rushed forward and took my hands.

"Chloe Mae Spencer. I have dreamed of this moment ever since our day on the lawn beside the grange hall. Remember?"

I nodded. "But I don't understand. Joe wrote that you were working in New Orleans."

"I was, but I hated it. At a family reunion in Baltimore, I convinced my father to send me to San Francisco instead. And when my brother cabled that you might be ready to leave this wasteland for California, I volunteered to escort you."

Drucilla sighed and batted her lashes. "Isn't that the most romantic thing you've ever heard?"

I shot a frantic look at Minna. She shrugged and grinned. Remembering my manners, I introduced Phillip to Minna and Jamie. Minna smiled and shook his hand. When Phillip reached out to shake Jamie's hand, the child glowered and stepped behind Minna.

While Minna showed Ian and Phillip where to put the luggage, Aunt Bea allowed Jamie to take her to see his sunflower plants. With the others occupied, Drucilla drew me into the library.

"Chloe, I have the most exciting thing to tell you." Drucilla paused, her face flushed with excitement. "I'm pregnant. Ian and I are going to have a baby in January."

I laughed aloud with joy. "Really? I'm so happy for you both." My exuberance turned to concern. "Are you feeling all right after the long train ride? Perhaps you should go upstairs and lie down."

"I will. I will. I promise."

Drucilla's eyes sparkled with a happiness I'd never before seen in them. "I guess I don't need to ask if you two are happy."

She smiled. "More than you can imagine." She slipped her arm into mine and led me to the sofa. "It was rough. With so many relatives in Boston, we had little real privacy. I can't wait to get to our home in Colorado."

"I am so glad for you. When you left, I suspected that your attitude toward Ian had changed."

She blushed. "Was it that obvious?"

I nodded and grinned.

"And now, what about you? Can you imagine this Phillip character going so many miles out of his way to escort you to California?"

"I don't know what he told you, but we weren't, I mean, he wasn't . . ."

Drucilla clasped my hand in hers. "Oh, I know. He explained everything. But you can't blame me for wanting my best friend to be as happy as I am."

Before I could reply, Ian and Phillip entered the room. Ian smiled down at Drucilla tenderly. "Drucilla, I'm going to saddle up a horse and ride out to find James. Maybe you should go upstairs and rest while I'm gone."

She glanced at Phillip, then rose to her feet. "You're probably right, dear. If you two will excuse us."

She flashed a knowing smile before gliding from the room on her husband's arm. Phillip sat beside me on the sofa. An awkward silence grew between us. I stared down at my hands; a tight vertical crease formed between his brows. At last Phillip spoke, "I hope you don't mind my coming here, Chloe. Perhaps I should have warned you before I arrived."

My mouth felt dry. "No, of course it's all right. I, uh, just don't know how soon I'll be ready to leave here."

"Didn't you tell Joe that the child would be starting school soon, and your job here would be done?" He placed his hand on the couch cushion between us and leaned closer.

"Well . . . yes. I'm just not sure when."

"Oh, I see." He drew back and stroked his beard. "Does your uncertainty have anything to do with the child's father?"

I jumped at the hot poker prodding my conscience. "No, of course not. We're friends, of course, but that's all."

He raised an eyebrow and nodded. "Then there's nothing to stop you. Leaving won't be a problem, will it?"

"No," I hesitated, "I guess not."

Phillip folded his arms across his chest and leaned back against the sofa. "Good. I'm glad. I guess your brother worried for nothing."

"My brother?"

A relieved smile crossed his face. "Yeah, Joe had convinced himself that you were falling for this McCall guy.

That's one reason he wanted me to see you."

I couldn't imagine how Joe had gotten such an idea from my letters; I'd always been circumspect whenever I mentioned James. After all, he and I had established the ground rules right in the beginning. We knew where we stood with one another. But now, after last night . . . I had so many questions. And I couldn't walk away without receiving some answers.

That evening, James invited Phillip to stay at the ranch as long as he wished. James played the perfect host to his guests at dinner. While he treated me with utmost respect, I sensed a coldness each time our eyes met. I decided that I had to talk with him—alone. But how was I to get him alone?

After Minna served her berry cobbler, James and Ian disappeared into the library to discuss business pertaining to their Colorado mining claims. Drucilla announced that she wanted to take a long, hot bath and then retire early. When Phillip asked me to take him on a tour of the ranch, Jamie insisted on coming with us.

The next morning Phillip arranged with Minna to care for Jamie while we rode over to Victoria. He said he'd heard about the interesting community from one of the passengers on the train from Chicago.

I demurred. "I'll have to check with James. He is my employer, you know."

Drucilla glanced up from her piece of dry toast. "He's in the library with Ian."

Squaring my shoulders, I marched to the library door and knocked. I had no idea what perceptions James had about Phillip and me. For that matter, I wasn't sure what perceptions James had about us.

Ian opened the door. James sat at the desk, the ranch's operating ledgers spread out before him, but he stood as I entered the room. I licked my suddenly dry lips. "I'm sorry to interrupt your business discussions, but, James, I need to talk with you."

"Hey," Ian replied before James could speak, "I need to check on Drucilla. Her morning sickness was worse this morning." He stepped into the hall and closed the door.

James waved me to the chair beside the desk, then returned to his desk chair. "How can I help you, Chloe?"

I took a deep breath. "We're friends, aren't we?" He nodded. "Even after the other night?"

James's face reddened. "Uh, I'm sorry about that. I was out of line. I don't exactly know what happened."

I hurried to his defense. "I don't either. But whatever it was, we can't allow it to destroy our friendship."

He stared at his calloused hands. "Chloe, I've been self-serving to keep you here in Kansas after Mary died. I tried to convince myself I was doing it just for Jamie, but, to tell the truth, your presence stabilized me when I thought I would fall apart. I'll always be grateful for that." I started to speak, but James raised his hand to stop me. "No, no. It's true. But Jamie is no longer a baby; he'll be starting school in the fall. And I can't justify keeping you from your dreams any longer."

"James, you didn't keep me from anything. I made an informed decision when I chose to care for Jamie. And if the identical situation arose again, I'd make the very same choice, right down to the other night."

Pain creased his brow. "Chloe, that's just it; that's why you have to go. Remember the day I told you I never wanted to marry again? Nothing has changed."

"I never thought . . ." I swallowed hard.

"Ian explained Mr. Chamberlain's mission. I think you should plan to leave with him." James reached over and took my hands in his. "Chloe, you are young and full of idealism. You'll make a wonderful bride for Mr. Chamberlain."

I yanked my hands away and leapt to my feet. "Obviously I remember our agreement better than you do. You promised to stop trying to marry me off. And that, Mr. James McCall, also has not changed!" I straightened imaginary wrinkles out of my skirt. "I came in here for two reasons. The first, for advice—and you gave it. The second reason is that Minna has agreed to watch Jamie while I accompanied Mr. Chamberlain to Victoria today, if that is all right with you."

James stood up slowly, his face crimson. "I think that would be nice for you, Miss Chloe. Be sure to visit the Victoria Manor. It served as a depot for the railroad and as a hotel for the English colonists until they could build their homes."

I tipped my head toward him. "Thank you, Mr. McCall. I'll be sure to take your advice—all of your advice. Good day." I whirled about and exited the room. After the door slammed behind me, I pressed my forehead against the door frame and fought back the tears. *Miss Chloe? Miss Chloe? I haven't been Miss Chloe to him since last fall. But then I called him Mr. McCall.*

I stormed up the stairs to my room and threw myself onto the bed. When the pillowcase was moistened with tears, I reached blindly toward the night-stand drawer, where I stored my clean hankies. I jerked my head off the pillow as someone placed one in my hand before I found the drawer knob. Through blurry eyes I looked into Minna's concerned face.

I threw myself into her arms and told her the entire story—except for the kiss. She stroked the back of my head and rocked me in her arms. "I thought it would be so easy to leave. Now I'm so confused. If James gave me one word of encouragement, one indication he might want me to stay for more than just Jamie, I would send Phillip packing on tomorrow morning's train."

"Here. Dry your eyes." She handed me a second handkerchief. "You and I have talked many times about the strange way God leads in our lives. What was that text in John 16 about asking for answers 'that your joy may be full'? Now is the time to ask Him to give you directions."

"I know you're right." I blew my nose into the lace-edged square. "But I can't understand James's aloof attitude. It's as if the friendship we've built over the year never existed."

"Did you ever think James might be just as confused as you?"

"No!" I shook my head vigorously. "James McCall is anything but confused. He definitely knows his own mind."

Minna smiled a knowing smile. "For now, why don't you put on a pretty dress, tie a bow in your hair, and have a fun afternoon with the nice young man waiting for you in the kitchen?"

I nodded and sniffed. "I guess that's all I can do, huh?"

She stood to her feet, kissed my forehead, and cradled my face with her hands. "God knows what is best for Chloe Mae Spencer, remember?"

As Minna left the room, she called back over her shoulder, "Wear that pretty pink gingham dress with the white embroidered collar."

I obeyed and splashed cool water on my face. After brushing my hair, I caught the sides up in a pink satin ribbon on the back of my head. I smiled at myself in the mirror. "You don't look half bad, Chloe Mae Spencer, for an old maid of almost eighteen, except for your puffy eyes, that is!"

Grabbing a bonnet and shawl from the wardrobe shelf, I glided down the stairs. On impulse, I knocked on the library door. When James opened the door, he inhaled sharply.

"Sorry, I didn't mean to disturb you." I flashed him a

brilliant smile. "I'm leaving for the afternoon now, with Mr. Chamberlain. Since my presence here is no longer needed, I'll plan on leaving for California on July five, if that's all right with you. That way, I'll be able to say goodbye to my friends at the Independence Day celebrations." As I spoke, the expression on James's face changed from surprise to pleasure to dismay, then darkened to a mood I couldn't identify so easily.

"That sounds acceptable. Will you inform my son of your departure, or should I?"

"Perhaps we both should speak with him, independent of one another."

He nodded. "As you wish. Have a pleasant afternoon, Miss Chloe." James waited until I turned and walked down the hall toward the kitchen before closing the library door.

Miss Chloe! What are we doing to each other? I set my jaw and stomped into the kitchen. "I'm ready to leave! Where is Mr. Chamberlain?"

Minna poked her head out of the pantry. "He's waiting in the buggy. Here's a lunch I made for the two of you." She handed me a basket bulging with food. "Don't worry about Jamie. Jake took him to the barn to play with Humble."

At the mention of Jamie, I swallowed a surge of angry tears. I set the basket on the table and tied my bonnet. I looked askance at the curls cascading down my back—perhaps I'd overdone it. I didn't want Phillip to assume our excursion to Victoria was more than a sightseeing tour.

Minna read my mind. "You look lovely. Did James say anything?"

I snatched the basket from the table. "Mr. Chamberlain and I will be back sometime this afternoon."

When I stepped out onto the porch, Jamie spied me and

waved. I waved back. Out of the corner of my eye, I saw a shadow move past one of the dining-room windows and a curtain flutter. Knowing it had to be James, I lifted my chin and marched down the steps to the waiting Phillip.

Victoria proved to be a fascinating community. We started our tour at Victoria Manor. We walked through the large waiting room, passed a small post office, and peeked in the general store on the first floor. Upstairs, we were told, were hotel rooms.

As we left the manor, Phillip asked, "Why would anyone construct such a large building out here in the middle of Kansas?"

"Well, according to James, the town founder, George Grant, and the Union Pacific Railroad Company built it for the wealthy and titled settlers Mr. Grant intended to lure to Kansas from England and Scotland."

Leaving the horses hitched to the post outside the depot, we strolled down the main street of the quiet little town. Many of its buildings were empty. "Mr. Grant hired the famous English architect R. W. Edis to plan Grant's 'city of dreams.' The plan called for streets one hundred feet wide and alleys twenty-five feet wide."

I read the sign on a small chapel, "St. George's Chapel. Established 1878." The gothic structure could have been lifted from the English countryside. "Do you think we can go inside?"

Phillip shrugged. "If it's open, sure." He took my arm and led me to the door. As the heavy wooden door creaked open, I felt like I was looking into one of Jane Austen's books. A rush of cool air brushed across my face as I entered the gray stone vestibule. The sanctuary walls, floors, and wooden pews were dappled with sunlight filtering through the jeweltones of the arched, stained-glass windows.

Forgetting Phillip, I slipped into one of the pews and

knelt on the cool limestone floor. He must have sensed I needed to be alone, for he wandered off in another direction.

While the silence and beauty of the room soothed my pain and confusion, a familiar text pulsated in my mind. "In all thy ways acknowledge him . . ."

Forgive me, Father, for forgetting my promise to wait on You. Will I ever learn to trust You? Breathing in the atmosphere of peace surrounding me, I turned my thoughts to James. Instead of feeling anger, I began to understand the turmoil he had probably experienced over the past year. Tears slipped quietly down my cheeks. *Be with him, Lord; help him to find someone to love.* I dabbed my eyes on my sleeve. *I want only the best for him and his son. I love them both so much.* As the truth of what I had admitted in prayer registered in my brain, my eyes flew open. *No, no. Not in that way. Just as a friend, Lord, or as a brother, not that way. Please, not that way.*

I must have cried aloud, for suddenly Phillip was beside me. "Are you all right?"

Disoriented, I looked up into his concerned face. I tried to say something, anything, but I couldn't.

He helped me to my feet and led me from the chapel. When we stepped out into the sunshine, Phillip asked, "What happened in there? You're as white as a sheet. Here, use my handkerchief." He handed me a large linen handkerchief monogrammed with a silk C, then steadied me down the steps to the street. "Perhaps we'd better call it a day. Perhaps you got too much sun."

I didn't try to explain. How could I? I wasn't even sure myself what had happened. By the time we arrived back at the carriage, I'd composed my thoughts enough to suggest we find a spot to enjoy our picnic lunch. "Maybe I'm weak from not eating much of a breakfast."

He accepted my explanation and helped me into the

carriage. "Mrs. Kline said that there's a grassy knoll across from Grant's villa."

We rode the short distance to the spot Mrs. Kline had described. There we spread out the tablecloth on the grass and removed the food from the basket. I nibbled on a lettuce-and-cucumber sandwich.

The mammoth limestone building cast an imposing shadow on the fields to the east of the villa, where Aberdeen Angus cattle grazed. Phillip pointed toward the herd. "James told me that, ironically, the cows are probably Mr. Grant's greatest accomplishment. His Angus herd was the first of what is now a major breed of cattle in the United States."

I smiled and nodded. *What did he say about the cows?*

Phillip pointed to the stables behind the main house. "Grant is said to have kept a prize stallion worth eighteen thousand dollars in that stable."

"Really?" I knew he'd said something about the stables, but I wasn't sure what.

"I read on a plaque back at the church that Mr. Grant's funeral was the first service held in the finished chapel. It seems that when Mr. Grant died, so did his dream."

"That's nice," I mumbled.

"Chloe, I don't know what's wrong, but do you want me to take you back to the ranch right away?"

Startled at the urgency in his voice, I snapped alert. Concern clouded his face. "You haven't heard a word that I've said since we left the church."

"Oh, uh, I'm sorry. I guess I'm not feeling too well. Would you mind very much taking me back to the ranch?"

Phillip's face froze into a humorless smile, which he maintained throughout the entire ride home in spite of my attempts to coax him back into his earlier mood.

At the dinner table that evening, James glowered from the head of the table. I ate silently, barely looking up from my plate. Poor Drucilla, peaked from her day-long bout with nausea, sipped a cup of comfrey tea. To spark conversation, Ian asked Phillip about our excursion. Phillip told about the sights we'd seen. "It's too bad poor Mr. Grant's dream died with him. So many of the original families gave up and returned to England."

Ian chuckled. "If they hadn't, we wouldn't be eating at this table right now. Father purchased the ranch from a discouraged English merchant."

Minna asked if we'd visited the German-Russian community of Herzog, across the river from Victoria. "My husband was a member of a Catholic church there. We didn't attend much because I was brought up Lutheran."

"We missed it, I'm afraid. Maybe next time." Phillip paused, then looked at Minna. "You know, I can't help but wonder why Grant's community failed and the German-Russian community right across the river thrived. You and your husband were among the first generation to arrive here, weren't you?"

"Yes, our ancestors immigrated from Germany to the Russian steppes in 1763. Then we immigrated to Kansas in 1876. We lived in a one-room, sod house for several years while we saved money for a frame house." The woman smiled through her wool-gathering. "Our people survived the harsh prairie life for two reasons: we were used to hard work, and we had no land to return to. So," she laughed and threw her hands into the air, "why am I considering going back to Russia, I'd like to know!"

We joined her laughter. Ian lifted his water glass to Minna. "Here's to a true pioneer." The rest of us seconded his toast.

Minna blushed. "Ah, where is my head? You are ready for dessert, no?"

The conversation ended early since we'd been up with dawn's first rays to prepare for the Fourth of July celebrations. While Jamie took his bath, I laid out his clothing for the next day. I had to tell him about my leaving, but when? I fluffed his pillow and turned back the covers. *If I tell him tonight, he'll have trouble sleeping. If I wait until tomorrow, I'll ruin his day.*

Sensing the boy standing in the doorway, I knew I couldn't put off the inevitable. "Come on, honey. Let's have prayer before I tuck you in."

"That won't be necessary, Chloe."

I turned to face James's bemused smile. Heat rose up my neck into my face. "Oh, I'm so sorry. I thought—"

"Don't be embarrassed. I know what you thought." His teasing grin frustrated me further. "Actually, it's been a long time since my mother or anyone else offered to say my bedtime prayers with me."

"Hi." Jamie appeared around the corner. He looked at both of us in surprise.

"I came to say good night."

"Really? Will you stay to tuck me in?"

James glanced over at me, then down at his son. "Doesn't Miss Chloe usually do that?"

"Yeah, but she won't mind." His eyes pleaded with me to agree. "Will you?"

I shook my head. "No, of course not."

We knelt together and prayed, Jamie and me on one side of the bed, James on the other. After the amen, the child hopped into bed. I tucked the covers around him and bent to kiss him good night.

"Son." James sat down on the edge of the bed. "Miss Chloe and I have something to tell you that you're not going to like very much."

I recognized the wide-eyed look in Jamie's eyes as he stared up into the man's face. It was the same look he'd given me when I explained to him about his mother's death.

"You've always known that Miss Chloe would be with us only for a while, that one day she'd leave and join her brother in San Francisco." James indicated for me to sit down on my side of the bed. "I thought we should tell him together."

Disbelief filled the child's face. "You're going to leave me? Did I do something bad?"

I shook my head no.

"Then why are you going away? You promised . . ."

I didn't know how to answer Jamie's accusation. My heart wanted to cry out, "I don't want to leave you, Jamie." Instead, I stared at the pattern of the bedspread.

James cleared his throat. "You're getting to be a big boy now, son. Next fall you'll start school. You no longer need a nanny."

Jamie grabbed his father's wrist. "Daddy, make her stay. Make Miss Chloe stay!"

"I can't do that, son. She has to get on with her own life."

The child turned his head slowly toward me, his lower lip protruding defiantly. "You promised!"

"Son, you're not being fair to Miss Chloe. She's been very good to you. When your mommy died and you needed her, she was there for you, remember?"

"Is that why she's leaving, because I said I didn't want her to be my mommy?" The boy sat up, his eyes filled with hope. "Is that it? If it is, I've changed my mind. I think you'd make a great mother, Miss Chloe. Please, Daddy, tell her, tell her that it's all right with us."

James avoided my eyes. "It's not that easy, son. For Miss Chloe to become your mother, I'd have to marry . . ."

"Then marry her, Daddy, marry her. Make her stay!"

"It's not that easy, son." The color crept up James's neck and face. Hoping to move the conversation to another topic, I plunged in.

"Jamie, I love you dearly, and your father loves you

dearly." I reached out to stroke the child's arm, but he pulled away. "And there is nothing in the world I'd like more than to have you call me Mother. But our loving you isn't enough for us to consider marrying one another. We could marry each other only if we . . ." The words caught in my throat, then came out in a husky whisper. "Loved one another."

Jamie bit his lower lip. "If I were old enough, I'd marry you, Miss Chloe. Then you would never have to go away."

"Thank you, Jamie. If you were a few years older, I just might have taken you up on that."

Jamie's eyes brimmed with tears as I stood, leaned over, and placed a kiss on his forehead. "Good night, cowboy," I whispered, then walked stiff-legged from the room. Once I reached my bedroom, I threw myself on the bed and cried myself to sleep.

Cause to Celebrate

The explosion of rifles and pistols brought me bolt upright. More explosions resounded across the prairie. War whoops and Texas yells erupted from the bunkhouse. Terrified, I leapt from my bed and ran to the window before I remembered the cause—July 4. Streaks of vermillion and gold filled the eastern sky, a great day for celebrating the birth of the nation.

In the mirror, I caught a glimpse of my rumpled dress, my tangled hair, and my face, puffy and streaked with yesterday's tears. The muscles in my neck and shoulders ached. After shedding my dress, I massaged my shoulders and stretched my neck from side to side, trying to loosen the knots. The sound of Minna preparing breakfast drifted up the stairwell as I returned to my room after bathing.

The day promised to be hot and sunny. Already the breeze felt warm through the open window. I slipped into a blue muslin skirt and white blouse, then brushed the snarls from my hair. I fastened it at the back of my neck with a blue taffeta ribbon.

Minna had breakfast ready and a picnic lunch packed by the time I got downstairs. I relieved her of the pancake turner. Flipping the flapjacks on the pan once more, I asked, "Who's next?" Ian, James, and the ranch hands were two servings ahead of Phillip.

"I guess those two are mine," he admitted. "Or did you change your mind, Jamie?"

The boy shook his head and bounded from the table.

Minna looked up from her plate. "What got into him?"

My gaze focused on James. He held his gaze dead center on his stack of pancakes, refusing to meet mine. Just then Drucilla staggered into the kitchen. "I passed Jamie in the hall. He seemed upset. What happened?"

James shoved his chair back from the table. "I'll see to the boy," he mumbled and fled the room.

"So." Drucilla sat down in the chair Ian offered her. "Is everyone ready to have fun today?"

Ian hovered over his wife. "Maybe you shouldn't go, dear. You look quite peaked."

"Nonsense. If I have any trouble, I promise to go over to Aunt Bea's to rest." She looked askance at her husband's pancakes. "I will forgo breakfast, however."

I fixed her a cup of comfrey tea, which she accepted gratefully.

When everyone finished eating, Minna and I made short work of cleaning the kitchen while the men hitched the horses to the rigs. Sam took Jamie in the wagon with him and the other ranch hands. The rest of us crowded into the carriage. Because of Drucilla's condition, I rode in the front seat between Phillip and James. With no armrests available, I folded my arms across my chest and maintained the rigid pose for the entire journey.

Sam had attached four-inch American flags to the front corners of the carriage and wagon, and Jake had wrapped the harnesses with bunting for decoration. As neighbors passed us on the road, I discovered the flags and the bunting were part of the Kansas tradition.

Aunt Bea met us on Main Street. The parade, the band, the float carrying a young woman dressed as the "goddess of liberty," and the Civil War veterans sporting chests full of medals atop bursting uniforms reminded me of Shinglehouse and, unfortunately, of Emmett. I was beginning to hate the Fourth of July.

In the afternoon relay games and races were scheduled. Phillip tried to interest me in the activities. When he suggested we take a walk, I reluctantly agreed. Once we were alone, he turned and faced me. "You don't want to leave Kansas, do you?"

I started to protest, then shook my head slowly. "I-I don't know."

"Either you do, or you don't."

"It's not that simple." I looked up at him, my eyes pleading for him to understand.

He searched my eyes for some time. I turned away from his gaze. "Oh, so that's how it is."

"Phillip, I honestly don't know how it is. I've never been so confused in my life."

His dry laugh lacked humor. "Ever since the day we talked on the lawn behind the grange, I imagined that one day, you and I would carry out our fantastic dream of becoming missionaries to Africa."

"Excuse me," I reminded, trying to add a lighter note to the conversation. "It was your dream to go to Africa, not mine. China was my calling."

He took my hand and placed it on his arm. "Right you are." We strolled down the boardwalk together, pausing to view the patriotic window displays. "Funny how life falls short of fantasy. Was there ever any hope for us? Or was that a fantasy too?"

I didn't know how to answer him. The revelation I had in the chapel the day before still wrestled with my reason. "Timing, Phillip. Just bad timing."

He didn't reply. There was nothing else to say. When we came to the end of the street, we retraced our steps.

Before we reached the park, he stopped again. "You still

haven't answered my question. Will you be coming with me to California?"

I shrugged. "It looks that way. I guess there's nothing for me here."

Phillip shook his head in disgust. "James McCall is a fool."

At the criticism of James, my Irish flared. "He's hurting for Mary's death. He loved her too much to marry again."

The man remained adamant. "Then he's twice a fool to risk losing a woman like you for a memory."

I started to reply, when Zerelda spotted me and called, "Come on, Chloe. We need another contestant in the women's baseball toss."

"I-I don't really feel like . . ." Protesting against Zerelda was like protesting the presence of a tornado. I allowed her to drag me over to the ball diamond. She didn't know yet that I was leaving. My throw came in second, and the crowd cheered as the judges handed me a red ribbon with gold lettering.

After the contest I drew Zerelda aside and explained as best I could my decision to leave, omitting the part about my feelings for James. She promised to come down to the railway station the next morning to see me off.

The men's baseball game had just started when Drucilla pleaded exhaustion. Since Ian was on one of the teams, I volunteered to take her back to Aunt Bea's place to rest. After the night I'd had, the idea of resting a while myself was appealing. My face and head felt hot. I suspected I was suffering from the curse of redheads—sunburn.

I helped Drucilla to one of the guest rooms, then headed for the room I'd used so many times previously. Stretching out in my camisole and crinoline on the bed, I let the afternoon breezes relax my tense body. Several hours later I partially awakened when Aunt Bea tiptoed into the room and covered me with a summer quilt. She asked a series of questions, which I must have answered. Then she left.

When I awoke, the room was dark, but familiar voices came from the parlor. I dressed and brushed my fingers through the tangles in my hair. A clock gonged nine times. *Oh, no, I must have kept everyone waiting. The men have to be back at the ranch for evening chores!*

Drucilla greeted me in the hallway. "Did you get a nice sleep?"

"Yes, but where is everybody? Is the picnic over?"

She laughed. "Hours ago. Ian is in the parlor talking with Aunt Bea. He thought it best that I rest here overnight before returning to the ranch." She thought for a minute. "Uh, Jamie went back with his father and the other men to do chores. Sam made me promise to tell you that they'll all be back in the morning to say goodbye."

"Goodbye? Oh, yes, goodbye. What about Phillip?"

"He drove Aunt Bea's wagon out to pick up your things, as well as his own." My mouth dropped open in surprise. "Don't worry, Minna promised she'd do the packing for you." Taking my arm, Drucilla led me into the parlor. "Do you have to leave so soon?"

"I guess so."

"Is it Phillip?"

I smiled and shook my head. The woman was an incorrigible romantic. "No, it's not Phillip."

Aunt Bea looked up as we entered the room. "Chloe, you must be hungry. How about a slice of pound cake with fresh blueberries on top and a glass of cold milk?"

My stomach growled. I nodded sheepishly. "I am a little hungry."

"How about you, Ian? Drucilla?"

Drucilla made a face and waved no. Aunt Bea laughed. "Just wait. Once your morning sickness passes, you'll eat everything in sight."

When Aunt Bea stood to go to the kitchen, Ian and Drucilla excused themselves to go to bed. As I ate, Aunt Bea asked me questions about my decision to leave.

"It was inevitable that I leave sooner or later. And with Mr. Chamberlain arriving when he did . . ."

"I always hoped . . ." The woman's voice drifted off into a wistful sigh. "I guess I've been reading too many storybooks. I do wish you well. And please write."

I reached over and gave her a hug. "I wouldn't think of doing less."

Phillip returned with my trunk just as I finished my dessert. He handed me a valise. "I left your trunk in the wagon. Minna insisted I give this directly to you. She said you'd need the stuff inside before morning."

I thanked him for his trouble.

He tipped his head. "Glad to be of service, ma'am."

While Aunt Bea showed Phillip to his room, I covered the blueberries and returned the cake to the cake holder. Aunt Bea then returned to say good night.

Setting the valise in the center of the table, I opened it. Packed on top were my hairbrush, my railway ticket, my Bible, and a plissé nightdress. "Bless Minna's heart." A practical blue-and-white seersucker skirt with matching jacket lay folded beneath the nightwear, followed by the appropriate undergarments.

I picked up my Bible and opened to the Psalms. "Trust in him at all times; ye people, pour out your heart before him; God is a refuge for us." *I like that. Trust at all times. I'm certainly learning to pour out my heart before You, Father. But the trust part? Just as I think I've gotten trusting in You down pat, my life turns upside down.*

My gaze fell on the railway pass. I remembered James's anger when I had asked him to purchase it for me. And I thought of all the times I'd almost used it. The words, "There is a time for everything," came to my mind. *Per-*

haps this is the time to move on, to look ahead, to let go. If God's plan for me doesn't include James McCall, will I be content?

Returning my belongings to the valise, I closed the case and carried it to my room. I didn't feel like sleeping yet after having slept much of the afternoon and evening. The cool breeze flowing through the open window lured me down the kitchen stairs and out into the starry night. I'd come to love the solitude of the prairie during my stay.

I set off at a brisk pace, but had no idea how far or how long I walked. I was too busy arguing with God about where I was heading to worry about where I was walking. And God was busy reminding me where I had been. Finally I argued myself into submission, and kneeling beside the dusty farm road that divided the shoulder-high corn crop, I conceded my will to Him.

I know You love me and that You will never leave me nor forsake me. And while in my mind I know I should be grateful for the outcome of today, my emotions don't agree. Please be patient with me, Lord.

I stood up and brushed the dust from my skirt, then lifted my eyes toward the eastern horizon. Somewhere beyond the darkness of midnight, my family was oblivious to my struggle. I rotated slowly to my right, where I could make out the scraggly silhouette of a tree.

The breeze coming in from the west fluttered the loose curls about my shoulders. Deliberately, I turned my face into the western breeze. East, north, or west, I finally trusted that my future rested securely with my Father. Contented and sleepy, I wandered back toward Aunt Bea's place.

At the edge of the cornfield, I heard a strange pinging sound. *Ping!* There it was again. I darted across the road to the chicken coop. *Ping!* The light from a lantern bobbed about the west side of the feed store. *Pa-ping!* This time it sounded like stones hitting glass. *Someone's trying to break into the store!*

I peered out from behind the coop. As the light danced away from the house, I could make out the form of a horse tied to Aunt Bea's lilac bush. I flattened myself against the building and held my breath. The intruder stood between me and the flight of stairs leading to the upstairs kitchen. Somehow I had to warn Aunt Bea and the others. I decided to circle the building from the other side. With a little luck, I could dash up the stairs before the thief knew I was anywhere around.

Silently, I sneaked around to the far end of the chicken coop. When I reached the front corner, I checked to be certain no one was in sight, then wormed my way between the carts, wagons, and other farm equipment behind the store. An open space of thirty or forty feet separated me from the store. Taking a deep breath, I broke into a run.

Halfway across the clearing, I heard someone call my name, not out loud, but in a raspy whisper. I glanced over my shoulder. No one was in sight. Without breaking stride, I darted behind the northeast corner of the two-story building, then paused to catch my breath. *Who called me? Was it my imagination? Perhaps Ian or Phillip heard the intruder and looked out of his bedroom window just as I sprinted across the clearing. That must be it.*

Satisfied with that explanation, I made my way around the east and south sides of the store. I crept up to the corner by the stairs and heard the ping of a pebble hitting a pane of glass. Again I heard my name being called.

"I know you can hear me," the voice rasped. "I've lobbed at least three stones right into your room. Come on, Chloe, come to the window. We need to talk."

Curious, I stuck my head around the corner to get a better view. When the horse whinnied, I recognized Honey.

Hope, anger, love, humor, and fear played tag in my emotions.

The man lifted the lantern above his head and hissed, "Chloe, it's me, James. Please let me talk with you. It's important."

Wary, I strolled out from behind the house. "What can be so important that it can't wait until morning?"

James continued to address the darkened window. "I'm here to beg you to stay. I didn't realize how much Jamie needs you."

"Jamie?" I circled behind him and leaned against the trunk of a giant elm tree. "As you said yesterday, your son no longer needs a nanny."

The frustrated man strained to catch sight of me in the window. "Chloe, you sound so hardhearted, not at all like yourself. The child cried himself to sleep last night."

"I'm sorry." I truly was, but I couldn't relent now. "Perhaps you can convince Minna to remain until he adjusts to someone new. At the dinner table the other night, she sounded like she might be having doubts about returning to Russia."

James turned around slowly, shining the lantern in my face. "How long have you been standing behind me?"

I tried to swallow my grin. "I don't know. How long have you been conversing with an empty window?"

He groaned and lowered the lantern to his side.

I sauntered toward him. "Why are you here?

The light bobbed closer to me. "To beg you to stay. What do I have to do to convince you that we need you?"

My throat constricted. "We?"

He stopped midstride. "Jamie, I mean Jamie. And, well, all of us at the ranch feel bad that you're leaving. We all love you."

The toe of my boot tapped out my irritation. "You mean to say that you rode all the way back to town in the middle of the night to tell me that I am well loved by your son and your hired hands?"

Abandoning restraint, he gave the lamp an exasperated swing into the air and bellowed, "What do you want from me?"

"A little sleep would be nice!" Aunt Bea, whose window was next to mine, leaned out of the window. "Do you think you two could move your peace conference to the other side of the house so I can go back to sleep? And if I may make a suggestion to both of you—a little honesty with one another would be nice!"

Mumbling an apology, James took my elbow and led me to the flight of stairs at the front of the store. I sat down on the third step. He remained standing on the outside of the railing. "By the way, why were you wandering about the countryside at this hour anyway?"

His question put me on the defensive. "I was doing what I always do when I'm restless—taking a walk."

"Hmmph! It could be dangerous, you know." He blew out the lantern and set it down beside the railing.

"Look, it's late. And your aunt is right. It's time we face our situation honestly." I took a deep breath and plunged on. "I've done a lot of thinking about us, not about Jamie or your hired help, but about you and me. The other night, when we ran into each other behind the house during hide-and-seek, I realized then that I couldn't stay on at the ranch after Minna left for Russia."

A sliver of moonlight backlighted James's profile, accentuating the thrust of his determined jaw. I waited for him to reply. When he didn't, I continued. "I'm not implying that the nature of our relationship has changed. It's a matter of propriety. I'm single. You're single."

He lifted his face to the sky, then turned to look at me. "So I'll marry you."

I blinked in surprise. "Excuse me?"

He enunciated each syllable. "I said I will marry you."

I coughed and sputtered in disbelief. The nerve of the man, the gall, the conceit! "I can't believe you. Why would I even consider marrying you?"

"For Jamie, of course."

I rose slowly to my feet. "James McCall, I love your son dearly." I ascended a step, then a second, until I stared him straight in the eyes. Squelching a flame of anger, I forced an even tone. "However, when I choose to marry, it will be because I love the man, not the child! Is that clear?"

His face was engulfed in shadows. "You are acting as if I insulted you. Obviously I care about you, or I'd never consider asking you to be my wife." He reached out and captured my wrist. "Wait, maybe I'm going about this all wrong."

"Maybe?" I lifted his hand from my wrist. One glance up at the darkened windows, and I forced my strident tone to a whisper. "That, my dear James, is an understatement. Now, if you'll excuse me, I am going up to my room. Good night."

"Chloe, wait. Let me explain."

I straightened my shoulders and continued up the stairs. He called after me.

"I've pursued you halfway across Kansas in the middle of the night. Doesn't that tell you something?" James hissed.

I paused and whirled about to face him. Pain and frustration scored his face. I fought the urge to reach out to him. I had to be certain. A lump filled my throat. "Yes, er, no. You're confusing me."

I opened the screen door. "Go away. Just go away." It was less a demand than a plea. Could he tell the difference? I wasn't sure. I ran down the hall, listening for his footsteps behind me as I ran. All was silent. I tiptoed into my room and closed the door. A quiver of panic fluttered in my stomach. *What if he leaves and never comes back? Oh, Father, what have I done?*

Curious, I ran to the window and leaned out. I knew if Honey were gone, so was James. When the horse whinnied softly, I allowed myself to breathe again.

A calm, steady voice spoke to me from beside the tree. "I'm still here. I'm not going anywhere until you give me your answer."

"Please, James, I-I-I can't just say Yes."

"Why not?"

"It's not that simple." Silence followed. I peered out the window. *Has he gone away? No, Lord, don't let him leave.*

From out of the shadows, I heard his voice. "Yes, it is just that simple. Either you love me enough to marry me, or you don't."

"Please go away. I can't think right now. We'll talk about it in the morning."

I slumped to the floor beside the window and waited to hear James leave. Only the sound of a tree frog broke the stillness. I drifted off to sleep to awaken suddenly to the sound of a whinny. Then I remembered. In the silence of my mind, I cried out. *Oh, Ma, I need you. I don't know what to do. I need you. I need you . . .* My thoughts evaporated into a yawn.

I was still crumpled on the floor when the first rays of dawn streaked across the sky. I yawned and stretched, wondering why I'd slept on the floor. Then I remembered. I peered over the windowsill. With his wide-brimmed hat over his face, James lay propped up against the tree trunk, sound asleep.

My muscles stiff from sleeping in an unnatural position, I hobbled across the room, exchanged my crumpled clothing for my nightgown, and crawled into bed. A fresh wave of sleep washed over me as my head sank into the downy pillow.

I awakened to someone knocking at my door. "Chloe, it's me, Zerelda." I strained to open my eyes.

"Zerelda?" I staggered over to the door and opened it. "What are you doing here so early?"

"Early? It's eight o'clock." She waved me aside and strolled in the room. "I came to say goodbye. What's all this about your changing your mind, again? And why in the world is James sitting outside your window eating a bowl of cornbread and milk?"

"Outside my window?" I dashed to the window and looked out. Zerelda leaned over my shoulder. James spotted us and waved. Suddenly I remembered I was wearing a nightdress. I dropped to the floor and peeked up over the sill. "Why are you eating outside?"

He grinned and waved his spoon in the air. "I vowed I wouldn't move from this spot until you answered my question."

"I have never heard of anything so, so—"

Zerelda whispered, "Romantic?"

I huffed at her. "So ridiculous." I crawled away from the window and slithered onto my bed.

My friend perched herself on the foot of the bed. "So what are you going to do?"

"Get dressed. Yes, that's what I'm going to do. I'm going to get dressed." I hauled the valise onto the bed and held up in front of me the dress Minna had packed for me. "Oh, no, I can't wear this today."

She examined the skirt with one hand. "Why not? It's a lovely outfit."

"It's one Mary gave me."

"Oh," Zerelda responded. "You stay right here, and I'll get another dress for you from your trunk. Which one would you like?"

I thought for a moment. "The light blue gingham one with the eyelet trim."

"Right." She leapt to her feet and ran from the room. By the time I finished brushing the tangles from my hair, Zerelda returned with the dress, a matching satin ribbon, and a white lace parasol. "Where did the parasol come from?" I eyed her suspiciously.

"Drucilla insisted you borrow it."

"Drucilla?"

"Of course, everyone's rooting for you two, you know. And you need it because James asked me to ask you if you would accompany him on a ride in Aunt Bea's carriage."

I glanced toward the window. "Is he still down there?"

"Of course."

The idea of continuing our discussion away from the family appealed to me. "Tell him I'd be delighted."

She ran to the window and shouted, "She said Yes to the carriage ride. Go clean up while she gets dressed." Zerelda whirled about and giggled. "I feel like a seventh-grader passing love notes between class sweethearts."

I stepped into my ruffled crinoline and laced the waistband. "How do you think I feel? I'm so embarrassed!"

The woman's eyes filled with love. "Don't be. Listen to your heart instead of your pride."

We argued over whether I should wear my hair down or in a braid circling my head. In the end, we compromised— I agreed to let her pull it back at the nape of my neck and pin it into a coil. She tied the satin ribbon into a bow and pinned it atop the coil.

As Zerelda lowered the dress over my head and buttoned it up the back, tears welled up in my eyes. Had it been only a year ago when my mother buttoned me into another dress? Zerelda adjusted the puff sleeves and stepped back to examine my appearance. "Turn around. That's right. Good, good! Don't forget the parasol and," she thrust a pair of lace gloves toward me, "these."

"Yes, Mommy," I teased.

"Just go. James is probably wearing ruts in his aunt's kitchen floor by now." She thrust my sunbonnet into my hands and pushed me into the hallway. "Go, go! Shoo!"

"I'm going. I'm going." The kitchen was empty, except for a plate of oatmeal cookies in the center of the table. Zerelda grabbed four of the cookies and shoved them into my hands. "Here, you wouldn't want to faint from hunger."

I groaned and cast her a exasperated look. "I have never fainted in my life."

"Well," she retorted, "you haven't had a very long life. You don't want to take any chances now, do you?" She peered through the window above the sink. "He's down there, waiting for you. My, does he ever look dashing."

"Dashing?" I brushed past her and pushed the screen door open. James stood at the base of the stairs, leaning against the side of the building. When he heard the door open, he straightened, swept his hat from his head, and smiled up at me.

He wore a black silk shirt open at the throat with a black bandanna carelessly knotted about his neck. His boots and breeches were also black, except for a large silver buckle at his waist. *Dashing is accurate.* I'd never considered the man particularly handsome, let alone dashing. His appearance had seldom entered my mind.

"Ma'am?" His smile didn't waver, nor did the amusement in his eyes. "Do I pass inspection?" I fumbled with the catch on the parasol to cover my embarrassment. He bounded up the stairs and took my arm. "You won't need the umbrella right away. Aunt Bea's carriage has a roof."

He whisked me down the stairs and across the yard to the stylish two-seater. He lifted me onto the black leather upholstered seat, then climbed in next to me. A wicked half-smile curved his lips. "Shall you drive, or shall I?"

I arched one eyebrow. "Please."

He flicked the reins over the back of the sleek ebony horse. The horse responded instantly. With one hand I clutched the armrest and with the other, the cookies, my bonnet, and the parasol, its shaft scraping against the front of the carriage.

James eased the parasol from my hand and placed it behind the seat, where a large basket rested. "Since you are so fond of picnics, I asked Aunt Bea to pack us a lunch. I hope you like leftover potato salad."

Along with the scent of the blossoming honeysuckle beside the road, I breathed in the pleasant aroma of shaving soap. Out of the corner of my eye, I could see a muscle flexing in the side of his face—James was as uncomfortable as I.

Despite the reference to the picnic Phillip and I had taken to Victoria, James had obviously gone to a lot of trouble to make everything nice. I could imagine my mother's voice telling me to be more gracious.

I touched his shirt sleeve. "That's a very nice shirt you're wearing. I don't think I've ever seen you wear it."

"I borrowed it from Ian this morning."

His taciturn answer left me confused. I searched for a reply. "Well, you look very handsome in it."

Sober faced, he attempted to return the compliment. "Thank you. And you, you look particularly fetching to-day."

Here we go again. I felt silly, like a child acting a part in a school pageant. *I've lived in this man's home for almost a year. We've discussed everything under the sun, short of personal hygiene and the rat infestation in London. I know more about his likes and dislikes than I know about my own brother's or father's. He is, by far, my best friend. Yet we're behaving like strangers. Particularly fetching? Oh, James.* A giggle escaped. I couldn't help myself. I hid my mouth behind a gloved hand and giggled again.

He reined the horse to a stop and set the brake. He didn't try to conceal his ill-humor. "What, may I ask, is so funny?"

At the peevish expression on his face that was so comical, I lost all self-control. I threw my head back against the seat and laughed aloud. I couldn't stop. The more I thought about the previous night's encounter and now, this morning's outing, the harder I laughed.

"What is so funny?" he demanded again.

Gasping, I pointed at his tense face. "You, me, this whole situation. It's ludicrous." Noting the crestfallen look on his face, I hastened to apologize. "Don't be insulted. I'm not laughing at you. I'm laughing at—" He stared incredulously as I dissolved into a fresh round of hysteria.

Somewhere in the middle of my second episode of laughter, he caught the humor of our situation. Beginning with a chuckle, James's mirth grew to match mine. The horse started to prance nervously, causing the carriage to jounce and sway unexpectedly. Weak from laughing so hard, I bounced against James. Still laughing himself, he caught me in his arms to steady me. My breath caught in my throat as I looked into his eyes. Somehow, I didn't feel like laughing anymore.

Pickles and Promises

James pulled firmly on the reins. "Whoa, boy, whoa." Aunt Bea's horse craned his neck toward the carriage, trying to see what might be delaying the journey. James turned to face me, his face serious. "Chloe, I meant what I said last night. I want to marry you."

"And I meant what I said. I won't marry you to give Jamie a new mother, as convenient as that may be for all concerned." I searched his eyes for answers to doubts I still hadn't voiced. "Remember when I told Jamie that no one could take his mother's place? The same goes for you. As much as I adored Mary, I can't and I won't be her substitute."

His face blanched, and he picked up the reins and urged the horse forward. "I'm not looking for a substitute anything, either a mother for my son or mate for me. If you remember right, I intended never to remarry."

I averted my eyes toward the passing grain field. "So what changed your mind?"

He tossed me a wry smile. "A certain freckle-faced redhead with green eyes and the most unpredictable sense of humor."

Before thinking it through I blurted, "Oh, James, I want to believe you. But frankly, it's too sudden, too convenient, like something out of a storybook." *How can I help you understand how I feel when I don't even know how I feel? And isn't love more than a feeling that's here today and gone tomorrow?*

I waited as James took a deep breath and released it slowly. "You're right. I'm going about this all wrong. You deserve a proper courtship."

"That's not it. We know each other too well to play childish games." I shook my head emphatically. "I simply need to be sure that you are thinking straight about me— about us. And maybe I need the same thing for myself. Marriage is serious business."

He stared ahead at the road, his face thoughtful. "Chloe, I can't pretend that I didn't love Mary Elizabeth or that I haven't missed her terribly . . ."

"Of course. I didn't mean—"

"And obviously the threat of your leaving caused me to reevaluate my position on several things." He glanced at me, then back at the road. "But please trust me enough to know that I would never ask you to marry me only to please my son."

I hid my smile behind a gloved hand. "But that's exactly what you did last night. Why the change?"

"You're not playing fair. I said what I did because I had no idea how you felt about me." He cleared his throat. "And I still don't know."

"I don't mean to play unfair. But I, I won't be buffaloed into anything. I've run ahead of God several times, and I can't risk doing it again on so important a decision."

James guided the horse to the side of the road near a grove of cottonwood trees edging Big Creek. After setting the brake, he hopped down and helped me from the buggy. His hands lingered on my waist.

"Chloe, I am not trying to rush you. I merely want to prevent you from leaving before we can find out where we stand with one another. If you leave Kansas now, we'll never know what might have been." He reached over the back of the seat, handed me a summer quilt, and grabbed a large basket.

Taking my arm, he led me to a grassy spot by the creek. As I walked beside him, I had to admit that what he said made sense. If I left for San Francisco with Phillip, I would never know for sure how I felt about James.

I'd never been so confused in my life. In escaping Emmett Sawyer, I had run ahead of the Lord—and I still bore the scars. I knew I didn't want to do that again. The happiness of three people—Jamie, James, and me—depended on my decision.

James set the basket on the ground. Together we spread out the quilt on the grass, and I settled myself in one corner. He knelt and raised the lid on the basket. "Are you hungry?"

My stomach tumbled at the thought of food, so I shook my head slowly. James dropped the basket lid and sat facing me. "Chloe, I . . ." Gently he touched my face, his eyes flooded with emotion. "Just tell me you'll give me a chance to win your heart. Give me time to prove to you that I love you for the beautiful woman you are in your own right."

Though his serious tone unnerved me, I resisted the urge to leap to my feet and run. Instead, I grinned at him. "You mean I'd be a good wife if I weren't so impetuous and stubborn, lacking the sense of a horsefly?"

"I never said—"

I chuckled. "Yes, you did, to Jamie after I broke my foot, remember?"

"I didn't mean—"

"But you said . . ."

"Chloe Mae Spencer, you have the most irritating ability to throw my own words back in my face." A thrill of fear mingled with wonder shot through me. Like steel bands, his fingers grasped my arms. "Yes, in spite of the fact you are impetuous, stubborn, and know how to unravel a romantic moment faster than a kitten can unwind a ball of yarn," he took a deep breath, "I love you! I want to spend the rest of my life proving that to you."

"I, I, I don't know what to say."

"Sh . . ." He released my arm and touched my lips with his finger. My breath caught in my throat. "Don't say anything," he whispered, his voice ragged with emotion. "All I'm asking is that you give us time." Leaning forward, he tenderly kissed the tip of my nose and hovered a breath from my lips. I closed my eyes in anticipation.

"No, I won't take unfair advantage of you."

My eyes blinked open; my face flushed with color. He turned and hauled the picnic basket across the quilt.

"I'll wait until you are certain of your love for me, if it takes forever." He opened the lid and peered inside. I couldn't see his face.

"And if I leave for California?" My voice broke.

He froze. The buzz of a honey bee filled the silence. In the back of my mind I could hear my mother's mantel clock ticking off the seconds. Finally James lifted a jar of potato salad from the basket and set it down in the middle of the quilt. After he took a deep breath, he stared into my eyes.

"The day you board the train for California, I will have your answer." He cleared his throat and reached into the basket for another container. "But for today, we are here together, so let's enjoy the good food Aunt Bea prepared for us."

He held up a jar of cucumber pickles. "Look, a jar of Aunt Bea's famous dill pickles. I so enjoy that woman's dill pickles. She wins blue ribbons at the county fair every year."

"She's a remarkable woman," I mumbled, removing my

gloves so I could help him serve the meal. I reached into the basket and withdrew a stack of honey-butter sandwiches. When he lifted a chocolate cake from the basket, I wailed, "There's too much food here! We could camp out for a week and never go hungry."

He laughed and placed a plate and napkin in front of me. "Well, I don't know about you, but I'm starving. Sleeping under trees all night works up an appetite."

I blushed. I still wasn't hungry. "I'm sorry."

He bit into a sandwich half and swallowed. "Hey, that was my choice, not yours."

I nibbled on a carrot stick. "Did anyone say anything to you this morning, about the noise and all?"

He laughed. "Aunt Bea had the picnic lunch ready for me when I came in for breakfast. I have no idea what time she got up to prepare it."

Our usually easy candor returned as we talked. My appetite returned. Before long we were laughing over the night's adventure.

"You should have seen yourself, talking to the empty window," I choked.

"I only wish I could have seen you scurrying around the back of the henhouse. It's a wonder those old birds didn't start squawking."

I laughed and reached for the pickle jar.

He reached for the jar at the same moment. His hands capped mine. "Here, let me loosen that cover for you."

I nodded. He held onto my hand, a smile formed at one corner of his mouth. "Do you know the first moment I recognized that I was in love with you?"

I shook my head slowly.

"The night you saved Honey's life. I ran in from the barn, took you in my arms, and said—"

" 'I could kiss you.' I remember."

"Standing there in the kitchen, face to face, I was

stunned to discover that I desperately wanted to kiss you—and not just for saving Honey's life. Then the day Saturn spooked, I couldn't believe your bravery. There you were, hanging on to the reins for your very life." He touched my hair at the nape of my neck. "Your hair was blowing in the breeze, illuminated by the sunlight." His voice grew husky, and he withdrew his hand. "After that, I would watch you bake bread in the kitchen, tussle with Jamie on the lawn, sit alone on the porch in the moonlight, and I'd fight against the truth growing inside me. And then the night playing hide-and-seek—that blew my defenses to smithereens."

He leaned back against a tree trunk, put his arms behind his head, and closed his eyes. "Yep, it sure feels good to finally admit it to myself and to you."

I watched the sunlight dapple his suntanned face. His breathing deepened into a snore. *I'm sure glad you're feeling so good. I'm a mess!*

While he dozed, I placed the leftover food in the basket, then collected the dirty dishes and carried them to the creek to rinse. Swooshing the dishes in the water, I glanced down at my shoes, then back over my shoulder. James had not moved.

Slipping out of my shoes and stockings, I dangled my feet in the water. The cold current calmed my spirit as my mind wandered over the past year and its changes. I thought of Jamie, then considered the future. *Can I actually wed Mary's husband? How will I feel when he talks about Mary fondly? Will I be resentful? Jealous? Where does Phillip come into all of this, or does he? And is all of this part of God's plan?*

I lay back on the grass and stared up at the horse-tail clouds floating by, my feet still submerged in the river. I closed my eyes and compared how I felt about James with my feelings for Phillip. James and I had built a year-long friendship. We'd weathered snowstorms, death, illness, political debates, flames, and snowball fights together. Somewhere, I'm not sure when, he'd become my confidant, my best friend. On the other hand, my relationship with Phillip Chamberlain was little more than a schoolgirl crush. *Perhaps another time, another place. . . .*

I felt rather than saw a giant shadow blot out the sun. Droplets of water splashed on my face. My eyes flew open in time to see the second shower falling. "Hey, what in the—"

Anticipating his next move, I bounded to my feet and dashed toward the carriage. James overtook me by the cottonwood tree, captured me in his arms, and looked down at me, his face now sober. As we faced one another, he stroked my head and shoulders. I gazed up into his face, mesmerized by the unfathomable look in his dark brown eyes. Then, without warning, he let go of my shoulders and stepped back. "It's time we head back to Aunt Bea's place."

I collected the dishes from the creek bank and put on my shoes and stockings while he folded the quilt.

On the ride home neither of us spoke. There was so much I wanted to say, but the words wouldn't come. I glanced up at the midday sun; there was still time to pack my belongings and board the westbound train for San Francisco. Suddenly I knew what I had to do.

When the carriage stopped beside the feed store, Aunt Bea's team of horses was already hitched to her wagon loaded with Phillip's luggage. As he helped me down from the carriage, James looked from the travel trunk, to me, then back again. Without a word, I ran up the outside stairs and into Aunt Bea's living quarters. I passed Phillip in the hall outside my bedroom door.

"Phillip, don't go yet. We need to talk." I ran into my room and removed the railroad ticket from the night-stand drawer.

I stared at the piece of paper. The words *San Francisco, California*, blurred before my eyes. "Oh, God, bless what I'm about to do."

Slipping the ticket into my pocket, I hurried back into the hall, where I'd left Phillip. He studied my face as I struggled to catch my breath. "You're not going with me, are you?"

I shook my head. "I can't, at least not now. I appreciate all you—"

"No," he interrupted, "don't apologize. I wish you the best. I considered staying over another day or two, but after last night, I knew it would be hopeless. Bad timing, I guess."

"Thank you for being so sweet about all of this."

His smile faded. "I'm not feeling particularly sweet at the moment," he said soberly.

"May I ride with you to the station?"

His face softened, and he nodded. "Before I leave, I need to thank my hostess for her hospitality."

"While you're doing that, I need to find James."

"Good luck." Phillip lifted one eyebrow. "He drove off in the carriage when you came inside."

My shoulders drooped. "Oh, well, I'll talk with him later, I guess. I'll wait in the wagon while you tell everyone goodbye."

Minutes later Phillip emerged from the house, along with Aunt Bea, Walter, and Ian. By the grins on their faces, I suspected Phillip had told them of my decision to stay. During the short ride to the depot, I asked Phillip to give my greetings to Joe and Cy. "And tell my big brother not to worry. I know what I'm doing."

At the railway station, I spotted Aunt Bea's carriage parked on the far side of the building but could see nothing of James. Behind us, the westbound train chugged to a stop, and Phillip tipped a waiting baggage man to load his luggage onto the train. Ian shook hands with Phillip, then volunteered to wait for me while I saw Phillip off.

"Thanks, but I'd rather walk home through the cornfield."

As Phillip and I strolled across the waiting platform, I glanced around, hoping to catch a glimpse of James. He was nowhere in sight. Beside the passenger car steps Phillip paused. "I wish I could talk you into coming with me."

"I know. Thank you for everything, Phillip. You're a good friend."

He reddened. "I'd hoped we could become more than just good friends."

I touched his sleeve. "Another time, another place, who knows what would have happened?"

When the conductor cried, "All aboard," Phillip lifted my hand to his lips. "May God be with you, Chloe Mae, and with that lucky man of yours." He stepped past the porter into the waiting passenger car and waved. The porter closed the door, steam hissed, and the giant locomotive inched forward. At that moment, panic rose inside me—by staying, I knew I'd made a decision that would affect the rest of my life. Choking back unexplained tears, I waved at Phillip until the caboose rattled past.

Blindly, I whirled about, smack into James's black silk shirt. "Going somewhere?" he asked, his dark eyes twinkling with happiness.

I looked up into his face and realized the moment had come. Slipping my hand into my pocket, I withdrew the ticket and placed it in his palm. "Here," I whispered, "I won't be needing this after all."

He glanced down at the ticket, and his breath caught. "Chloe," he gasped, taking both of my hands in his, "does this mean . . . ?"

I nodded slowly.

His eyes filled with tears. "Are you sure?"

Again I nodded. For a moment, I thought he intended to kiss me right there on the station platform. Instead, he glanced about at the audience we'd acquired. Placing my hand on his arm, he led me to the carriage.

After we'd climbed on board, I paused. "Wait, James, there's something we need to talk about right away." A look of concern swept across his face. I continued. "We've talked so many times about God. We've studied His Word together. We've argued. We've prayed." I searched James's eyes, praying for his understanding. "So I think you know why it's important to me to be certain we are letting God lead us."

He nodded slowly and took my hands in his. "When I asked Mary Elizabeth to be my wife, I was wildly and madly in love. I gave no thought to anyone but us. With you, I am older and better understand the obligations that go into a marriage relationship."

I waited, afraid he might say the very thing I'd accused him of earlier—that his decision to marry me was based on logic, not love. He knitted his brow. "My love for you has an added dimension." He searched for the right words. "My love is, is mingled with respect and admiration and most important, friendship. You've become vital to my happiness, Chloe."

James studied my face as he continued. "God's leading? I know without a doubt that it was no accident that brought you into our lives. I have no idea where He will lead us tomorrow, but as long as we continue to walk side by side, anywhere's all right with me. Does that answer your question?"

I nodded and sniffed back my tears. We rode in a companionable silence until we reached the corner where we'd turn to the feed store.

"I don't feel much like heading for Aunt Bea's right now."

"Me either."

As we headed out into the country, James glanced my way every now and then and grinned like a ten-year-old. At the deserted Adams' place, he looped the reins around the brake handle and suggested we walk down the overgrown pathway.

My arms encircled his neck as he grasped my waist and lowered my feet to the ground. James drew me close to him, searching my eyes as he spoke. "I love you, Chloe Mae Spencer."

I swallowed the lump in my throat. My words came in a barely audible whisper. "I love you too."

"Enough to become my wife?"

"Enough to become your wife and the mother of your children."

He crushed me into his arms, and I buried my face in his black silk shirt. After some time, James leaned back and tilted my face toward his. "When I saw you at the train station with Phillip Chamberlain, I was afraid you'd decided to leave with him. I was sure I'd lost you forever."

"No," I said softly, "I couldn't."

"Is it too soon to ask you again?"

I shook my head slowly.

He smiled and tenderly cupped my face with his hands. "Will you marry me?"

"Yes." I smiled up into his eyes. Strong, gentle hands drew me to him. His warm and reassuring kiss erased my past fears while confiding promises for our future. Unwillingly, he stepped back, one hand lingering on my neck. I kissed his hand, then took it in mine.

"What about Jamie? How are you going to tell him about us?"

James chuckled. "Oh, that shouldn't be difficult; he was

the first to suggest I come after you."

"Really?"

"Speaking about telling families, I want to receive your parents' approval before we get married. I plan to write to your parents as well as mine tonight so that the letters can be posted in the morning."

A warm peace filled my mind. Knowing that James wanted to do everything right assured me that our love had God's blessing. I remembered Bertha and Conrad Schnetzler, a couple I had met on the train to Chicago. Even after thirty years, her face glowed when she gazed down at her husband's sleeping form. *Will it be the same for us?*

I glanced toward James, trying to picture him with gray hair and early-morning stubble. The imagined image made me giggle. He eyed me questioningly. "What's so funny?"

I blushed. "It's hard to explain. I was just trying to picture you thirty years older."

"Thirty, forty, fifty years—a lifetime is ours to enjoy." Swinging me around to face him, he grabbed my other hand. My skirt billowed as we twirled like kids in the buffalo grass. "Come," James broke into a run toward the carriage and hauled me after him. "I want to tell the whole world that you've agreed to become Mrs. James Edward McCall."

When we burst into Aunt Bea's kitchen, James shouting the news of our engagement, Ian sat at the table reading the local newspaper. Drucilla stood beside Aunt Bea helping dish out bowls of chili. The two women squealed with delight while Ian glanced up from the paper, a look of total boredom on his face. "That's news? Drucilla and I have known for weeks that you loved one another. I'm glad you two finally figured it out."

James laughed and cuffed him on the shoulder. "My know-it-all big brother."

Drucilla moved protectively nearer Ian. "So when's the wedding?"

We looked at one another and shrugged. James winked at me. "We haven't discussed a date yet."

Ian stretched and folded the newspaper. "Well, I hope it's soon, little brother. I just got word from Putnam, our banker. He wants to meet me in Denver on September one to sign the title papers for the third mine."

James glanced at me. "Do you think we'll hear from your parents by then?"

Before I could answer, Aunt Bea came up behind me and put her arm around my shoulders. "You would if you sent a wire. That would give them plenty of time to respond with a letter."

"You know," Ian stroked his chin, then glanced up at his wife, "with Drucilla's being pregnant, you two could go instead of me and make it your honeymoon trip."

Aunt Bea gave me a squeeze. "I'd be glad to care for Jamie while you're gone. By the way, where is the child now?"

James laughed. "He spent the night in the bunkhouse with Sam and the boys. Today they were to take him out checking on the new calves. And of course, Minna is still there with him."

Ian stood and slapped James on the back. "Then it's settled, little brother. Mr. and Mrs. Putnam are members of Denver's upper crust, the 'sacred thirty-six.' They'll probably throw a dinner party in your honor."

Drucilla jabbed her husband in the ribs. "They'll be on their honeymoon, dear! Why would they want to attend a dinner party?" She leaned across the table, her eyes dancing with excitement. "You're going to love Denver. Ian has told me all about the 'Queen City of the Plains.' "

Birthday Surprises

July 6, 1899.

Dearest Ma and Pa,

By the time you read this letter, you will have received James's telegram. In spite of the unusual circumstances, James and I are eager to receive your blessing before we become husband and wife. . . .

I love him, Pa. You met him, Ma, so I know you can understand why. . . .

I went on to tell my parents about James's proposal. I also asked my father's forgiveness one more time. This time, however, I ended my plea with, "While I crave your forgiveness, I know my heavenly Father has forgiven me and has given me peace. Psalm 86:5 has been a blessing to me." I mailed the letter at the station on our way back to the ranch.

Jamie wasn't at the house when we arrived. Minna told us he'd gone out with the men and wouldn't be home until suppertime. When Minna learned of our engagement, she patted my hand and nodded her head knowingly. "It's about time you young-uns discovered what I've known all along."

James draped his arm around my shoulders. "You were right, Minna. There's no doubt about that." He turned to

107

me. "This is the woman who insisted I go after you. Between her and Jamie, I didn't have a moment's peace."

Self-conscious, I slipped my arm about James's waist. "I hope you're not sorry."

Kissing the tip of my nose, he responded, "Chloe Mae Spencer, if necessary, I plan to spend the rest of my life assuring you of my love. Now, if you will excuse me, I have business in the library. I believe Drucilla went up to her room to lie down."

"I hope she's all right. I'm worried about her; she's looking peaked." I looked up at James. "After I unpack my luggage, I'll see if she needs any help."

James and I walked to the library door. "If you see Ian, tell him I'm going over the ranch ledgers and can use his help." He kissed my cheek before I ran up the stairs to my room. Once inside, I threw open the curtains and raised the window.

My trunk and my valise sat at the foot of my bed. I laughed to myself as I unpacked my clothing. *How many times have I done this?* When I lifted the white wedding dress Ma had made for me months before, a thrill coursed through me. She made it for me after I ran away and before she knew about James. *Ma, did you sense when you met James that I would be needing the dress in the near future? No, probably not. You just sent it out of love.*

Reluctantly, I hung the dress in the wardrobe and closed the doors. After arranging the rest of my clothing in the bureau, I hurried down the hall to Drucilla's room and pressed my ear to the door. Hearing no sounds coming from within, I decided she must be sleeping, so I tiptoed back down the hall past Jamie's room.

I couldn't resist opening the door and peeking in at his private domain. The circus train from his Uncle Ian snaked back and forth along the length of the window seat. His lead Civil War soldiers marched in formation along the edge of his bookshelf. The Confederate button he'd found at the soddy held special honor in the center of the parade ground. I smiled to myself. *How will it feel the first time he calls me ma? Will he want to call me "Ma"? Or will I remain Chloe to him?*

I decided whatever he chose to call me would be all right. I closed the door and strolled down the hallway to the head of the stairs. The door to James's room stood partway open. Noticing that the library door at the foot of the stairs was still closed, I stepped inside the darkened room. Leaving the door ajar, I crossed to the window and tied back the lavender brocade draperies. Sunlight danced across the royal blue Oriental carpet at the foot of the bed, spilling onto the shiny light and dark oak parquet flooring. I pushed the lace panels aside and opened the window.

I trailed my fingers across the foot of the rosewood four-poster bed, examining each of the giant dusty pink-and-lavender cabbage roses as I walked. I glanced back at the matching Queen Anne chairs upholstered in lavender silk. I could almost imagine Mary sitting there with her feet elevated on the pettipoint footstool and sipping chamomile tea.

Still thinking of Mary, I strolled over to the headboard to study the six framed wildflower prints and the blue velvet ribbon of silhouette ovals over each of the marble-topped bed stands. At the sound of footsteps, I glanced toward the framed mirror, half-expecting to see Mary behind me.

James strode into the room behind me. Flustered, I sputtered an apology. "I didn't mean to invade your privacy. I came in to open the window, to air out the room. I really am . . ."

"Sh . . ." He slipped his arms around my waist. "It's all right. I don't mind."

Tears welled up in my eyes as I stared at our reflection in the mirror. I inched away from his touch. "It's almost as if she's still here," I whispered.

James handed me a clean handkerchief from his pocket. "Chloe Mae, I can't wipe the memory of Mary from my life. We will both have to live with that fact. As to Mary's personal items, her clothing has already been sorted and distributed; I plan to let Drucilla take what she wants of the other items, then pack the rest away in the attic for Jamie."

"I would never want you to stop talking to me about Mary. She was my friend too." I rested my hand on his arm. "And I think Drucilla would appreciate having something of her sister's. And now, to change the subject, I should see whether Minna needs help preparing dinner."

When Jamie arrived home that evening, James called him into the library. There, we told him of our decision to marry. The boy stared at the floor while James told him about our plans to honeymoon in Denver.

"Can I go too?"

James grinned at me, then knelt down in front of Jamie. "I think it would be best if you stay here with Minna. We won't be gone long."

The boy's face darkened, and he glared at me. "I don't want you to marry my dad! I don't want you to go away." Pushing away from his father, Jamie raced from the room. His feet pounded up the first flight of stairs and on to the attic.

Startled, James shook his head. "I don't understand. He was all in favor of the marriage the other day."

The child's outburst left me shaken. "Maybe we should reconsider our decision, at least until Jamie can come to terms with it."

James opened the center drawer of his desk, then slammed it shut. "Nonsense! He's a child. Let's continue on with our plans. Maybe he'll come around."

"I don't know . . ." I shook my head slowly.

James guided me toward the hallway. "I'll talk with him after dinner. By that time he should have calmed down."

I wanted to believe James. I wanted to believe that time would make everything all right, but I wasn't so sure. I still hadn't uncovered the incident that caused him to stop speaking for almost a year.

At the dinner table, James and Ian conversed about the newest mine in Colorado. Drucilla and Minna talked babies and morning sickness. I listened, glancing every now and then at the empty chair across from me. When Minna asked me a question, I snapped alert.

"I'm sorry. I was wool gathering. What was it you asked?"

Minna smiled. "That's all right, dearie. I just wanted you to reassure Drucilla that her appetite will come back, and with a vengeance."

I smiled at the expectant mother. "That's what they tell me, anyway."

"Take my word for it," Minna assured. "You'll crave the weirdest foods. Ian will turn green from the very thought."

I eyed the empty chair once more. In my imagination I could see the boy crouched behind the brown trunk, sobbing into his quilt. "Excuse me," I mumbled, "I think I'd better go check on . . ."

Minna placed her hand on my wrist. "Leave him be, child."

"He needs me . . ."

James glanced down the table at me. "Minna's right. He needs to be alone for a while."

I bit my lip to hold back the tears. With my fork, I picked at the serving of apple cobbler on my plate.

When the men excused themselves from the table, I

glanced pleadingly at James. "I'll go up and check on him in a few minutes," he assured me.

"James . . ." Minna stood and started stacking the dirty plates. "Maybe I should go. Jamie and I have become pretty close these last few days, you know. Just yesterday he told me how happy he was that you and Chloe might marry."

I turned toward the woman. "He said that?"

She nodded. "I don't think it was the idea of your marriage that upset him. It must have been something else you said."

"What?" James threw his hands into the air. "I told the boy we were getting married and would be honeymooning in Denver, that's all."

Minna raised an eyebrow. "And?"

Exasperated, James ran his fingers through his hair. "And? And nothing! He asked if he could go along, and of course, I told him No."

"Oh, James, that's what is bothering him." Minna shook her head and clicked her tongue. "You left him to come West. You and Mary left him to go back to Boston, and his mother never returned. Chloe, you've left him a number of times too." She gathered a stack of plates in her hands. "Even Ian and Drucilla have come and gone out of his life. And he's heard me talking about returning to Russia."

She bustled into the kitchen, calling over her shoulder, "The poor child! Is it any wonder the thought of you two leaving him for your honeymoon scares him?"

"The poor little boy," Drucilla wept into her table napkin. Drucilla wept a lot lately.

James and I stared guiltily at one another. He walked toward me, but I turned toward the hall door. I had to go to the child and reassure him. Ian reached out and stopped me. "Minna's right. Let her try."

James put his arm around my shoulders and drew me

out onto the front porch. The screen door slammed behind us as we strolled to the far end of the porch. I leaned against the porch post and stared at the western horizon.

"Why didn't I think of it? Of course he would be afraid. It makes sense." I shook my head from side to side. "I'm going to be a horrid mother!"

James tilted my chin up so that our eyes met. He smiled tenderly. "This is what being a parent is all about, Chloe. It's more than baking cookies and wiping dirty faces. You know that."

"I know."

"And you'll be a wonderful mother, love."

"I hope so." I buried my face in his shoulder. He wrapped his arms about me and held me for some time.

As the sun neared the horizon, James suggested, "Let's take a walk to the stream."

Taking my hand in his, we strolled down the steps onto the lawn. I glanced up toward the attic. A light glowed from the window. *Minna's still with him.*

When the last streaks of daylight faded, we circled back toward the house. Minna met us at the front door. "Jamie is up in his room. Perhaps you both should go see him."

James thanked Minna for her help, and together we climbed the stairs. Gently, I knocked. When I didn't hear a reply, I opened the door a crack. "Jamie, are you still awake? May we come in and kiss you good night?"

"Yes," a small voice whispered out of the shadows.

James knelt beside the pillow while I sat at the foot of the bed. "Son, remember when I went away to Boston? You thought I'd never come back, but I did."

"What about Mommy?" Jamie asked. "She never came back."

James stroked the child's head. "She wanted to—ever so much, but she was too sick. She couldn't help being sick."

"But why do you have to go away without me?"

James glanced toward me for support. I shrugged. "Well, son, someday you'll understand that parents don't take their children on their honeymoon."

The child persisted. "But why?" I fought back the urge to smile.

"Well," James hesitated, "new couples need some special time to get to know each other."

Jamie's scowl deepened. "But you know Chloe already, and she knows you too."

James rolled his eyes toward the ceiling. "Son, it's just the way it is. We'll be gone for a week. Minna will be here for you."

I leaned forward. "So will Sam. Maybe we can arrange to have Billy and Benny come over one day. Would you like that?"

The child sat up in bed. "And can they bring their ponies so we can go horseback riding together?"

"I'll ask Mrs. Paget for you."

James cast a look of relief my way, then returned his attention to his son. "Jamie, you are my son—forever. I know you're afraid we may never come back to you, but by God's grace, we will—I promise."

A tear trickled down Jamie's face and onto his pillow. "I'm sorry for what I said, Miss Chloe. Oops, I can't call you Miss Chloe anymore, can I?"

I grinned and patted his hand. "You can if you wish."

He thought for a moment. "May I call you just Chloe for a while?"

James started to speak, but I interrupted. "Sure, if you feel comfortable with that, so do I."

After Jamie said his prayers, we kissed him good night, stepped out into the hall, and closed the door. James took my hand and said quietly, "Chloe, don't you think it would be better for him to get used to calling you Mother, right from the start?"

"When he's ready, he will."

"I hope you're right." James shook his head.

During the next few weeks, I spent as much time as possible with Jamie. We built forts in the tall buffalo grass and defended them against enemy invaders; we collected herbs and dried them; we played tag on the lawn with the goats. Most evenings we sat on the porch and listened to James tell stories about growing up in Boston and about Jamie when he was a baby. Later, after Jamie went to bed, James and I would spend time together.

My birthday dawned scorchingly hot and muggy after a thunderstorm the night before. At breakfast, Minna announced that she was preparing a special picnic supper to enjoy by the creek. "I've invited Sam and the hands to come along, as well as Zerelda and her family."

"Ooh," Drucilla sighed with anticipation, "that sounds heavenly. My ankles are swelling the size of tree stumps."

"I have a few plans too," James added. "I need to drive into town, and I was hoping my son and my favorite gal might come along." He winked and grinned at Jamie.

Minna stood and wagged her finger at James. "Just a minute. You can go if you promise to be back here by five."

"Yes, ma'am." James acted suitably submissive.

After the meal, Drucilla insisted that she and Minna would clean up. I skipped up the stairs, two at a time. At the landing I pulled myself up short with the thought, *Not very dignified for an eighteen-year-old woman!* Sounds of the horses' clopping feet and rolling wagon wheels drifted in through the open windows. *Aw, who cares?*

I slipped into my coolest dress, grabbed my eyelet-trimmed bonnet, and bounded down the stairs and out the front door. Jamie waved to me from the back of the farm wagon. "Hurry, Chloe! Daddy said we can go to the park if we have time."

Catching a glimpse of James coming out of the carriage house, I slowed to a decorous walk. He helped me onto the wagon seat and climbed on board after me. As we rode, Jamie told us about the plans he and Bo had made for the week we would be gone on our honeymoon.

"Son, remember Bo has his own work to do too."

Listening to the father and son talk, I hugged the moment to me, like a dream that might slip away. *We're just like a family. No, we are a family!*

We went directly to town, where James treated us each to a phosphate at the drugstore. I laughed as Jamie slurped the icy concoction, his eyes wide with enjoyment. I remembered my first soda at the ice-cream parlor in Shinglehouse and the look of pure satisfaction on my father's face as I sipped the sweet, tongue-tingling liquid through the straw.

When James finished his drink, he excused himself to make a few purchases. After he returned, we moved next door to the general store. James handed the clerk the list of foodstuff Minna had requested and promised to return for it in an hour.

"Here, try one of these." The clerk handed me a rosy blushed peach. "Yesterday's train brought in a shipment of peaches from Georgia. Ready to preserve or eat."

I bit into the plump, juicy piece of fruit. "Umm!" I'd never tasted anything so delicious. I held the peach out toward James. "Here, take a bite."

"Playing Eve?" he teased as he sank his teeth into the succulent fruit.

"Wrong fruit." I blushed and handed the rest of the peach to Jamie to finish.

James told the clerk we'd take two bushels. When the clerk bent his head to add the peaches to our list, a wicked grin formed at the corners of James's mouth. "Can't prove that statement, can you?"

"Hmmph! We'll see about that!"

Jamie handed the pit to his father. "Can we go to the park, Daddy?"

"We have one more stop to make; then we'll go to the park," James replied.

We strolled along the boardwalk, gazing in the store windows as we passed. I paused in front of Mrs. Gowdy's Dress Shop. In the window, a dressmaker's form wore a gown of emerald green satin with ecru lace down the bodice. A matching feather hat, purse, shoes, and elbow-length gloves were displayed on the ledge in front of the dress. The accompanying sign read, "Come in today for your fitting for the Harvest Ball."

"This is the place." James took my elbow and steered me into the shop. A bell jangled as we pushed open the door, and a large-boned woman with frizzy blond hair peaked out from behind a yellow-striped curtain. "Mr. McCall, how are you today?"

"Millicent, I'd like you to meet my bride-to-be, Chloe Mae Spencer."

"We've already met." Millicent swept around the counter to where we stood. "Your aunt brought her in last year for a fitting. So, how are you doing, honey?" She lifted my arms and twirled me about slowly. "You look as lovely as ever."

I felt color creeping into my cheeks. "Thank you."

She patted my cheek and then turned toward James. "So, have you come for the dress?" She waved her hand toward the window. "As you can see, it's finished."

"Sure is beautiful."

"What dress?" I hissed at James.

"The one in the window, dear. I ordered it made for you the day you agreed to marry me."

Millicent bustled over to the window and removed it from the dummy. "Come on, sweetheart, let's see if it needs any alterations. I understand this is your eighteenth birthday."

I groaned and followed her into the back room. "Is there anything James didn't tell you?"

"Not much, actually."

As my cotton dress dropped to the floor, she slipped the green satin over my head. One by one, she fastened the tiny fabric-covered buttons up the back. Puffing the sleeves, she stood back to admire her work. "It fits perfectly, like a glove. Speaking of which . . ."

She dashed out into the store and retrieved the accessories from the window. While I slipped into the shoes, she fluffed up my hair and fastened the hat. I stood and looked in the mirror at a stranger. "It's, it's gorgeous . . ."

Beyond the curtain, James called, "Hey, when do we get to see it?"

I slipped on the gloves and walked out from behind the curtain.

James whistled and reached for my hands. "You look even more beautiful in it than I imagined."

Feeling conspicuous, I mumbled, "James, you shouldn't have."

"And why not?" He took one of my hands and twirled me around. "Jamie, my boy, isn't she the most stunning beauty west of the Great Lakes?"

"Yes, sir. You sure do look good, Miss Chloe, er, Chloe."

Realizing it was time to be gracious, I curtsied. "Thank you, kind sirs, for your gracious compliments."

"You will be the toast of Denver, Mrs. McCall-to-be."

Millicent grunted. "It's about time Hays' fashions hit Denver, instead of the other way around. Oh, by the way, here's the dress you left, Mr. McCall, for me to use for sizing."

I glanced at Mary's favorite pale-blue silk dress, then walked toward the back room. "I'd better change back into my everyday dress so we can go to the park."

At the park Jamie and I sat on one end of the seesaw while James rode on the other end. We squealed with mock horror when James kept us up in the air until we cried "pumpkin pie."

James took turns pushing both Jamie and me on the swings. All three of us slid down the slide. And after a dizzying ride on the merry-go-round, we headed back to the general store for our supplies and to the dress shop for the boxed dresses.

We stopped at the station for the mail, then drove to Aunt Bea's. While the men loaded the wagon, Jamie and I ran out to the barn to see Muffin and her current litter of kittens.

Jamie and I sat on the ground playing with the six fluffy creatures when James came around the corner. "Jamie, Aunt Bea says you can take one home with you, if you like."

The child's eyes lighted up. He snatched the tiniest kitten into his arms. "Oh, yes! This is the one I want. I call him Mutt." The gray-striped kitten yowled a protest.

"Come on, son, it's time to head home. We don't want to be late for Chloe's birthday supper."

Jamie thanked Aunt Bea for the kitten while James helped me into the wagon seat. Then Jamie hopped into the back of the wagon.

Aunt Bea touched my arm. "Chloe, before you go, I have a birthday gift for you." She handed me a small black-velvet box. "This was James's grandmother's. I want you to have it."

I opened the lid and gasped. Inside, a brooch watch surrounded by hand-tooled, silver filigree rested on a pillow of white satin. "It's beautiful. Thank you."

She stood on tiptoe and kissed my cheek. "Wear it in good health."

"Thank you. Thank you so much." I slipped the velvet box into one of the dress boxes for safekeeping.

She stepped back, away from the wagon. "See you in two weeks for the wedding."

Guests, Invited and Otherwise

Jamie leapt from the wagon before the wheels stopped rolling. "Look, look, Aunt Minna," he called. A terrified Mutt dangled from his hand as he ran.

Minna stepped out onto the porch and waved. Wiping her hands on a towel, she bent down to inspect the newest member of the family.

James brought in the groceries while I carried the dress boxes upstairs. I placed the box containing Mary's dress on James's bed, then hurried to my own room. When I lifted the top off the box, the breeze through the window ruffled the tissue paper. The satin rustled when I held the dress up in front of me to admire in the mirror. The vibrant green satin deepened my fiery red hair to a rich auburn hue. Opening the velvet box, I held the brooch up to the neck of my new dress, admiring the silver filigree.

At the sound of horses racing into the yard, I ran to the window to see Sam and the other men leap from their horses and stampede into the house. "They're comin'. They're comin'!" Sam shouted.

I peered down the road and saw no one, only a white cloud bank filling the western sky. Along with the approaching cloud came a high-pitched hum. *Tornado? Hurricane? What?*

I ran down the stairs onto the porch, where Sam stood

with James, Minna, and Ian, pointing toward the fast-approaching cloud. "Hurry, grab every quilt, every blanket, even your petticoats, ladies. Cover the garden plants and the shrubs. Jamie," Sam shouted at the stunned boy watching from the doorway. "Close every window and door in the house and in the bunkhouse and barn!"

James and Ian burst past me, down the steps, and toward the barn. Already, I could see Bo and Darcy stabling the horses while the rest of the men grabbed shovels to dig a trench around the house and the barn.

"What is it? What's happening?"

Minna pointed toward the sky. "Grasshoppers!" I stared at the glistening white cloud. The sunlight reflected off millions of insects wings, like a delicate veil separating the earth from the sun. "Quick!" she shouted. "Go gather twigs and wood—anything that will burn—and dump it into the trenches."

Drucilla stuck her head out of an upstairs window. "What's happening?"

"Grasshoppers! Help Jamie close the windows, then stay inside." I ran into the house, taking the stairs two at a time. By the time I reached my room, I'd unbuttoned my dress. It fell to the floor, followed by my crinolines. I hauled my brother's breeches out of the bottom drawer of my dresser and put them on, along with Pa's shirt. I put on a pair of my old work boots that Ma had included in the trunk from home and bounded down the stairs. *Oh, dear Father, help us. Please help us.*

By the time I ran out the front door, some of the men were carrying armloads of dried wood to the newly dug trench. "What good will this do?" I shouted as I dumped my first load.

"Hopefully," Ian replied, "the smoke and the fire will keep the grasshoppers from landing inside the circle and devouring every living plant around the house."

I wiped away the sweat trickling down the sides of my face. "What about the crops?"

"I knew this year's crop was too good to be true." He shrugged and went in search of more firewood.

I'd just dumped my eleventh armload of tinder when James shouted, "Light the fires. Here they come."

Instantly, the men threw lighted matches on the kerosene-doused wood. Snakes of fire spread along the ditch until the blaze encircled the house and barns. We ran for the house and up the stairs to the second-floor windows, where we watched millions of grasshoppers drop to the earth, like enormous snowflakes. Their weight snapped off small tree limbs. The cornstalks crumbled beneath the devouring hoard. Their sheer volume smothered the fire in the trench.

The sound of the insects crunching their way across the lawn, leaving denuded trees and bushes in their wake, filled the air. James groaned and leaned against the windowsill. "Gone! Everything's gone."

I put my arm around his waist, as much for my own comfort as his. We held onto one another until the insects had marched on toward the east. The Confederate renegade William Quantrill and his bandits couldn't have left the area more devastated than this omnivorous army. Not only did the grasshoppers strip all the vegetation bare, but they fouled wells, streams, and ponds, as well.

The words, "There shall no evil befall thee; neither shall any plague come nigh thy dwelling," played over and over in my mind. *I don't understand, Lord. You promised if we trusted in You, these things wouldn't happen to us. Where are You when we need You?*

Defeated, I helped Ian and James collect the quilts and blankets we had spread over the plants in what had been our kitchen garden. Beneath the covers, the produce had been devoured to the ground. Minna sputtered as we shook the quilts and aired them on the clothesline. "Looks like we'll be having a washing bee tomorrow morning!"

James paced back and forth on the side porch, staring out at the barren prairie. "It's gone! Everything is gone."

Ian walked over to his brother. "Not really. With a little rain, the grass will come back. We'll buy extra feed for the cattle this winter, but we'll survive." Ian threw his arm around James's shoulder. "Come on, let's go inside and eat a slice of the strawberry-cream birthday cake Minna worked on all morning."

Minna brightened. "We're going to have our picnic anyway, on the dining-room floor. We'll move the table and chairs to one side and spread out tablecloths on the carpet."

Jamie bounced up and down beside Minna. "May I help blow out the candles?"

She grinned and glanced over at me. "That's up to the birthday girl, don't you think?"

He danced to my side. "May I, Chloe? May I?"

"I'll think about it. In the meantime, why don't you go down to the barn and tell the men there's a party brewing?"

"Yippie!" Jamie bounded down the steps and across the yard. The rest of us headed inside to wash and change clothing.

In spite of the tragedy, we found ourselves laughing during supper over some of the events.

Sam pointed at Minna. "I thought I'd die laughin' when you did the jig out there."

"Well," the woman huffed, "you'd dance too if you had one of those nasty creatures crawling down the back of your dress!" The image of Sam dancing in a calico dress produced a gale of laughter.

Minna's smile faded. "This wasn't the worst grasshopper attack I've seen since I arrived in Kansas. That was in 1878. Farmers reported the pests were four inches deep in some places." She took a sip of apple cider. "Many

farmers gave up and moved on afterward. We'll probably
lose a few families this time too."

James turned to Sam and Ian. "I suppose we'd best go
into town tomorrow and report the damage. Aunt Bea will
want to order extra grain."

The men continued talking while Minna rose to her feet
and slipped out of the room. She returned with a cake
ablaze with candles of all sizes. "All right, that's enough
talk about grasshoppers and ruined crops. This is Chloe's
eighteenth birthday. Let's sing happy birthday to her."

Jamie helped me blow out the candles as promised.
Minna's rich, creamy frosting took the edge off our dis-
couraging afternoon. When I told her so, she confided, "It's
made with goat's milk."

I choked on my last forkful. "No! That's impossible."

She grinned devilishly. "Ask Jake." I glanced over at
the hired hands sitting together along the outside wall.
Jake winked at me and smirked.

The hall clock gonged midnight before James carried
his son upstairs to bed. After sending Drucilla upstairs to
bed, Ian insisted on helping Minna and me clean up the
dining room and rinse and stack the dishes in the kitchen
sink. Ian joined me in urging Minna to leave the dishes in
the sink.

I called after her from the bottom of the stairs, "The
dishes will still be there in the morning. As my ma used to
say, 'Dirty dishes are your best friends; they never leave
you.'"

Minna looked back over her shoulder. "I don't think she
meant that as justification for indolence."

I laughed. "Maybe not, but it sure works for exhaustion,
doesn't it?"

I wandered through the downstairs rooms, blowing out
the lantern flames as I went. *Neither shall any plague . . .*
I shook my head to dislodge the thought. *God has let me*

down. I trusted Him, and He let me down. When I arrived
back at the foot of the stairs, I resisted the urge to take one
last glimpse at the devastation. Instead, I hurried to my
room. I didn't read my Bible that night. I didn't kneel to
pray. As I slipped beneath the cool muslin sheet, a cold
chill permeated my tired body from the inside out. Like a
child refusing to believe the truth, I squeezed my eyes
shut and pounded the pillow beneath my head.

The cleanup began early the next morning. As soon as
the men finished chores, Bo and Shorty cleaned the well.
Ian, Sam, and James headed to town on horseback. I gave
Jamie permission to help Darcy and Jake rake up the
dead grasshoppers decomposing in the August sun. Drucilla
fussed about being useless while Minna and I washed all
the soiled bedding and hung it out to dry.

The men returned from town to report that the grasshoppers had eaten a wide swath of devastation across
the entire county. They followed the depressing announcement with one of a different nature. The news of the
tragedy had spread across the Midwest with the swift-
ness of the Union Pacific. The telegraph agent at the
railway station was busy receiving messages from
farmers north and south of Ellis County, promising shipments of hay and grain to needy farmers. Help was
promised from as far away as Omaha, Nebraska, and
Dallas, Texas.

"I've never before seen people work together like this."
James shook his head in amazement. To myself, I said, *It's
lucky somebody cares in this God-forsaken place! God-
forsaken? Can a place be God-forsaken? The famous explorer Zebulon Pike thought so. After last night, I'm beginning to think the explorer might have been right.*

Minna puffed with pride at James's statement. "That's
the way of the prairies, young man. We call it 'being
neighborly.' "

James laughed. "That's what Aunt Bea said."

"Good woman, that Beatrice McCall," Minna muttered, padding out the back door to check the quilts drying on the line.

"You'd better get them in soon," Ian warned. "Old Simon, the barber, predicted a thunder boomer tonight."

As promised, the rain came—cool, refreshing rain that pounded against the barren ground. By the end of the week, green sprouts of buffalo grass broke through the sod. Because the garden flowers had been devoured by the grasshoppers, Minna insisted on making me a bouquet of paper roses for the wedding. I watched her dip sheets of parchment paper in warm tea and lay them out to dry.

"The delicate ecru color will contrast nicely with your white gown," she explained. "I'll add a ruffle of matching lace and pink satin bows, and you'll have a posey that will never fade."

On August 30, the morning of the wedding, Drucilla insisted I take a long, relaxing bath using her lemon verbena bath salts. Downstairs, I could hear Ian and Sam moving furniture around in the parlor to make room for our wedding guests. Sarah Reinhardt, a neighbor of Aunt Bea, sat at the pump organ, wheezing out the notes of the "Bridal Chorus."

As I passed from the bathing room to my room, I could hear Zerelda and Minna arguing about the centerpiece for the table. I dried my hair as best I could with the Turkish towel, then tried to write a letter to Hattie. Restless, I paced to the window and back again to the wardrobe. I didn't like being confined to the second floor. I checked and rechecked my traveling case to be certain I'd packed everything I'd need on the honeymoon.

When I thought I couldn't stand the isolation any longer, Jamie burst in, carrying a copy of *Pilgrim's Progress*. He shoved the book into my hands. "Aunt Drucilla said I'm getting underfoot and that I should ask you to read to me."

"Why aren't you playing with Billy and Benny? I heard Mrs. Paget's voice in the dining room."

Jamie plopped himself in the middle of my bed. "Mr. Paget is bringing them later when he comes for the wedding."

Hopping onto the bed beside him, I opened the book and began to read. We had just reached the Slough of Despair when Aunt Bea burst into the room. "Oh, darling, isn't this a perfectly beautiful day? 'Happy the bride the sun shines on,' you know. So why aren't you getting dressed? Your guests are beginning to arrive."

I glanced toward Jamie. "Maybe Billy and Benny are here now."

Aunt Bea nodded. "Yes, I saw the Paget wagon pulling in right behind me."

Jamie leapt from the bed and bounded from the room, all interest in reading forgotten.

"Here's an envelope James insisted I give to you." Aunt Bea handed the large brown envelope to me. I recognized my mother's delicate scroll immediately. I worried my bottom lip as I tore open the envelope. A bouquet of notes tumbled out onto the bed along with the hated coin.

Tears slid down my face as I pushed the coin aside and opened each of the notes. My brothers and sisters had each written a message or drawn a picture for me for my wedding day. Only Pa's message was conspicuously absent.

Aunt Bea rocked in the rocker by the window while I located my mother's message.

My dearest daughter Chloe,

What a delightful surprise your telegram was, as was the letter you wrote soon after, regarding your engagement and wedding. If I had to pick a son-in-law, I couldn't have done better. James was so considerate to stop here on his way West. Even Ori talked about the handsome stranger for days after he left. Please, darling, tell your young man that Pa and I give our wholehearted blessing to this union. My only regret is that I can't be there to witness your beautiful day.

Happy eighteenth birthday, darling. Remember your birthday verse in Proverbs 31:12. It is a prophecy, my daughter. While Pa refused to write a letter (you know how stubborn he can be!), he did insist I include the gold coin. Before you become discouraged, take a closer look at it. And now, my darling, be happy together. Our prayers are ever with you.

Lovingly, your mother and father,
Annie and Joseph Spencer.

I picked up the coin and turned it over to study the face. *Something's different—the date! It's not the same coin! Pa didn't return the same coin but instead gave me a different gold piece to commemorate James's and my marriage.* Tears trickled down my cheek. *Why does he find it so hard to say, "I forgive you"?*

My stomach lurched. Though I hadn't eaten since breakfast, it wasn't food I wanted—it was peace of mind. Ma's letter had both eased my fears and stirred them up. I glanced at the Bible on the night stand, where it had remained unopened since my birthday. I longed to read Proverbs 31:12 to see what my birthday text might be, but memories of God's desertion surfaced in my mind.

I sighed. *Why do I take two steps forward in faith and three steps backward?* Slipping the coin and the notes back into the envelope, I put them in my valise. I sniffed and glanced over at Aunt Bea. "They're from my family. I think I'll read them later, on the train to Denver."

Aunt Bea stood, placed her hands on her hips, and tilted her head to one side. "So, how can I help you, child?" Before I could reply, she eyed the tangle of curls tumbling around my shoulders and grabbed my brush from the top of the dresser. "Come, sit here on the footstool while I brush your hair. Drucilla is bringing us a curling iron. We'll heat it over the kerosene lamp."

I laughed and held out a handful of hair. "Curls? I hardly need more curls."

"Hush, child, the woman knows what she's doing." Aunt Bea beckoned me over to the footstool, and she sat behind me on the rocker. "Such beautiful hair. Did you inherit it from one of your parents?"

"From my father's side." Aunt Bea lifted the hair off my neck to brush from underneath. "You're lucky you aren't my daughter. You would have inherited either thin, dishwater blond hair from my husband or straight brown hair from me."

I smiled up into her face. "I'm sure that's the worst trait I'd inherit from you, Aunt Bea."

"Oh, now don't go sweet-talkin' an old woman."

Drucilla knocked on the door with one hand and instantly opened it with the other. "My, my, you still aren't dressed?" She threw open the doors to the wardrobe and spread my dress and my chemise out on the bed. "You will, of course, need something old, Grandma's brooch; something new, the dress; something borrowed, my white satin slippers; and something blue. What can you carry that's blue?"

"I have something blue right here." Aunt Bea reached into her purse and handed Drucilla a linen handkerchief with blue-lace trim. "Do you have a sixpence for her shoe?"

Drucilla handed me my new camisole and corset. "We can do without that part of the tradition since this is Kansas, not Londonderry."

"What are you two talking about?"

Drucilla stared at me with disbelief. "Good luck, child. Good luck. I even have a tiny pouch of rice for you to carry in your glove."

"Rice?"

Drucilla clicked her tongue. "To guarantee you many sons."

I peeked around the edge of the screen. "What about daughters? Do I need to carry wheat or something?"

Drucilla rolled her eyes toward the ceiling. "The rice works for girls too."

"Well, I'm glad to hear that." I laughed and ducked back behind the screen.

A moment later Drucilla peered over the top of the screen. "Come out here and let us lace that corset."

I stepped out from behind the screen. "Tighter? I can't breathe as it is."

"It can't be helped." Aunt Bea ordered me to take a deep breath while she tugged on the laces. When I was certain I'd never be able to take a deep breath again, she patted my arm. "There, that should do it."

Zerelda entered the room in time to see the two women lower my wedding gown over my head. "Oh, Chloe," she gasped, "it's beautiful. I can't believe that your mother embroidered each of these silk daisies by hand."

As the soft folds of the dress settled down around me, I could smell the aroma of Ma's favorite perfume, lily of the valley. I piled my hair on top of my head while Zerelda and Aunt Bea buttoned the tiny pearl buttons at my wrists and Drucilla took charge of the ones up the back.

When the last button was fastened, the women stepped back so I could see myself in the mirror. A row of delicate tatted lace edged the high-necked collar. Matching lace and strings of silk embroidered daisies ran in alternate rows from the neckline to my waist. The cuffs went from my wrist to my elbow, where the sleeves puffed to my shoulders. The skirt fell in graceful folds around my ankles.

My eyes misted. *If only Ma were here to see this moment. If only Hattie . . .*

"Sit down, Chloe," Drucilla ordered. "I want to style your hair into ringlets. My mother used to do this with Mary's and my hair every Sunday morning."

First fastening the ringlets atop my head with combs and hairpins, Drucilla then circled my face with a halo of whisper-thin ringlets. While Zerelda and Aunt Bea sighed appropriately, Drucilla stood back and examined her masterpiece from various angles. "Aunt Bea, would you go to my room and fetch the veiling on my bed?"

"Veil? I don't know anything about a veil," I protested.

"Hush, this curl by your right ear refuses to hang right." She moistened the hair with water from the washbasin, then wrapped the strand around her finger.

Aunt Bea returned with a confection of white veiling like I'd seen only in catalogs and ladies' magazines. Drucilla clustered the veiling on my head and pinned it in place. She snapped her fingers toward Zerelda. "The bouquet. Where's the bouquet?"

Zerelda stepped into the hall and returned with Minna's paper-flower creation. The three women stepped back to admire the finished product and gasped in unison. Drucilla pointed at my feet. "Your shoes! You forgot to put on your shoes and stockings."

"Oops!" I wriggled my bare toes and grinned. Minna came running up the stairs to tell us the preacher from Victoria had arrived.

I wrestled with my cotton hose, stepped into the white slippers, and took a deep breath. "I'm ready," I whispered.

"Here." Drucilla handed me a pair of white lace gloves and held the bouquet while I slipped them onto my hands.

Aunt Bea kissed my cheek, then lowered the veil over

my face. "Be happy, child. Be happy."

My friends escorted me to the landing, where Zerelda called to Jamie. Jamie stepped from his father's room, his hair slicked down and his boots polished to a high shine. He had been delighted when I had asked him to walk me down the aisle. The child stepped out of his father's bedroom and proudly extended his arm to me.

"Wait until the three of us are in the parlor before you start down the stairs," Zerelda warned.

Jamie nodded solemnly. Knowing Zerelda, he'd been reminded of his duties several times during the previous hour. The women each blew me a kiss, then descended the staircase. The organist switched from a brutalized rendition of "Annie Laurie" to the "Bridal Chorus." I glanced at Jamie, he at me.

"This is it, cowboy," I whispered.

He looked up at me and grinned. "Careful on the stairs. You don't want to stumble, Mom." *Mom, he called me Mom!*

Fresh tears sprang into my eyes, and I bit my lip to keep from crying. "I love you, Jamie."

His grin widened. "I love you too."

We walked down the stairs and into the parlor. Smiling faces greeted us—Shorty, Sam, Zerelda, Amy, Darcy, Aunt Bea, Bo. As I approached, they cleared an aisle for me. I spotted a short little man who I assumed was the preacher.

My paper bouquet shook in my hand. I hesitated a moment. *Oh, Father, please help me. I know I love James, and he loves me, but right now I'm so afraid.* I glanced down at Jamie. He threw me a broad smile. I looked ahead of me down the neighbor-lined aisle. Drucilla and Ian, our matron of honor and best man, stood on each side of the smiling minister.

As Jamie urged me forward, James stepped out into

the aisle and faced me. He wore the gray woolen suit he'd worn the day he returned from Boston. I'd never seen him look so handsome. His eyes glistening with tears drew me to him.

As I took tentative steps forward, he came to meet me. With all the decorum of a wizened lawyer, Jamie lifted my hand from the crook of his arm and placed it in his father's hand. Then the child sidled up to Aunt Bea.

Tenderly, James bent and kissed my fingertips, then placed my hand on his arm. We took two steps forward, standing toe to toe with the preacher.

"Dearly beloved, we are gathered here . . ." The minister's voice faded. I felt lightheaded. Tiny pinpoints of light danced before my eyes. I licked my parched lips, focusing my eyes on the minister's mouth, since I couldn't hear his words. I must have swayed, for James looked down at me.

"Are you all right?" he whispered. Quickly he took my right hand in his and encircled my waist with his left arm, drawing me to his side. "If you need to, lean on me."

James had no idea how much I needed to hear those words. While I needed his physical strength, I needed his spiritual and emotional strength as well.

"Do you, James Edward McCall, take this woman, Chloe Mae Spencer, to be your lawfully wedded wife?" At the mention of our names, my mind began to clear. I looked up into James's soft brown eyes. ". . . and cherish her till death do you part?"

There was no hesitation in his answer. "I do." His firm, mellow voice comforted me.

The minister continued. "And do you, Chloe Mae Spencer, take this man, James Edward McCall, to be your . . ." I blinked back my tears as I gazed into my husband-to-be's eyes. ". . . and cherish him till death do you part?"

My reply came out in a husky whisper. "I do."

I could hear the minister continuing with the ceremony, but I only saw James. "By the powers vested in me by God and the state of Kansas, I now pronounce you husband and wife."

High Society

Mr. and Mrs. James McCall. Mr. and Mrs. James McCall. The words swirled through my brain as family and neighbors engulfed us. Drucilla straightened my veil while Ian tried to clear a pathway through the crowd of well-wishers. The organist tried her best to play the "Wedding March," but no one was marching—no one was going anywhere.

The temperature in the parlor must have hovered somewhere near one hundred. I couldn't breathe. Men I hardly knew were kissing me. Older women were pinching my cheeks and sobbing. Suddenly a voice at the far end of the room bellowed, "Clear an aisle for Mr. and Mrs. McCall. There will be a receiving line on the front porch, where punch and cake are also being served." I peered over the heads of our guests to see the diminutive Minna standing on a footstool.

"Punch and cake" must have been the magic phrase, for Minna barely stepped off the footstool before the crowd swept out of the room, leaving only the immediate family behind. Drucilla and Aunt Bea kissed me while Ian and Jamie congratulated James. Once we'd exchanged kisses all around, James scooped Jamie into his arms, took my hand, and led me out onto the porch.

We cut the foot-high wedding cake Minna had spent the

morning decorating, then mingled with our guests as Minna and Zerelda served the cake.

Later, when the crowd finally thinned, each of the ranchhands shook James's hand and kissed mine. Bo blushed and stammered his congratulations. Sam started to kiss my hand, but changed his mind and kissed my cheek. "Forgive me, Miss Chloe, but you are the closest I'll ever have to a daughter, I s'pect."

Then to James he said, "I hope it's all right, boss, but Mr. Ian promised the men the night in town to celebrate the doings. They've worked hard these last few weeks, cleaning up after the hoppers and all."

James smiled. "That's a good idea, Sam. I should have thought of it myself."

Sam grinned. "We'll be back in time for mornin' chores, so don't worry none."

"Sam, I never worry with you in charge. You're one top-notch foreman."

"Thanks, boss." Sam tipped his hat to me and ambled down the steps toward the bunkhouse.

As the last carriage pulled out of the yard, I leaned my head back against James's chest. He brushed his lips across my ear.

"Hold on, you two lovebirds." Aunt Bea bustled out the front door. "I just want you to know Jamie is upstairs packing a valise. If it's all right with you, he's decided to come home with me for the night."

James grinned and kissed his aunt. "You're a real gem, Beatrice McCall."

"She sure is." Ian and Drucilla joined us on the porch. "And we're going with them. I've convinced Dru to see a doctor tomorrow, just to be certain everything's all right with this baby. We'll ride in with Aunt Bea, then when you leave for Denver tomorrow, we'll bring your carriage back to the ranch."

"Oh." Aunt Bea's eyes twinkled with mischief. "Minna is spending the night at Zerelda's place, so I guess you two will have the ranch to yourself."

I blushed and averted my eyes.

Drucilla brushed a kiss on my cheek and whispered, "Be ready for a shivaree."

"A what?"

She darted a glance over her shoulder at Ian, then back at me. "A shivaree," she hissed. "It's the custom here in Kansas."

It was shortly after midnight when I discovered the meaning of the term *shivaree*. James and I awoke to a horrendous clanging outside. Lights danced on the ceiling over our bed, as if a huge bonfire burned outside our window.

"Prairie fire!" James leapt from the bed, rushed to the window, and leaned out. A clamor of voices, bells, and clanging pots greeted him. "What in the world?" He threw back his head and laughed. I tossed back the covers and ran to his side.

Below our window were a dozen lanterns and twice as many people. They were banging pans, shouting, whistling, and ringing school bells.

"Yeah!" Zerelda shouted. "Three cheers for the happy couple!" The crowd complied.

Ian yelled. "Come on, you two. We won't go until you feed us." Again the crowd shouted and clanged their noisemakers.

A voice I didn't recognize shouted, "Let's kidnap the bride!"

I grabbed hold of James, envisioning being thrown across the back of a horse and dragged across the prairie. "James, do something."

He laughed and squeezed my waist. "No one's going to take you from me, my sweet. But I do think we'd better give them something to eat, or they may keep up this racket all night long."

James lighted a lantern, and I threw on my dressing gown and brushed my hair back from my face. At the bottom of the stairs, I left James to open the front door while I hurried to the kitchen to see what grub I could rustle up.

Our friends surged into the house, hollering and banging their noisemakers. Zerelda led the way past James into the kitchen. Minna had already sneaked in through the back door during the commotion.

When she saw the look of panic on my face, Minna laughed. "Don't worry about a thing. I have all the goodies stashed in the pantry. And your guests brought the cider. What else do we need?"

I stood in the middle of the kitchen, bewildered. "What is all this?"

Zerelda grabbed my arms and whirled us about the room. "This, my dear, is a Kansas shivaree! We're here to serenade the bride and groom."

I paused to catch my breath. "So that's what Drucilla tried to warn me about before she left."

"Yes, and Ian was furious with me for warning you." I whirled about to see Drucilla standing in the doorway. "He fussed all the way to town."

The party lasted until three in the morning, when all the partyers except Ian and Drucilla had straggled home. Ian thumped his brother on the back. "Well, we'd better head back to Aunt Bea's. She decided to stay with Jamie and leave the celebrating to the rest of us."

I glanced at Drucilla and noted the dark circles under her eyes and her pale complexion. I sidled over to James and slid my arms around his waist. Then I looked over at Ian. "Why don't you and Drucilla stay here the rest of the night? It's too late to drive back to town now."

James gazed lovingly down at me. "She's right, Ian. Go on up to bed, and we'll see you at breakfast."

Drucilla smiled gratefully at us. "Are you sure you don't mind?"

"Mind? We insist."

Ian hugged his brother, then guided Drucilla up to their room. I gazed about the kitchen strewn with cookie crumbs, spilled cider, and dirty dishes. I sighed and shook my head. James drew me into his arms. "Aren't you glad it's our wedding day and no one expects us to clean up this mess?"

"But I can't leave—"

James lifted his eyebrow. "Aren't you the one who told Minna something about dirty dishes being your best friends?"

"But, I can't expect—"

His lips came down on mine, and I melted into his embrace. All thoughts of dirty dishes fled my mind. As he straightened, he whispered, "I have finally found a way to get in the last word."

"Oh!" I wriggled to break free of his grasp. Instead, he swung me into his arms and carried me up the stairs to our room, pausing long enough to turn down the wicks on the lamps as we passed.

I awakened to a gloriously sunshiny morning. James sat in one of the Queen Anne chairs, pulling on his boots. I smiled and stretched. "Good morning, sweetheart."

He looked up, then crossed the room in three long strides. "Sh, it's early yet. Go back to sleep. I need to give a few last-minute instructions to Sam before we leave for Denver. He and the men plan to take feed out to the herd."

James had a large herd of black Angus cattle. With the pasture devoured by insects, the men needed to haul hay and grain to keep the animals alive.

"I should get up and . . ."

"Just go back to sleep. If you're worrying about mess in the kitchen, Minna was here at dawn. All the work is done."

"James, why didn't you tell me?"

He kissed the tip of my nose. "Hey, I didn't know anything about it until I went downstairs a half-hour ago. So, now you have no excuse for not going back to sleep."

Feeling deliciously indulged, I yawned, stretched, and allowed myself to be coaxed into going back to sleep.

"Sleep, my love." James threw me a kiss and strode from the room.

I arose midmorning and puttered about. When I was about to close my valise, my gaze rested on the Bible Aunt Bea had given me. *Oh, well, might as well take it along.* I stuck it in the top of my case and clasped the bag closed.

The hall clock gonged twelve. I glanced at the brooch watch pinned to my bodice and smiled—right on the minute. Taking one last look about the room, I hurried downstairs to help Minna with lunch. A short time later, James and Ian returned to the house, and Drucilla joined the four of us at the table. After we finished eating, I insisted on helping Minna clean up the dishes while the men loaded our luggage into the carriage.

When we were alone in the kitchen, I asked Minna, "Have you reconsidered going back to Russia?"

She wrung out the dishcloth and turned to wash the surface of the table. "I don't know. But I do know I can't take advantage of your husband's hospitality indefinitely."

"Take advantage? Minna, you've made yourself indispensable to all of us, not the least to Jamie. Besides, look around you." I leaned across the table toward her. "This is a big house. I can't take care of this place alone. Even with Zerelda coming in two or three times a week, I had my hands full."

"Yes, and now with Zerelda in the family way, she will

be pretty busy with the twins and her new baby."

"Pregnant? No! She never told me."

Minna laughed. "She didn't tell me either, but an old woman like me knows."

James popped in the back door. "Are you ready to go?"

Speechless from Minna's announcement, I nodded.

James eyed me curiously. "Do you have a bag other than the one I carried out? Is something wrong?"

I shook my head. "Oh, I need to get my cape and my bonnet upstairs."

He grinned and shook his head. "They're already in the carriage, as are Drucilla and Ian. So if you're ready . . ." His eagerness to leave proved contagious. He planted a kiss on Minna's cheek. "Thanks for everything, Minna. You've been a peach. Oh, if you need anything while I'm gone, see Ian."

I kissed Minna on her other cheek. "Are you sure?" I whispered.

A wicked grin filled the woman's face. "As sure as I can be."

James grabbed my hand and started toward the door. "Sure about what?"

"I can't believe it." I ran alongside my husband, down the steps, and to the carriage, my two steps to his every one. He lifted me into the carriage and climbed in after me. By the time I located my bonnet and tied the ribbon under my chin, the horses were in motion, and I was on my way to Denver.

Aunt Bea and Jamie met us at the train station. Ian and James had gone to the telegraph office to send a telegram to our contact in Denver while Drucilla and I rested on the bench beside the depot.

The moment he saw us, Jamie waved and ran to meet us, carrying a basket half his size. "Here." He eagerly shoved the container into my lap. "Aunt Bea says it's a long way to Denver, and you might get hungry. So we packed you a lunch." He straightened his shoulders and announced, "I made the gingersnaps all by myself!"

"You did?" I peered under the blue gingham napkin covering the food. "May I taste one now?"

"No, you have to wait until suppertime," the boy scolded.

Aunt Bea laughed. "I had as much trouble with him as he is having with you. I see you survived the shivaree."

I felt the color creeping up my neck and into my face. "Yes. It certainly is an unusual custom."

Drucilla huffed. "It's a barbarian custom, if you ask me."

Aunt Bea chuckled. "Be glad they didn't kidnap you for ransom. One time they hid the bride for twelve hours and charged the groom a dollar an hour to get her back. Of course they gave the money to the bride as a dowry."

I knew my face revealed my horror, but I couldn't help it.

"Now don't go jumping to conclusions." Aunt Bea patted my hand. "They did it because the groom was a wealthy skinflint who married the daughter of a poor itinerant preacher."

The familiar sound of a train whistle sent a tingle of excitement through me. I craned my neck for a glimpse of the arriving locomotive. When the men returned, James picked up Jamie in his arms, and together they watched the locomotive belch steam and cinders into the sky.

I turned to kiss Aunt Bea goodbye, then Drucilla and Ian. I saved my last kiss for Jamie. "Goodbye, cowboy, we'll see you in one week. Seven days."

"I know, I know." He threw his arms about my neck. "Have a nice honeymoon. But Aunt Bea and I decided last night that I won't take you or Daddy on my honeymoon either."

I laughed and squeezed him tight. "Be good for Minna.

And don't forget to study your times tables every day."

"Aw," he groaned, "do I have to?"

I grinned at James, then back at his son. "No, I guess you need a week's vacation too."

"Great! Isn't she great, Dad? I know I'm gonna like her as a mom."

James kissed his son and set him down. "Don't expect such favored treatment every day, son."

A teasing dimple formed at the corner of the child's mouth. "I won't."

"Good!" James tousled his son's hair. At the conductor's "all aboard," my husband grabbed our bags. "Well, it's time. One week, son. Take good care of Mutt."

I followed James to the first passenger car, where the conductor helped me board. James led the way through the almost empty car to our seat. "Is this all right?"

"Looks fine to me."

"We can go back to one of the other passenger cars if you like." His eagerness to please touched me.

"Let's start out here and see how it goes," I suggested.

After stashing our luggage in the rack overhead, he indicated for me to take the window seat. He had little choice. I'd already been leaning across the seats and hanging out the window to wave goodbye to Jamie and the others. As we settled into our seats for the long ride west, James took my hand in his and caressed the back of my hand with his thumb. "Are you as happy as I am, Chloe?"

My eyes twinkled up into his. "Do you need to ask?"

He smiled. "No, I can see it in your face."

The White Caps west of the city blurred past as the train gathered speed. The hills were once again white, this time denuded by grasshoppers instead of buffalo. I glanced down at our intertwined fingers and thought of Mary. She had loved the man sitting beside me. Now she was gone, and my hand rested in his.

Grim thoughts sprang into my mind. *How long will we have together?* I shuddered and shoved the gloom out of my mind. *Today I'll be happy, God. I don't have time to worry about You and Your capricious games!* Even while I thought the angry words, promises of God's love and constant care refused to die.

James must have noted my change of expression. "Is something wrong?"

I took a deep breath and squeezed his hand tighter. "I was just wondering how long we will have together."

"How long?"

"Yes, how long."

James slipped his hand from mine and put his arm around my shoulders. "Does it matter? Thirty years, three years, seventy years—if I learned anything from losing Mary, it was that the secret to happiness is enjoying each day you have together."

My voice caught in my throat. "But you and Mary expected to grow old together, and it didn't happen."

James gently kissed my forehead. "Life has no guarantees, darling. Believe me, if he could buy an elixir that guaranteed long life, my father would have cornered the market by now. He is so obsessed with dying that he's forgotten how to live."

I snuggled closer to my husband. "I'd like to meet your father and mother someday. You've never told me much about either of them."

The tone in James's voice became clipped. "My mother is a paragon of etiquette. She would as soon swallow poison than be forced to use the wrong fork at the table. But seeing nine- and ten-year-old children going to work in the shoe factories before dawn and returning home after dusk evokes no reaction from her."

I waited for him to continue. "As far as Ian and I are concerned, she couldn't do enough—the best tailors, the best teachers, the best horses, the best Boston had to offer in art, literature, and culture." He paused. "Don't misunderstand, I love her dearly. But she's unbelievably cold to anyone outside her narrow circle of friends and family. Fortunately for Mary and me, Mary's family was acceptable, or we never would have been allowed to court, let alone marry."

I knew without asking that the daughter of an herbalist would never meet their approval.

We talked for some time, but eventually the rocking of the train lulled us both into silence. James leaned his head back against the seat and closed his eyes. I shifted to free his arm so he could rest more comfortably. For a time I stared out the dusty window at the unending prairie. A windmill and a clump of trees pinpointed each lonely homestead that we passed. White-faced cattle watched us rumble by as they grazed on the sparse grass.

Night settled over the prairie. I looked at James and smiled. His head rested against the seatback. Leaning my head against James's shoulder, I decided to see whether I could doze for a while.

It seemed that I had barely closed my eyes when I heard the woman across the aisle gasp. When I looked her direction, she pointed to my window.

I had awakened to the first rays of dawn and caught my first glimpse of the famous Rockies. At first I thought the mountains were clouds. But as the train angled northwest toward Denver, my heart leapt at the sight of the rising sun outlining the jagged peaks. I shook James's arm. I knew he'd never before been this far west.

"Honey, look. Look at the mountains. Aren't they incredible?"

He opened his eyes. "Oh, my," he exclaimed, "Ian always said they were magnificent, but magnificent doesn't do them justice."

The mountains seemed to grow as we approached Denver. As the city's skyline came into view, James told me more about Denver. "This town's famous for its health resorts. Royalty from all over the world come here for 'the cure.' "

I pressed my face to the window, not wanting to miss a thing. "I was overwhelmed with Chicago, more for its size, though, than its beauty."

James laughed. "The Colorado mines have cast the town in silver and gold. Of course, it's not Boston."

Long before, I'd learned that to Ian, Drucilla, and James, no city compared to Boston. I jabbed him in the ribs. "You and your Boston. Does Boston have mountains like these surrounding it?"

James bristled. "No, we have just the entire Atlantic Ocean at our front door."

Our banter ceased with the train's arrival at the station. A hansom cab awaited us, taking us to the Brown Palace Hotel, where James had reserved the bridal suite. When James signed the register as Mr. and Mrs. McCall, I blushed, but the desk clerk maintained his detached demeanor.

"Excuse me, sir. There's a message for you." The clerk retrieved a note from the box marked 313. "It was delivered earlier this morning."

James opened the note and smiled. "Mr. Putnam wants me to call him right away. You have a telephone here at the desk?"

"Of course, sir." The man waved us toward the wall opposite the desk.

James thanked him and strode across the lobby. Since I'd only heard about the incredible black box, I tagged along after James. He cranked the handle on the side of the box and waited. "Four-o-seven, please."

He smiled and kissed the tip of my nose. "You look

darling, Mrs. McCall.

"Mr. Putnam, please. Mr. James McCall of Hays, Kansas. Yes, I'll wait. Thank you."

"What do you hear?" I whispered.

He put the receiver up to my ear. I listened to strange crackling sounds, then a voice. "Phineas Putnam here."

Startled, I shoved the receiver back at James.

He smiled and craned his neck toward the mouthpiece attached to the box on the wall. "Yes, this is James McCall. We just arrived at the Brown Palace Hotel, sir. Yes, a pleasant journey. Thank you. Tomorrow morning at nine, at your office. That would be most gracious of you. Thank you, sir."

James returned the receiver to the hook on the side of the box. "He's sending his driver to pick me up tomorrow morning."

"How far away was Mr. Putnam?"

"He lives on Seventeenth Avenue, about five miles from here."

I gasped. "Imagine being able to hear someone's voice from five miles away!"

James laughed. "It's only a matter of time until the continent will be crisscrossed with telephone lines. You'll be able to stand here in Denver and speak with someone in Washington, D.C."

I believed James, but I couldn't begin to understand. We returned to the desk for our room key, and the clerk signaled for a porter to carry our luggage. As we passed the taproom, James whispered, "Look at the floor. Ian says it's studded with three thousand silver dollars."

The biggest surprise came when we stepped into a wrought-iron cage, and the uniformed operator asked what floor we wanted. After the porter told him, the cage began to rise. I grabbed James's hand and squeezed my eyes shut. My small-town roots were evident to anyone watching, but I didn't care. All I could think about was living through the next few moments.

When the elevator stopped on the third floor, I could hardly wait for the gate to open and to escape. The next morning, it was only to please James that I agreed to ride the lift down to the dining room for breakfast. Because James had business at the bank all morning, he hired a carriage and driver to take me on a tour of the city. In the afternoon, we shopped for school clothes for Jamie, as well as for ourselves.

On our third day in Denver we visited Elitch Gardens, a seventeen-acre amusement park and zoo. We laughed at the antics of the clowns and gasped at the feats of the acrobats. After touring the zoo, James led me to an open field. People lined up for rides in the two hot-air balloons that hovered over the closely cut grass.

"You want to go up in one?"

I looked at the blue, yellow, and purple balloon, then looked at my husband. His eyes sparkled with excitement. "Obviously you do."

"Sweetheart, if you'd rather not . . ."

Be a good sport, I told myself, taking a deep breath. "All right, let's try it."

James paid for our tickets, and we joined the line. Off to one side of the field was a hearselike vehicle pulled by four horses. James followed my gaze. "It's an ambulance in case there's an accident of some kind."

"Oh." My stomach churned like a gristmill. I could hear my mother's voice, "If God wanted men to fly, He would have given them wings." Though I had scoffed at her attitude then, she sure made sense now.

The couple ahead of us climbed into the gondola of the red-and-white striped balloon. Our turn was next; I grasped James's arm in terror. *Maybe this isn't such a good idea after all.*

"Honey." He gently pried my fingers from his arm. "You're cutting off the circulation to my fingers."

I looked over at my husband. The eagerness evident on his face made him look like a child of ten. I told myself, *I can do this. I can do this.*

James helped me into the gondola, then climbed in beside me. The balloon operator smiled at me. "It's all right, lady. I do this for a living, remember?"

Mute with fear, I nodded and gripped the side of the gondola.

"The process is really very simple. Hot air rises; cool air falls. So when I fire the burners, the hot air fills the balloon over our heads and lifts us into the air." I heard the swoosh as the flame shot up, and the balloon began to rise. I squeezed my eyes shut as the operator continued explaining the process to James. "When we're ready to come down, I reverse the process."

"I'm ready, I'm ready!" I squealed.

"Not yet," James cried. "Look, look, an eagle's-eye view of the city. See over there. That's the dome of the county courthouse."

I opened one eye and peeked down at the building, then squeezed my eyes shut again.

"Over there, sir," the balloon operator pointed, "is the Rocky Mountain News building. And over on your left is the University of Denver, founded in 1876."

I opened my eyes in spite of my fears. If I was going to die, I was going to die—so it didn't make sense to miss out on the excitement in the meantime. "What is that building over there?"

James and the operator glanced at me, surprised. "The Tabor Opera House. Rumor has it that when the building was being built, Mr. Tabor objected to the bust of William Shakespeare being carved in the arch of the main entrance and demanded that his own likeness be put there instead."

The view of the mountains was spectacular. Even from our incredible height, the mountains towered over us. The longer we soared over the city, the more accustomed my stomach became to the swaying of the gondola. As our ride came to an end, I whispered to James, "I could learn to like this mode of travel."

The balloon operator averted his face, pretending he hadn't heard. But I did detect a satisfied smile on his lips as he set the gondola down precisely on its mark.

Before we left on our honeymoon, James had suggested that I pack my wedding dress. On our fourth day in Denver, I discovered why. James and I spent the morning at a photographer's studio having our wedding pictures taken. The photographer took a second set of photographs with me wearing my new green satin gown and James wearing a tuxedo he'd brought for the dinner party at the Putnams' place the following evening.

Throughout the afternoon and all the next day, I dreaded the dinner party at the Phineas T. Putnam residence. What did I know about high society? I'd never been invited to one of Mrs. Chamberlain's afternoon teas, let alone to a dinner party at a millionaire banker's mansion.

At Home

James cut a dashing figure in his tuxedo and spats. I wondered if he would ever wear them again once we returned to the ranch. Then I looked in the gilt-framed wall mirror and laughed. *How often do you think you'll wear your green satin ball gown on the Kansas prairie?* I grimaced at the large green plume on the tiny hat perched on the side of my head, feeling rather like a chicken trying to pass for a peacock. We stepped into the lobby just as the Putnams' hansom pulled up in front of the hotel.

During the ride in the hansom, James did his best to ease my nerves. "Keep in mind that, while it is not true of our host and hostess, who are pure Mayflower stock, most of the people at the party tonight are a generation away from their grass roots. Their social veneer is thin. So don't allow a bunch of whist-playing matrons to unnerve you."

"I'm not sure I understand. Are you saying they might look down their noses at a rancher from Kansas?"

"We're the McCalls of Boston, should anyone ask."

I chuckled into the black ostrich-feather fan he'd insisted I buy during our shopping spree. "Oh, I get it. We're going to outsnob the snobs."

He grinned and squeezed my hand. "That's one way to put it. Many of these people would look like country bumpkins next to Boston's Back Bay crowd."

"And in Europe, I suppose Bostonians would be considered hopelessly provincial."

He shook his head and chuckled. "I think you've gotten the point all too well."

"Why, Mr. McCall, I do believe you yourself are a pompous prig!" When he opened his mouth to protest, I closed it with a kiss. When I drew away, I grinned devilishly. "Now I know how to get in the last word."

I leaned back against the seat to appreciate the view of the gigantic homes lining Seventeenth Avenue. "They must have large families here."

"No, only large bankbooks and egos to match. It's a matter of having too much money too soon. Even with the government's demonetization of silver in '96, fortunes are being made every day."

I shook my head. "Incredible. And I thought our home was huge when I first arrived in Hays."

He stretched his arm out on the back of the seat behind my head. "Can you imagine living in a city where robberies, suicides, and murders occur almost every day?"

I shook my head and snuggled closer. "All for the love of money?"

He wrapped his arm about my shoulders. "And the supposed security it brings."

When we reached our destination, I discovered the magnitude of the Putnams' dinner parties. I'd expected a guest list of eight or ten. By the number of carriages parked outside, there had to be fifty guests, at least. A butler met us at the front door. He bowed and led us to the atrium and garden, where our host and guests were sipping what I assumed were alcoholic beverages. Having been brought up to firmly believe in teetotaling, I shot a worried glance at James. He winked and led me down the steps to meet our host, Phineas T. Putnam.

"So nice of you to come. I do hope Herbert arrived at the

hotel on schedule." The graying, balding man shook James's hand.

"Right on time." James took my hand. Before James could introduce me, Mr. Putnam turned to me.

"And this must be your lovely new bride. We're so glad you decided to grace us with your presence."

The man's bushy white mutton-chop whiskers fluttered as he spoke. I gulped back the urge to giggle. "Thank you, Mr. Putnam. We appreciate your kind hospitality."

He kissed my right hand. "Phineas, my dear. Call me Phineas. She certainly is exquisite, James."

A waiter appeared at Mr. Putnam's elbow to ask James what we might like to drink. At James's request for mineral water, the waiter bowed and disappeared.

Mr. Putnam led us across the room to a well-padded, middle-aged woman with swirls of black curls kept in place by a diamond-studded tiara and matching combs. Her midnight-blue satin gown glittered with sequins and jewels in the candlelit atrium. "James McCall, my how you've changed. Last time I saw you, you were chasing crabs on the beach at Newport."

"I'm sorry, but I don't think I . . ."

"Of course you don't remember me. I am the former Gladys Tarrington, of the Newport Tarringtons. Your mother used to bring you children out to the beach every August to escape the city heat."

James smiled and shook his head. "I'm sorry but . . ."

"My parents owned the estate next to yours. By the time you would have been old enough to remember me, I would have met and married dear Phineas and moved to Baltimore. And after the bonanza silver strike, we moved to the wild West."

The waiter returned with our mineral water. The hostess glanced toward me and smiled. "But here I am running on about ancient history, when I haven't allowed you to introduce me to your fetching bride."

After James introduced me, she shooed James away and captured my hand. "Come, my dear, let me introduce you to Denver's finest." In spite of my determination not to like any of these people, I genuinely liked Mrs. Putnam, though I found her friends less than gracious.

One matron decked out in gold satin and a boxcar load of diamonds arched her eyebrow and smiled down her nose at me. "So, Chloe, are your parents into commodities or banking? My husband is in bonds, gold bonds, that is."

I glanced about, hoping James would rescue me. Seeing no hope of rescue, I smiled a half-devilish grin at the woman. "Oh, my father is in oil."

"Oil?" The woman's eyebrows almost disappeared into her hairline. "Honoria." She snagged a chatty blond woman from the next cluster of guests. "You must meet Chloe McCall. She's the bride of that devastatingly handsome young man over there talking to William Chandler. Her parents are in oil." She pronounced the word *oil* with awe.

The woman reminded me of Drucilla when she had first arrived in Kansas. I sucked in my cheeks to keep from laughing. "He's a pipeline inspector for John D. Rockefeller in Shinglehouse, Pennsylvania."

Her brow knitted. "A pipeline inspector. I don't understand."

"He inspects the pipes for leaks and damage."

The women's smiles faltered. They looked at one another, then skillfully excused themselves, leaving me to fend for myself. I sighed with relief. *James may be a blue-blooded Bostonian, but my blood still runs Pennsylvania red.*

After the seven-course meal, James excused us early. "We have a long trip back to Kansas."

On the ride back to the hotel, James asked me if I had enjoyed myself. He laughed when I told him about my encounter with the "oil" lady. "I can't say I really enjoyed the evening, but it was an experience I'll always remember."

He hugged me and nibbled on my ear. "Chloe Mae, when you hit Boston for the first time, you're going to set those Beacon Hill matrons on their bustles."

A few hours later, we left for the depot. As the train pulled out of the station and headed east, I took a last look at the majestic mountains.

I removed my hat and settled down into the seat next to James. "So are you ready to go home to the humdrum life of being a farmer's wife after the excitement of life in the big city?" he asked.

I sighed contentedly and leaned my head against his shoulder. "More than ready."

"Me too." He closed his eyes and leaned his head against the window. I studied my husband's profile in the moonlight: the shock of curls on his forehead; the slight bump in his proud, aristocratic nose; his lips; his chiseled jaw. I wondered how I could ever have doubted my love for him or his love for me. In such a short time, he'd become my life, my joy, my strength.

The words "I will never leave you nor forsake you" surfaced in my mind. I pushed them aside. Closing my eyes, I rested in the knowledge that James was my companion now. He was the one who'd always be there for me—unlike a God I couldn't see, hear, or understand.

The hours between dawn, when I awakened, and nine o'clock, our estimated time of arrival in Hays, dragged interminably. We took on and deposited mail, freight, and passengers at every watering hole and crossroad in western Kansas. Finally I spotted the White Caps, and I knew we were almost home.

Jamie and Ian met us at the station. On the ride to Aunt Bea's, then home, Jamie couldn't keep his hands off us; he had to keep reassuring himself that we had returned. I don't know how many times he asked me to tell him about the telephone call and the balloon ride.

"Someday, Daddy, will you take me up in a balloon?"

"You bet."

During a lull between the child's questions, I leaned forward and tapped Ian on the shoulder. "You haven't said how Drucilla is feeling."

He shook his head. "Not too well. Here she is in her fifth month and still can't keep much food down. I'm worried."

"Has she been getting out in the fresh air?"

He nodded. "We take walks together every morning and evening."

"I'm so sorry. I wish I knew how to make her more comfortable."

He glanced over his shoulder at James. "I'd hoped she would be feeling better before I left to check out the new mine. She's not going to like staying behind."

I sniffed. "I don't blame her. I wouldn't want James gadding about the continent while I languished in bed bearing our child!"

Ian scowled at me. "I'll be back before the baby's born."

"Maybe."

With the first glimpse of the farmhouse, my stomach tumbled with anticipation. As the carriage came to a stop beside the picket fence, I gave an unladylike leap from the carriage and ran up the back steps into the kitchen. "We're home! We're home!"

"My, my," Minna dropped her dustcloth and threw her arms around me. "You've been gone only a week."

"It seems like forever. Hmm, what smells so good?"

"A pot of vegetable stew, that's what. Now," she held me out at arms' length, "just let me take a look at you. Rosy cheeks, sparkling eyes—it looks like marriage agrees with you, child."

I blushed and hugged her again.

She looked askance at my traveling outfit. "Why don't you run upstairs and get into something more comfortable?" In a whisper, she added, "And get out of that whalebone corset. That's the last thing a slip of a gal like you needs. Never did cotton to those rib-crunching garments—not natural!"

I laughed and obeyed. It seemed strange to think of the room at the head of the stairs as mine. My luggage sat at the foot of the bed next to James's luggage. When I opened the rosewood wardrobe, I discovered my clothes neatly hanging on the left, James's on the right. Mary's Bible was gone from the marble-topped table by the window. The silver dresser set had been replaced by a note addressed to me.

Dearest Chloe,

   I gave the silver dresser set to Drucilla as a keepsake. Minna moved your clothing to the drawers on the left. Open your top-drawer.

   Love, James.

In the drawer a velvet-covered box sat on top of my hankies, scarves, and gloves. Inside the satin-lined box lay a silver-backed brush, comb, and mirror set with my new initials engraved on the brush and mirror. I picked up the mirror to examine it more closely. "Oh, they're beautiful . . ."

"I'm glad you like them." I whirled about to find James leaning against the doorjamb.

I laughed, threw myself into his arms, and planted a kiss on his lips. In my enthusiasm, I knocked him off balance, and he staggered to catch himself to keep us both from tumbling down the stairs. "Woman, you're dangerous."

I giggled. "You don't know the half of it. We Irish lasses know how to keep our men guessing."

He loosened himself from my grasp and ambled over to the dresser. "You don't need to remind me of that. But there's something else in here you missed." He removed a wooden box from beneath my lace shawl and opened it for me. I gasped with surprise at the silver picture frame that matched the dresser set. Inside the frame was the wedding photo we'd taken in Denver. "I have a larger print in my valise to put downstairs in the parlor on the mantel."

"You said the photographs wouldn't be ready in time to bring back with us. You said the photographer would have to mail them."

James shrugged. "Well, he would have if I hadn't paid a little extra for faster service."

I laid the mirror on the dresser and carefully lifted the silver frame from the box. Three extra prints, in the form of postcards, fell out. James bent to pick them up.

"I got these for our parents and for Aunt Bea. She's been such a good egg through all of this." He dropped them back into the box.

My eyes misted and I swallowed hard. "You are the most thoughtful man I've ever known. I love you, Mr. McCall."

"I love you too, Mrs. McCall."

I rushed from the room and down the stairs to show Minna and the others the photograph.

While Jamie wasn't excited about his new school clothes, he did enjoy assembling the paper hot-air balloon kit we purchased for him at Elitch Gardens.

Jamie started school the following Monday. James arranged to drive the wagonload of neighborhood children to school while another neighbor brought them home. The boy came home from school each day bubbling over with excitement. On the whole, he seemed to have adjusted to the major changes in his life surprisingly well. Our lives seemed to be falling into a comfortable routine, except for Drucilla's health problems.

I wrote home telling the family about our wedding and our honeymoon in Denver. I knew my mother would laugh over the Putnams' pompous guests. I told about the balloon flight, the elevator ride, and the telephone call. "Thank you again for the notes and letters. I miss you all. Ma, the dress fit perfectly. And, Pa, thank you for sending my very own gold piece. I will treasure it always. I am including a wedding photograph James had made especially for you. Love, Chloe."

Awakening one morning before dawn feeling queasy, I hurried down to the kitchen to prepare a cup of peppermint tea to settle my stomach. I was surprised to find Drucilla, her hair frazzled, her face pale, seated at the table and sipping a cup of tea. "Couldn't you sleep either?" she asked.

"No, something I ate last night didn't settle right, I guess."

"Hmmph!" she snorted. "You're probably pregnant."

I laughed and disappeared into the pantry for the peppermint leaves. "Not likely. So has the swelling gone down in your legs?"

"Are you kidding?" Her tone of voice revealed her discomfort. "You should see my ankles! I could join the circus as the elephant lady."

"It's almost over. Once little Ian arrives, you will forget all about the discomforts of pregnancy." I rubbed my fingers across my forehead. *I don't really need this today.*

"Easy for you to say," she mumbled and sipped at her tea. "Did you know Ian is talking about making a trip to Columbine, Colorado, before the baby is born? With my luck, he'll be snowed in and won't make it back in time!"

"Oh, I don't think he'll do any such thing. He knows how

you feel about being left behind." I'd heard bits and pieces of Ian and James's conversation regarding the latest mine they'd purchased. Though the first two mines were not producing great wealth, the managers Ian had left in charge were sending through regular reports. But the reports from the manager of the Renegade Mine on Hahn's Peak, near the Colorado border, didn't match up with the projections made at the time of the sale.

"I'm not so sure." Tears started down Drucilla's cheeks. "Oh, Chloe, we had a big fight last night. I told Ian that if he left me here to have this baby alone, he could keep right on going and never return."

"Oh, Dru, I'm so sorry." I rushed to her side and knelt beside her. I didn't know what else to say.

Squeezing her eyes shut, she pushed her hair from her forehead and wept. "I remember how my sister felt being left behind in Boston when James and Ian headed west. James will never know how devastated Mary felt, alone and pregnant. The night before she left for Kansas, Mary confided that she was afraid she'd die and never see him again."

I had never thought what it must have been like for Mary to stay behind when James left for Kansas. At the time, I couldn't understand the woman's stubborn determination to reach him—regardless of the consequences to her or her newborn's health. "But you're not Mary; you're you. You don't have consumption."

"I know," she wailed. "And I didn't mean what I said about Ian leaving and never returning either. Even if something terrible happened to me or to the baby, I'd want him back."

"Then tell him so."

She pushed her chair away from the table and rose unsteadily to her feet. "He's so angry with me that he's upstairs packing right now."

"Go to him. Tell him what you told me."

Drucilla turned and stumbled blindly from the room. Just then the teakettle whistled and I reached for a hot pad when I heard a scream and a thump, thump, thump. *Oh, dear God, no. No!*

I ran into the hall to find Drucilla crumbled at the foot of the stairs, holding her stomach and sobbing. From upstairs, Ian, Minna, and James came running.

"What happened?" Minna shouted.

"My baby. My baby is going to die!"

"No, honey, not necessarily. No . . ." I cradled her in my arms. "Ian! James!" I shouted. "Help me get her upstairs to her room. James, I need my medicine bag. Minna, I left the teakettle on the stove."

Ian lifted Drucilla into his arms and carried her up the stairs. James ran ahead of him to our room for the bag, and Minna disappeared down the hall to the kitchen.

How far she'd fallen I did not know. Halfway up the staircase, I remembered that I should have checked for broken bones before I moved her. *Oh, dear Father, I need Your help now. Forgive me for being angry with You. Don't hold my sins against Drucilla and her baby. How ironic,* I thought as I ran down the hall after Ian, *I prayed the same prayer over Mary the night on the train.*

A voice as plain as my own said, "And I answered that prayer too." Startled, I glanced around to see who had spoken. No one was there. Shaking my head in disbelief, I entered the room. One look around the room told me that Drucilla hadn't exaggerated. Ian's valise sat at the foot of the bed, half packed. A gray woolen suit lay on the floor where he'd dropped it when she screamed.

"Ian, I need to examine her."

"Definitely!" His head bobbed.

"I think Drucilla would be more comfortable if you left the room, and I know I would."

"Oh." His face reddened. "I'll go see what's keeping James."

"Thank you. It will only take a minute."

As Ian opened the door, James handed him my medicine bag. Ian passed it on to me, then left. I took out the stethoscope I had purchased soon after I arrived in Kansas and placed it on her protruding stomach. "Does it hurt anywhere particular?"

She rolled her head from side to side. I could hear a steady, healthy throb. Sighing with relief, I removed the stethoscope. "Right now, your baby's fine."

Drucilla burst into tears. "Oh, Chloe, you wouldn't deceive me, would you?"

I choked back my own tears. "Not in a million years. But I do think you'd better stay in bed until we're sure you didn't damage the placenta. That means I don't want to see you out of bed for anything, got that?"

She nodded. "May Ian come back in now?"

"That was my next recommendation, along with a cup of comfrey tea to help calm your nerves." I walked to the door and opened it. "Ian, Drucilla is asking for you." Turning back to Drucilla, I shook my finger. "Now remember, if you need anything, call for help. I'll be up to check you again after a little while."

Ian hurried to his wife's side. Before leaving the room I said, "Ian, I need to see you and James in the library when you're finished here. You can stay until Minna arrives with Drucilla's tea."

I closed the door behind me. James hovered outside the room. "James, what is going on? Drucilla told me that Ian plans to leave for Colorado today. Why is this the first I'm hearing about it?"

"It was only yesterday afternoon that Walter delivered a wire from Putnam." I marched down the hall toward our room. He fell into step beside me.

"Wire? What wire?"

"The one telling us of the irregularities in the reports coming in from the Renegade Mine."

I entered our room and whirled about to face him. "Didn't you think it was important enough to mention it, say at the dinner table or before we went to bed?"

"I didn't want to upset you."

I tapped my foot impatiently. "James, I resent being treated like a hothouse flower."

"I wasn't treating you . . ."

"Yes, you were. One of the things I've appreciated about us is that we can and do talk about anything. And now you didn't tell me about this wire." I folded my arms and waited for his reply.

"You're right." He stepped closer to me and took my hands in his. "I was treating you the way I would have treated Mary. She never wanted to discuss 'men's stuff,' as she called it."

His honesty stripped my anger from me. "Both of us know I'm not Mary."

He kissed my fingertips gently. "No, you're Chloe Mae McCall, and I love you just the way you are." He lifted a wave of my hair and let it filter down my back. "Do you know how beautiful you are?"

I brushed his hand away. "Don't try to change the subject."

"Chloe, I'm sorry." He led me to one of the Queen Anne chairs. "Old habits die hard. You're going to have to help me establish new ones that fit our marriage more comfortably. We're going to have to help each other."

I looked up into his concerned face. "You're right. And I'm sorry too. I don't want to butt into your business, but I don't want to be shut out either."

"I never want to shut you out."

"The honeymoon must be over." I bit my lip. "We just

had our first fight."

"No, no, no." He kissed the tip of my nose, then my cheeks and my lips. "I don't want the honeymoon ever to be over for us."

We heard a knock at our bedroom door. James sighed. "Guess I'd better open it, huh?"

I grinned and nodded.

"James, Dru needs Chloe right away."

I flew to the door and opened it. Ian fell into step behind me as I rushed down the hall. "What's happening? Is she in pain?"

"I'm not sure. Minna won't let me into the room."

Bursting into Drucilla's room, I found Minna sitting on the far side of the bed, comforting Drucilla. Minna looked up at me. "I think she might be threatening to miscarry."

I took Drucilla's hand. "Are you in pain?"

She nodded her head and squeezed her eyes shut. I grabbed the stethoscope from the night stand, where I'd left it, and listened for the fetal heartbeat. It was racing faster than when I'd measured it previously. As I examined her, I found other signs of a potential miscarriage. "Minna, ask Ian to go for Doc Madox right away."

I stayed with Drucilla until Ian arrived with the doctor, then waited in the hallway with Ian while the doctor examined her.

Ian paced the hallway. "Do you think she'll lose the child?"

"I honestly don't know."

When the doctor opened the door and stepped out into the hallway, we rushed to him. "I gave her medication to help her sleep. Now, nature has to heal whatever was injured in the fall.

"Mrs. McCall, keep a close eye on her. If she goes into labor, you know what to do." He shrugged his shoulders. "We've done all that's humanly possible. It's up to God and the baby now."

God, I thought as I saw the doctor to the front door. *God?* Discouraged, I wandered up the stairs to my room, slammed the door, and threw myself on the bed. After a while I slid off the bed to my knees. *All right, You win. I admit that I need You. I don't understand You, but I do need You. Help me to believe in You like I once did.*

I picked up my Bible and opened it to the spot where I'd inserted a bookmark. Ecclesiastes 3. "To every thing there is a season, and a time to every purpose under the heaven: a time to be born, and a time to die . . ." I forced myself to read farther. "A time to weep, and a time to laugh; a time to mourn, and a time to dance . . ." I read on, pausing at verse 11. "He hath made every thing beautiful in his time . . ."

In God's time. I'd never thought of God's time being different from mine. The concept wrapped itself around my imagination and refused to let go. I mulled the idea throughout the rest of the day. About three in the afternoon, I realized that my stomach had settled down, and Minna's stew simmering on the back burner smelled mighty good.

Jamie arrived home from school with a drawing of Mutt. He told me about the Christmas play for which the students had begun practicing. "And I get to be a snowflake. Can you make me a snowflake costume?"

I promised to try. While Jamie changed out of his school clothes, I checked on Drucilla. She was still sleeping off the doctor's medication.

Later that evening, after I put Jamie to bed for the night, James invited me to join him and Ian in the library. Ian began, "This is the situation, Chloe. There's a good chance that we are being robbed blind by the present manager at the mine."

James turned to me. "One of us needs to go to the mine

and clear up the problem. Ian had planned to travel out and back before the baby came, but now . . ."

"Now," I interrupted, "it would be a terrible mistake for him to leave. Even after Drucilla's out of danger, she is terrified she will never see you again." I paused and glanced toward James. I didn't want to hurt him, but both men needed to understand Drucilla's fears. "Drucilla remembers the pain Mary suffered being left in Boston . . ."

"No!" James shook his head. His eyes read disbelief. "She never said she didn't want me to go. She never told me . . ."

"That's right. She didn't tell you how she felt because she knew how badly you wanted to leave Boston. When you left, she was certain she'd never see you again."

"If I'd known, if I'd only known." James buried his face in his hands.

I put my arms around his shoulders. "If you'd known, the outcome might have been exactly the same. Your presence couldn't have stopped the consumption, nor would it have guaranteed her a full-term pregnancy."

"I hate to be practical at a time like this." Ian stood and paced to the door and back again. "But we have a problem here and now. What should we do?"

James lifted his face. "Sell the mine. Get rid of it. It's not worth it."

"What?" Ian whirled about and stared at his brother.

"I said sell it."

"We'd lose our shirts!" I watched the game of toss-and-catch go on between the two brothers.

James glared at his brother. "I don't care. Since you can't leave, I'll hop a train to Denver, make a deal with Putnam, and be back before the end of the week."

I shook my head. "There must be a better way."

Chocolate Mousse and Other Surprises

"No! No, no, no!" James stormed across the library. "The mines are Ian's interest; the ranch is mine. That's how we divided it, and that's how it's going to stay."

"He's your brother. He needs you." I'd never seen James so upset. "If we don't help him, he'll lose a lot. And we'll lose too, since the ranch and the mines are under both your names."

"No!" He pounded his fist into the palm of his other hand. "Besides, what do I know about mining?"

I counted to ten under my breath. I had to remain calm. "You are a Harvard graduate in business. He's not asking you to do whatever miners do. He needs you to find the irregularities in the books."

Distraught, James ran his hand through his hair. "I could be gone until spring, you realize."

I leveled a steady gaze at him. "We could be gone until spring."

"Oh, no. You don't know what life is like in a mining camp. It's especially rough on a woman."

"I was brought up on hard work. While we weren't as poor as dirt farmers, everyone had to work."

"Besides, it's not just you and me. Jamie needs you here."

"He needs us. So he'd go with us, of course."

169

"No! And that's final."

Before I could press my point, James strode from the library, and the front door slammed behind him. Defeated, I dragged myself upstairs. After changing into my nightgown, I loosened my braid and brushed out my hair. *Sorry, Ian, I tried.*

I peered out the window into the night, hoping to catch a glimpse of my husband. Remembering Pa's rule about not going to sleep angry, I considered getting dressed again and trying to find James. *No,* I told myself, *he's not angry at me. He's angry at the situation.*

I took my Bible to bed since I didn't intend to sleep until James returned. Opening the book to where I'd left off in Ecclesiastes, I began to read.

When I awoke at dawn, the wick had been turned down in the lamp beside the bed, and my Bible was gone. I ran my hand across the other side of the bed and found it empty. Concerned, I sat up. There, in the chair by the window, James sat asleep, his chin on his chest, his legs sprawled out in front of him, and the open Bible in his hands.

I slid out of bed and tiptoed down the hall to the bathroom. By the time I returned, James had awakened. I smiled at him as if nothing had happened. "Good morning, darling. Have a good sleep?"

He grunted and scratched his beard. "Does it look it?"

"My, aren't we grumpy this morning!" I bit my tongue as soon as the barb was out.

"Sorry! You're right." He stood up and stretched. "For that matter, you're right about a lot of things. We can't afford to just throw away the mine and its profits. However, I still think it would be best if I went to Colorado alone."

My heart sank. I didn't feel like picking up the argument where we'd left off. I felt lightheaded; my stomach felt queasy. The evening before, in all the excitement, I hadn't eaten much. "Please, James, not now. Just hold me and tell me you forgive me for being so persistent last night. I can't handle your being upset with me."

"Oh, Chloe." He took me in his arms and cradled my head against his chest. "I was angry because you were right. I prayed about it last night, and I know I have to go."

My words came out in little gulps. "We have to go! You can't leave me behind. Please."

He sighed and shoved his hands in the back pockets of his trousers. "I don't know what I'm going to find when I get there. I can't take a wife and young son into such an uncertain situation."

I wrapped my arms about myself and walked to the window. Tears streamed down my face. I couldn't fight any longer. I refused to nag or cajole or throw a childish tantrum. If he wanted me to stay in Kansas, I would have to accept his decision. Turning slowly to face him, I wiped my tears on the sleeve of my nightgown. "All right, James. I trust your judgment. I'll do whatever you say."

A look of relief swept across his face. "You will?"

I nodded, walked slowly to the wardrobe, and opened the doors. "I trust your judgment. I wouldn't have married you if I didn't. When will you be leaving?"

"Uh, well, I figured if I left next Tuesday, I'd have time to review Putnam's findings and still make it to the town of Columbine before the weekend."

So soon? The sight of his clothing arranged neatly on one side of the wardrobe brought a fresh flood of tears. "Tell me what clothes you'll want to take with you, and I'll be sure they're ready. I need to replace the button on your blue denim workshirt. I know you'll want to take that with you."

I removed my brown gingham dress and my everyday petticoats from the wardrobe. "While in Denver, it wouldn't hurt if you bought a few new pairs of woolen stockings. I've darned . . ." When I turned, I discovered he'd left the room. Fighting the tears, I hurriedly dressed and went to waken Jamie for school. As I was coming out of Jamie's room, I met Ian and asked about Drucilla. He grinned, his eyes sparkling with relief. "She seems to be doing a lot better this morning. She wanted me to ask you when she can get out of bed."

I frowned. "Tell her not to be in too big a hurry. And tell her I'll be up to see her after breakfast."

He thanked me and went back into their room.

At the breakfast table nothing was mentioned about the mines. Trampled fences in the south pasture occupied the men's attention.

Once Jamie was off to school, the kitchen cleaned, and Drucilla convinced that a few more days in bed would be worth it, I took a stroll to the stream. I was surprised to see new grass peeking through the stubble left by the grasshoppers. *To everything there is a season.* I smiled to myself. *Even for grasshopper invasions?*

The men were gone from the house until suppertime. When Jamie saw them riding into the yard, he bounded from the house. "Daddy! Daddy! Guess what? Teacher read a poem to us about a little girl who brought her lamb to school. She says I can bring Humble to school on pet day if you say it's all right."

"Really? You'll have to check with Jake about that." James dismounted and lifted his son into his arms. "It sounds like you had a great day at school."

"Oh, yeah. It was all right."

I watched and listened as they walked Honey to the corral. Jamie reported every detail about his school day. What would happen to that strengthening bond if James couldn't return until spring? On the other hand, Jamie loved school. Would it be fair to tear him away from something he enjoyed so much? *Oh, well, it's out of my hands anyway.* I returned to the dining room, where I'd been polishing the silver tea set.

That evening, while we gathered around the dinner table, James said he had two announcements that would affect us all. "Minna, come in here, please." She'd gone to the kitchen for a platter of bread she'd forgotten. As she stepped into the room, James strode to her side and put his arm around her shoulder. "First, Minna spoke with me this afternoon. She's decided to stay on with us indefinitely."

I jumped up from the table and gave her a hug. "Oh, I'm so happy. Why didn't you say something earlier? I had no idea."

She shrugged. "I first wanted to be sure I wouldn't be in the way."

"In the way? Never." I hugged her again.

"And second." James cleared his throat. "Chloe and I have talked about it, and we have decided to leave the ranch in Ian's care while we spend the winter in Columbine, managing the mine."

I gasped and shot a worried look toward Jamie. His face gleamed with happiness. James intercepted my thought. "Jamie will, of course, come with us. He and I talked about it this afternoon, and he's excited about living near a real gold mine, aren't you, son?"

The child nodded eagerly. James slipped his arm about my waist and continued. "If Drucilla continues to heal, we will leave for Denver on Tuesday, then head to Columbine before the week is out, according to how quickly I can go through Putnam's files."

I knew it wasn't a good time to bring up objections, but I did so anyway. "What about Jamie's schooling?"

James waved his hand. "He'll attend the school in Columbine, if there is one. If not, we'll take books and school supplies. You've already proven yourself an excellent teacher. To your credit, his teacher says Jamie's far ahead of the other children his age."

"And Daddy says I can go on a hot-air balloon ride for my birthday." The child's eyes danced with excitement. His seventh birthday would occur while we were still in Denver.

James squeezed my waist. "Don't worry, sweetheart. It was your idea in the first place, right?"

The week disappeared in a flurry of activity. I dashed off letters to my family, telling them I would send our new address as soon as possible. Since Drucilla knew Ian would not be leaving her alone, her spirits lifted, speeding her recovery. Ian thanked us repeatedly for helping him save the Renegade Mine.

"Don't worry," he assured James, "the ranch is yours when you return. Nothing will turn me into a cattleman. Can't understand how you can tolerate the mangy beasts, myself."

As for Jamie, all he could talk about was going hot-air ballooning in Denver and exploring a real gold mine. Come Tuesday, we boarded the train for Denver. Within ten miles, I realized I'd never before traveled with an energetic child. Being with him every day, I hadn't noticed the changes that had taken place in the boy since the trip from Chicago. He made me tired just watching him bounce around the partially filled passenger car, getting acquainted with the other passengers, talking with the conductor whenever the man strolled through the car, and trying to see all there was to see outside every window at the same time. Except for a distant windmill or a white-faced bovine, I couldn't see what the child found so interesting.

Seeing the strain in my eyes, James leaned back against the seat and closed his eyes. "Don't worry, he'll tire himself out in no time."

My new husband had many talents, but prophesying wasn't one of them. Jamie's frenzy continued throughout the evening. His enthusiasm spilled out to everyone in the car. Even the grouchy old man in the last seat who snarled at the conductor took time to teach Jamie some magic tricks. A bad mistake, for then the boy had to practice his new tricks on the rest of the passengers, including his father and me. Jamie was the first to spot the Rocky Mountains and the first to see the lights of Denver. When we deboarded, you'd think the car had been populated by family members by the way the passengers fussed over him.

One elderly woman patted my arm. "You have a lovely son there, an exceptional child, and a perfect gentleman, I might add."

I thanked her and glanced up at James. He shrugged and signaled for a cab. The driver loaded our luggage in the back of the carriage while we settled ourselves inside the closed carriage. I shivered from the biting wind sweeping down off the mountains. Jamie had questions about everything we passed. "May I ride on a trolley while we're here?"

"We'll see." James sent me a worried look when an involuntary sigh escaped my lips. "Right now, I think Chloe needs to rest. You look exhausted, darling. You're awfully pale. Are you all right?"

"I'm fine." I smiled through half-lidded eyes. The mild cramps that had started during the train ride were, in a way, a relief. A niggling fear that I might be pregnant could be laid to rest. I was grateful that I hadn't mentioned the possibility to James—he never would have agreed to my traveling with him.

"I booked us in the Teller House this time." James held my hand. "Phineas recommended it to me. It's smaller and newer—seventy rooms, but the owner spared no expense in the construction and decoration of the place. I hope you like it."

I laughed. "Of course, I'll like it." I tried to hide my grimace as the muscles in my abdomen contracted.

"Are you sure?" He brushed a stray lock of hair from my forehead. "You don't look so good."

"It's just female woes. I brought along some comfrey tea, which should help."

"Ah, well, if you need anything, ask. Do you understand?"

I nodded and leaned back against the seat. James drew my head to his shoulder. "I booked a suite, a room for Jamie and one for us, with a parlor in between. I'll take Jamie with me whenever possible so you can rest."

"Thank you."

When we arrived at the Teller House, James hurried us through registration. Jamie squealed with delight, and I fought back a wave of nausea as the elevator carried us to our fourth-floor suite.

The bellboy unlocked the door and handed James the key. "The master bedroom is on your left. The second sleeping room is on your right, and the bathroom facilities are through that . . ."

Without waiting for further direction, I raced in the direction he pointed, closing the door behind me.

As I ran, I heard James drop coins into the man's outstretched hand. "Thank you for everything. I'll take it from here. Just leave the luggage by the door."

Turning on the faucet, I leaned over the sink. The cold water I splashed on my face helped.

James knocked gently on the door. "Chloe, are you all right? Should I call a doctor?"

I could hear Jamie behind him asking, "What's wrong with Mama? Is she sick? Is Chloe gonna die?" I loved the way the child fluctuated between calling me Mama and calling me by my first name.

I dried my face on a thick white Turkish towel and opened the door. Two worried faces stared at me. I gave them a weak smile. "I'll be fine. And no, I'm not going to die, nor do I need a physician."

"Do you want anything from the dining room? I could get you a sandwich or a bowl of . . ."

I turned green at the suggestion and shook my head emphatically.

James knitted his brow tighter. "I guess that wasn't a good idea, huh?"

"Why don't you take Jamie downstairs to breakfast while I rest awhile? I'm sure I'll feel better after a little nap."

The two looked at me uncertainly. "You sure you'll be all right here alone while we're gone?"

"I'll sleep the entire time, honest."

James hurried over to the door and picked up my valise. "Let me carry this into the room for you so you can get out of your traveling clothes."

"Thank you. And you two, have a good time together."

I closed the door behind me and stumbled to the massive headboard. After slipping out of my dress and into a nightgown, I turned back the elaborate brocade coverlet and snuggled between the sheets. I closed my eyes and willed myself to sleep.

I awakened at sunset feeling wonderful. It bothered me that all my discomfort was gone—it was too good to be true. Opening the door to Jamie's room, I found James asleep on the double bed, his arm cradling his son.

I was sitting in the parlor reading a copy of the *Rocky Mountain News* when they awakened. James suggested we see if the dining room was still serving. My stomach responded to his suggestion with a positive growl.

All through dinner, Jamie told me all about their afternoon of sightseeing and trolley riding. "They don't give hot-air balloon rides on Wednesday, only on Saturday and Sunday. But Dad isn't sure we'll be ready to leave for Columbine before the weekend, so I still might get to go."

I glanced toward James. "Is that so?"

James nodded. "I called Putnam this afternoon to let him know we were in town and to give Jamie a chance to talk on the telephone. Phineas told me it will take some time to assemble facts here in Denver before I can discover the origin of the problem at the mining office."

The waiter removed our dinner plates and handed us dessert menus. My eyes lighted on the last two items, a napoleon and chocolate mousse. I smiled to myself as I remembered the desserts I'd never gotten to taste in the Chamberlains' luxury Pullman car. I knew very well that it would be reasonable to have one dessert one night and the other the next, but I didn't feel particularly reasonable. I grinned sheepishly at James over the menu.

He glanced up from his menu in time to catch my imploring look. "What? What would you like? Order anything you'd like."

I lifted two fingers over the top of the menu and looked pleadingly into his eyes.

"Two? Are you sure?"

The waiter bowed. "The desserts are of a generous proportion, madam," he warned.

James laughed. "If the lady wants two, she gets two. Just which two are we discussing?"

"The chocolate mousse and the napoleon."

James nodded. "The lady will have the chocolate mousse and the napoleon. And, son, what would you like?"

The waiter arched his eyebrows and scribbled my order on the pad while Jamie licked his lips and studied the menu a while longer.

"While my son is deciding, I'll take a slice of mile-high carrot cake."

Jamie grinned and closed the menu. "May I have a strawberry ice-cream sundae?"

James closed his menu, "I guess that will do it for us. A slice of carrot cake, a strawberry sundae, a chocolate mousse, and a napoleon."

"Very good, sir." The waiter bowed, collected the dessert menus, and went to fill our order.

"I can't believe a restaurant that doesn't list the prices for the food," I hissed across the table at James.

James replied in an affected British accent, "Very continental, don't you think?"

I swallowed my answer when the waiter wheeled the dessert cart to our table. My eyebrows rose higher than the waiter's had previously when I saw the size of the napoleon. After he left, I whispered, "You guys may have to help me eat these."

James chuckled and took a bite of his cake.

By the time I finished the outrageously delicious mousse, I knew I would never be able to eat the entire napoleon. Cutting the pastry in three portions, I shared it with the men in my life. I resisted the urge to lick my fingers clean. "The napoleon was tasty, but the mousse, m-m-m, the mousse was superb. Oh, yes, I need you to order one more thing, James."

Surprised, he asked, "You do?"

"Yes, could you ask the waiter for a wheelbarrow? There's no way I can walk out of this place. I ate too much."

We laughed and made our way into the hotel lobby, where we found Mrs. Putnam arguing with the desk clerk. "There you are. This despicable little man refused to tell me where you'd gone." She glared over her shoulder at the red-faced clerk. "And here you were in the hotel all the time!"

She rushed to us, hugging and kissing us like long-lost relatives. Jamie stared in fascination at the dead fox draped across the woman's shoulder, then at the massive ebony plume curling and fluttering over the top of the mountain of curls piled on her head.

She pinched the boy's cheeks and cooed, "Oh, you beautiful child!"

A pout formed on his face. "Girls are beautiful. Boys are handsome."

"You're so cute! Isn't he darling?" She laughed and patted him on the top of his head.

"So what are you doing here, Mrs. Putnam?" James asked.

"Gladys, darling, Gladys! I'm here to take you home with me." The woman took my hands in her diamond-and-ruby-studded fingers. "When Phineas told me you were feeling ill, my dear, I couldn't let you stay here in an impersonal hotel." She gazed about the elaborate lobby with disdain. "We have a guest cabin by the duck pond behind the main house. It is yours for as long as you need it." She patted James's hand affectionately. "And whenever you're in town, I expect you to use it."

James cleared his throat. "Gladys, this is so generous of you. I don't know what to say."

"Say you'll come home with me now. It's really quite simple. Why should you settle for this?"

Settle? I lifted my gaze to the monstrous crystal chandelier over our heads and swallowed back the urge to giggle.

James shook his head. "I can't let you do this, Gladys. We can't put you out."

"Put us out?" Her eyes saddened a moment, then brightened once again. "Having you there would be a pleasure. The place has been so quiet since our son, Phineas junior, joined a law firm in Washington, D.C." She bent down to face Jamie. "We have a full stable of riding horses and bridle trails right on the property. Do you ride English or Western style?"

Jamie shrugged and looked toward his father.

"Western, son."

She straightened and put her hands on Jamie's shoulders. There was something poignant about her invitation. "Please say you'll stay with us."

James and I exchanged a glance. "All right. I checked our trunks in at the station. Jamie and I'll go up to the room and pack our valises while you two relax in the lounge."

I turned to James. "Are you sure you don't need my help?"

"You relax."

The guest cabin was everything Gladys claimed—and more. Calling the place a cabin was an uncharacteristically modest understatement. The parlor had three separate seating areas. There wasn't a kerosene lamp or gas light in sight; electric-powered chandeliers and lamps illuminated every room. The three bedrooms were each the size of the entire hotel suite we had vacated. I learned later that the Putnams had hired a maid, a cook, and a butler for us before we accepted their hospitality.

As James and I settled down to sleep that night, he said, "Moving here is going to turn out to be a blessing. I haven't had a chance to tell you, but tomorrow I need to take the train to Colorado Springs. I need to talk with the former owner of the Renegade Mine."

I eyed him suspiciously. "How long will you be gone?"

He touched the wall switch, and the light flicked off instantly. "A day or two at the most. I'd considered taking Jamie with me, but with the riding stables and our hostess to keep him busy . . . I could get back sooner if I went alone."

"That makes good sense. Jamie is never any trouble, you know that. And I am feeling much better tonight." My eyes grew accustomed to the darkness. Filmy white curtains filtered the moonlight coming in through the French doors.

James turned over, and within a few minutes, I could hear his gentle snore. I thought about the events of the day, especially my illness. I was never sickly: whenever my brothers or sisters had caught a bug at school, I always escaped. Lying in the darkness, I reviewed the last few weeks. And my suspicions grew. *You just might be pregnant, girl. And your discomfort today was a warning to take it easy.*

I slid out of bed, put on my dressing gown, and opened the doors leading to the garden. I strolled down the flagstone pathway to the water's edge, where moonlight danced on the surface of the pond.

Thoughts tumbled relentlessly through my mind. *Shall I mention my suspicions to James before he leaves tomorrow? Sooner or later, he's going to figure it out, you know. No, he has enough worries on his mind with this business deal.* A niggling thought worried my brain. *He might send me back to Hays. Maybe I'll wait until we reach Columbine before saying anything.*

The next morning, breakfast was served in the solarium, a cozy room off the kitchen furnished in painted wicker furniture and yellow-flowered chintz. While James and Jamie ate a hearty meal of French toast, piled high with blueberries and whipped cream, I fought down my nausea with a cup of peppermint tea. When James asked me why I wasn't eating, I rolled my eyes. "You ask me that after last night's indulgence?"

"That will teach you." He laughed, then turned toward his son. "Last night I arranged with Mrs. Putnam for you to go riding this morning with the groomsman."

Jamie looked pleadingly at me. "Will you come with

me, Chloe? Please?"

I blanched, then regained my composure. "I'd love to, honey, but I'm still not feeling that great. Can we go together another time?"

He grinned. "Sure. Maybe when Daddy gets back we can all go as a family."

"Good idea, son." James arose from the table. "I've got to get going. I'm riding to town with Phineas; then I'll leave directly from his office for Colorado Springs."

Jamie looked up from sipping his hot chocolate. "You're going away, Dad?"

"Just for a couple of days. I'll be back in time for your birthday ride in the balloon on Sunday," James explained.

The child's eyes lighted up. "You mean I'm gonna get to fly?"

"That's right. The three of us will have a great day together at Elitch Gardens." James kissed my forehead, then kissed Jamie's cheek. "I gotta get going."

I started to get up from the table. "Right now?"

"Right now." He leaned down and kissed me properly. "I'll be back as soon as possible. You two take care of one another. I'm going to miss you terribly."

I nodded, afraid if I tried to speak, I would shout at him, scream, pound his chest with my fists, tell him that I was carrying our child and I needed him to stay with me. *Get a hold of yourself, Chloe. Be reasonable!* I didn't feel reasonable; I was on the verge of tears.

"Honey," he looked into my eyes. "What's wrong? I'll be gone only two days and a night, I promise."

"I know. I'm being silly." I sniffed back the tears. "I love you, James."

He drew me to my feet and enveloped me in his arms. "I love you too, sweetheart."

He threw a second kiss to Jamie and left. The next two days proved to be a blessed reprieve for me. Except for a twinge of nausea when I first got out of bed in the morning, I felt terrific. After his ride, Jamie and I fed the ducks and swans in the pond. In the afternoon, Gladys insisted on taking us to the city park, then to an ice-cream parlor for a dish of maple-nut ice cream.

That evening, I begged off from attending the opera with the Putnams, saying I didn't want to leave Jamie alone in unfamiliar surroundings. Besides, I'd never been to the opera in my life, and I had no intention of going without James at my side.

Before dismissing the butler for the night, I asked him to build a fire in the fireplace. Changing into our robes and nightwear, Jamie and I curled up in front of the fire with a book of watercolors depicting African wildlife.

After Jamie dozed off, I watched the flames dance and thought of the child that might be growing inside me. Filled with a strange elation, I placed my hand on my stomach.

It had been easy to say I wanted to bear James's children, but now I wasn't so sure. Because of Jamie, I'd become a mom before I became a mother. My own mother's weary face surfaced before me. I thought of how hard her life was, bearing so many children. For all I knew, she could be expecting another. Thinking of her made me feel depressed. *Now I will no longer be a carefree girl. Now I will get wrinkles. Now my hair will lose its shine. Now I'll become ragged and old.*

During the night, Jamie awakened me. The fire had died; the ashes lay cold and lifeless beneath the iron grate. He kissed me good night and padded off to his bed. I staggered to my room and crawled under the covers, robe and all.

Where Eagles Soar

James arrived back in Denver on schedule. When Jamie and I met him at the station, I cried.

"Why are you crying?" He looked at me strangely. "I told you I'd be back."

"I don't know." I sniffled and reddened. "I can't help it. I'm so glad to see you."

That evening he tried to explain what he'd discovered about the mine. After repeating himself three times, he looked at me askance. "Is anything wrong? Are you still feeling ill?"

"I'm fine, as healthy as a horse. Speaking of horses, did Jamie tell you about his riding lesson? The groomsman said he had a real knack for the saddle." I could see my husband wavering between pursuing the subject of my health and letting it pass for the time being. I heaved a sigh when he did the unexpected.

"A knack, huh? Jamie didn't tell me that. He told me he learned some new tricks."

On Saturday, we took the train and then a carriage for a drive and picnic lunch up in the mountains. We ate our lunch at an overlook. Autumn tones of gold and orange dotted the forest. The city of Denver looked insignificant against the sweep of jagged peaks and plunging valleys surrounding us on three sides. Pale golden prairie grass started at the base of the mountains and swept eastward as far as the eye could see.

After lunch we hiked to a waterfall. James and I sat along the bank while Jamie tried to catch a fish with a stick, a string, and piece of beef jerky for bait. Late in the afternoon, ominous clouds forming over the tops of the western peaks urged us back to the valley. Jamie worried all the way to Denver that a storm would prevent his promised balloon ride.

Morning dawned to a cloudless sky. At Jamie's urging, we were the first in line at Elitch Gardens. Excitement crackled around the boy. The balloon operator caught the child's spirit, patiently answering each of the child's questions.

As the balloon touched down, Jamie hugged his father. "Thanks, Daddy. When I grow up, I want to be a balloonist and fly every day."

James took his son's hand. "Well, you never know, son."

We spent the day at the gardens, enjoying the acrobats and the magicians and watching the animals in the zoo. The next morning we said goodbye to the Putnams and boarded the Union Pacific for Steamboat Springs. Breathtaking scenery unfolded around us as our train wound its way up the mountain. The change of scenery gave me a new vitality. On this trip I was almost as bad as Jamie, jumping from one side of the train to the other to get a better view of the passing drama.

Toward evening, the train pulled into Steamboat Springs, a wild and bawdy mining center that boasted fifteen bars and no churches. We spent the night in the only hotel in town, but the music and shouting from the bar downstairs prevented all but the lightest of catnapping. The next morning we boarded a train that ran on a mining spur north to the town of Hahn's Peak.

I clutched the side railing until my knuckles turned

white as our open-air passenger car bounced and swayed around death-defying curves and over rickety wooden trestles at what seemed like incredible speeds. Even Jamie had the good sense to sit still and hold tight. The only other passenger on the train was a grizzled old prospector with a gold front tooth. Grit, as the character called himself, told tales of panning for gold across the West. "Yep, started out as a dumb kid in '49; been at it ever since."

"Did you ever find any gold?" Jamie asked.

"Yep, plenty of times," the old man said. "Staked claims and sold claims, then moved on to the next bonanza. The fun is in the seekin', not the spendin', son. Here." Grit reached into his shirt pocket and handed Jamie a shiny chunk of ore. "Gold. Known more men destroyed by the mere sight of it than I've ever seen destroyed by dy-no-mite or fire in the hole."

"Fire in the hole?" Jamie's eyes lighted up almost as much as mine.

"Yep. That's when the miners hit a gas vein. The flame from the lanterns sets off a fireball through the tunnels."

We saw the mountain called Hahn's Peak before we saw the town. After leaving me at the general store, James and his son went to rent a team and wagon for the four-mile ride to the town of Columbine, our destination. I inspected the bolts of sturdy fabric and heavy yarn designed for service, not style. Beyond the dress and shirt fabrics was a stack of canvas bolts, yards and yards of canvas.

Instead of an abundance of farming equipment, mining gear lined most of the walls. A white-haired woman wearing three dresses, one on top of the next, and a patched sweater over all, entered the store. I could feel her watching me out of the corner of her eye as the clerk mumbled aloud the items on the woman's shopping list.

"You have here three-penny nails. I got an extra ship-ment in, and right now, they're on sale ten for a nickel."

She shook her head. "Nope, can't afford it. I only need three to repair the back step."

I looked away to hide my surprise. *What is a nickel? Buy ten, buy twenty,* I thought.

The friendly clerk tapped his pencil on the counter. "You can pay me the rest next time you come to town."

"Nope. Pay as I go, that's my motto." She nodded her head proudly. "Now are you going to sell me those nails, or do I have to send clear to Denver for 'em?"

The clerk grinned and totaled her order. "That will be one dollar and twenty-two cents." She unsnapped her purse and counted out the exact change.

"There, that should do me for a while." As the woman stepped out into the sunlight, she turned and smiled shyly at me. I returned the courtesy. A few minutes later, James and Jamie drove up in a wagon. In the back I could see our trunks and valises, along with a generous supply of grain and hay for the horses. I waved and hurried out of the store as James stepped down from the wagon.

"The blacksmith said we should buy our supplies here in Hahn's Peak. The prices in Columbine are even higher. I bought the team and wagon with the understanding that he'd buy them back when we leave."

I groaned. My back ached. My head ached. I didn't feel like staying around Hahn's Peak any longer. I wanted to get to our new home and stretch out on a real bed.

James read the ill humor on my face. "It will only take a couple of minutes to buy a few essentials to get us through the next few days. Then, when you're refreshed, we can come back down for whatever else we need."

I nodded and took his arm. James called back over his shoulder to Jamie. "Stay here and watch the wagon, son."

Back inside the general store, I sat in one of the wooden

rockers by the pot-bellied stove while James greeted the clerk and gave him a list of the food staples we'd need.

The clerk rushed about the store, collecting the items requested, all the while talking about the benefits of living in an up-and-coming town like Hahn's Peak. James leaned over my shoulder. "Must be the town's chamber of commerce."

A dog barking drew my attention out the window. Jamie stood beside the wagon playing go-fetch with a gray-and-brown mutt. James turned to the clerk. "Whose dog?"

The clerk shrugged. "Used to belong to old Ned before he headed into the hills one night and never came back. Now Rags belongs to the man who feeds him."

"Who's that?"

The clerk grinned. "Anybody and everybody. Usually eats out of garbage cans."

James turned back to the counter as the clerk tabulated our bill on the cash register. James glanced at me, then back at the clerk. "Do you think anybody would mind it we adopted the dog?"

The clerk replied, "S'pect not. Will that be all?"

James reached in his pocket to take out his money. "Say, how much for one of those rifles?"

My ears perked up—I hated guns. As the men dickered over the price, the clerk picked up a brown cardboard box from behind the counter. "I'll throw in an extra box of shells."

James agreed to the price and counted out the cash. The man's eyes widened at the roll of money in my husband's hand. Calling a stock boy from the back room to load our purchases into the wagon, the clerk then walked us to the door. "I wouldn't carry that much cash around with me if I were you," he cautioned. "Men have been killed for a whole lot less. The bank's down yonder."

We thanked him for the advice. "You know, the man

makes sense, about the money, I mean," I said.

"I agree. We'll stop by the bank and the assay office on our way out of town." Turning to his son, James said, "So I see you've met Rags."

Jamie looked up and grinned. "Look, Dad, he can fetch the stick when I throw it." The boy tossed a small stick fifteen feet down the road. The gutsy little dog charged after it, then returned and laid it at Jamie's feet.

James bent down and examined the dog more closely. "I'd say Rags is still a pup; he has a lot of growing to do to fit those feet. Son, do you think Rags would like living with us?"

"Really?" The boy danced first on one foot, then on the other. "He can come home with us?" Jamie knelt down and hugged the animal. Then he paused and looked up at his father. "What about when we go back to Kansas? Will I have to leave him here?"

James lifted the dog into the wagon. "Let's worry about that when the time comes, son."

We climbed into the wagon, Jamie in back with the dog, and drove up the dusty street to the bank. Jamie, Rags, and I waited in the wagon until James returned. When I was certain I could wait no longer, James came out of the bank with a dapper, gray-haired gentleman. The dark gray suit with a light gray-and-red-silk vest he wore hung from his gaunt frame. His thin mustache drooped a good three inches below his clean-shaven jaw.

"Mr. Avery, I would like you to meet my wife, Chloe, and our son, Jamie."

I smiled and extended my hand. Instead of shaking it, he kissed it.

"This is Attorney Prentice Avery. He handles the papers for the Renegade Mine."

I smiled politely and slipped my hand out of his grasp. "Ah, then I am sure James will be seeing a lot of you while we're here in Colorado."

The lawyer's gray eyes gleamed with intelligence and cunning. "I look forward to seeing more of you also, Mrs. McCall."

I gave a tiny, insincere laugh. "Thank you."

The men shook hands and parted. James hopped onto the seat beside me and urged the horses forward. The road to Columbine began to climb before we passed through the edge of town.

As we rounded a bend, I spotted a woman limping along the side of the road, a pack over her back. As we drew closer, I recognized her as the woman I'd seen in the general store. James slowed the wagon. "Ma'am, are you going far? Can we give you a lift?"

She turned and smiled. "That would be mighty neighborly of you. I'm Ula VanArsdale. My husband Noah and I have a small place a mile this side of Columbine."

He helped her onto the seat beside me. "Do you walk into Hahn's Peak often?"

"About every week. We own a rooster and few laying hens. Since our horse died last spring, I walk to town to sell the eggs."

"That must be difficult in the snow."

The woman's gnarled hand massaged her left knee. "It is, but I can't complain; I don't suffer near as much as Noah. Getting out of bed is a chore for him some days."

I eyed her speculatively before I spoke. "Does applying a deep-heat garlic poultice help? My pa swears by it."

She turned to me. "Is your father a doctor?"

I hastened to explain. "He's not a medical doctor, but an herbal doctor."

"Too bad he doesn't live around here. The closest doctor is at Steamboat Springs, if you ever find Doc Yancy sober." She pursed her lips. "Do you know anything about medicine?"

I glanced at James, then back at our traveling companion. "A little."

"Praise God!" She chuckled and grinned at me. "If I were a prophet, I'd say you're about to learn a whole lot more, moving to Columbine. People in these parts are dying for the likes of you. How do you make this garlic poultice?"

As James halted the wagon in front of the cabin she called home, I explained the simple process. "Three-quarters cup of finely chopped garlic and a cup of lard in a jar . . ."

When I finished giving her the directions, James helped the woman down from the wagon. "You just rub it on the joints?"

I nodded. "That's right. Loosens congestion in the chest too."

Rags barked at a chicken running by the wagon, but Jamie grabbed the dog before he could give chase.

James glanced cautiously at Rags. "Nice to have met you, Mrs. VanArsdale. We'd better get going before you have one less hen."

I waved as we drove back to the main road. "She's quite a character."

"Colorful," James muttered.

I jabbed his ribs. "You're sounding like a Boston prig, Mr. McCall."

"Sorry." He reddened.

I leaned closer and purred, "I'm just teasing."

Taking a deep breath, I coughed. "I'm finding it difficult to breathe up here."

James nodded. "It's the altitude. Ian says you get used to it."

"I hope so."

The town of Columbine was everything Gladys and

Phineas told us—and less. It seems mining camps go through four stages of growth: first, the tents; second, the log cabins for the avid prospectors and merchants who only want to strike it rich and leave as quickly as possible; third, with the arrival of the sawmill, frame structures with false fronts; and fourth, if the town promises permanence, brick and stone buildings. Columbine appeared stuck in stage two. Thrown-together shacks stood side by side with sturdier log cabins. The mouths of caves dotted the hillside surrounding the town.

Jamie leaned over the seat. "Where's our gold mine, Dad?"

"According to the map, it's two miles east of the town."

Jamie wrapped his arms around Rag's neck. "Will we live at the mine or in town?"

"In town, at least for a while."

Ill-clothed, unshaven miners stared openly at us as we rolled down the main street of Columbine. Tavern keepers peered out at us over swinging bar gates. A brightly painted woman sashayed out of one of the buildings and leaned against a watering trough. "This is Columbine?" I whispered, eyeing the garishly painted hotel sign swinging over one of the noisier establishments.

James followed my gaze. "Don't worry, we're not staying there tonight. Phineas wired ahead for rooms at Dinah's Boardinghouse."

Both Dinah and her boardinghouse turned out to be clean, comfortable, and respectable. So respectable that Jamie had to leave Rags tied outside by the kitchen door all night.

While James settled Jamie in the room next to us, I scrubbed myself clean of the day's dirt and sweat, then tucked my aching body beneath the bedcovers. James returned, washed up, and turned off the kerosene lamp on his side of the bed. As he climbed into bed, he gave an exhausted sigh.

I knew the time had come. While I'd been able to hide my morning sickness, I no longer doubted my condition. I had to tell him about the baby.

I inched closer to him, my voice mellow and pleading. "Honey . . ."

"Hmm?"

"Honey, I have something important to tell you."

He groaned. "Can't it wait until morning?"

"I suppose." I rolled back onto my side of the bed.

He sighed. "I'm awake now. You might as well tell me."

"I-I-I think I'm pregnant." His silence filled the room, suffocating me. I held my breath until he spoke.

"Pregnant?"

"Uh-huh. Are you angry?"

"About your being pregnant? Of course not. The timing is what scares me." More silence followed. I lay on my back, staring into the darkness. James took me into his arms. "How long have you known?"

"Since we arrived in Denver."

"What?" He sat upright in the bed. "Why didn't you say something earlier?"

I answered in barely a whisper. "I'm sorry. I was afraid you'd leave me there, or worse yet, send Jamie and me back to Hays alone, without you."

"You're right. I would have!" Leaping from the bed, he relighted the lamp and loomed over the bed like an avenging angel. "I can't believe you kept this from me. Do you realize how isolated we are out here? Columbine is no place for a pregnant woman!"

"I'm sorry," I whispered.

"How far along are you?"

"Probably a month to six weeks."

"You were pregnant when we left Kansas? Didn't you know?"

I shook my head.

"You're a midwife. How could you not know?"

I shrugged and pulled the quilt up to my chin.

"And your illness on the train? You said . . ." He paced to the bedroom door and back.

I grimaced. "I think I almost lost our baby. I'm sorry."

"Stop saying you're sorry. I can't believe this." He rubbed the back of his hand across his forehead. "I suspected. That's why I kept asking you if you were all right."

"I'm sor—"

"Don't say it." James sat down on the edge of the bed and grabbed hold of my shoulders. Tears glistened in his eyes. "Don't you understand? I can't bear the thought of losing you. It's a nightmare starting all over again."

Realizing the enormity of my decision not to tell him sooner and the obvious fears he would have after losing three infants and his wife Mary, I choked back a rush of tears.

"If I lose you too, I-I-I . . ."

I reached up and brushed his hair from his forehead. "I'm not Mary; I'm Chloe. And I'm healthy and strong, remember? Besides, women have been bearing children in remote regions for centuries."

"And dying from it."

"I come from strong Scotch-Irish stock."

He laughed. "I don't know what you inherited from the Scottish side of the family, but your feistiness is definitely Irish." He took a deep breath and stared into my eyes for a moment. "So, what happens next?"

I caressed the side of his face. "We find a place to live until you finish your business at the mine. Then we head back to Denver, hopefully before winter sets in, and come June fifteen or so, we have a baby."

He smiled wryly. "That's pretty much the picture, I suppose." His face darkened. "Promise me one thing—

don't keep anything from me again, especially now, under the circumstances."

"I promise."

"And promise me you will take care of yourself. No heavy lifting, no overexertion, no heroics."

The next morning, James insisted I sleep in while he, Jamie, and Rags went to check out the Renegade mining camp. I didn't object. I spent the morning writing letters to my family. As I added a P.S. to each of the letters announcing my pregnancy, I grew accustomed to the idea, almost eager.

I was downstairs in the parlor talking with Dinah, the proprietor, when James returned. James sat down beside me on the sofa as Dinah excused herself. "There's a two-room cabin we could use. It was built by the mine's original manager, but it's now in terrible shape." James frowned. "The current manager, Otis Roy, keeps a room in town."

"A little soap and hot water will turn it into a home in no time."

He shook his head. "It's small and isolated. I stopped at the sheriff's office and found out there's an abandoned two-bedroom cabin west of town that will suit us much better."

"Wonderful." I rose to my feet. "I'll go pack."

"Wait a minute." He caught my hand in his. "I hired the sheriff's wife this morning to clean it thoroughly. She was glad for the money. We can move in tomorrow morning."

I pulled my hand away and jumped to my feet. "Can we at least go see it today?"

He laughed. "Of course. That's why I didn't unhitch the team."

"Let me get my hat and shawl." I ran to the door, then stopped. "Where's Jamie?"

James stood up and dusted his hat with his sleeve. "I left him and Rags at the cabin to get used to the place. He asked me to convince you to let Rags sleep inside at night, in his room, of course. Did I take on an impossible task?"

I shook my head. "Unless the animal grows too big for the cabin, that is." It wasn't that long ago I was arguing with Ma about letting Patches sleep at the foot of my bed on cold nights.

One glance at the place, and I lost heart. The cabin was nestled near a granite outcropping. Nearby was the gorge that carried the spring runoff, but in October, the river was little more than a trickling stream. Rough-hewn logs of varying sizes formed the railings, posts, and beams for the small front porch.

Rags bounded around the side of the house, barking, with Jamie close behind. "How'd ya like it, Mama? Wait till you see inside." He scaled the porch steps and held the door for me.

I gazed about the small living area dominated by a gigantic stone fireplace. Clustered around a multicolored rag rug was a brown leather sofa, worn golden, and a couple of equally aged upholstered armchairs. A small keg used for storing nails sat between the two chairs. A cookstove, a cabinet with an open cupboard of dishware, and a sturdy homemade table with two benches stood near the only window in the room. Beneath the glass-paned window was a work counter and sink with a hand pump.

Jamie eyed me eagerly. "Do ya like it?"

I continued my inspection. On the wall opposite the fireplace were two doors with a desk and crude chair in between. A rough-hewn ladder leading to the open loft above leaned against the wall. The bare walls displayed only one ornament—a black bear skin. I decided to look for the possibilities. *Gingham tiebacks for the window, matching pads for the benches, a dried weed arrangement in the middle of the table, baskets of every size hanging from the open beams. Bright flowered covers for the chairs, a few throw pillows, and—the bear's carcass has to go!*

I heard footsteps behind me. James linked his hand in mine. " 'Fraid it's not the Putnams' guest house."

"It's perfect. Which room will be ours?"

"Over here." We had to sidestep over our trunks to reach the door. "No indoor plumbing."

I'd noticed the boardwalk leading from the cabin to the outhouse as we came inside. "I didn't grow up with such luxuries, remember?"

The bedroom was larger than I expected, or maybe it looked larger because of the lighter toned wooden floor and bedstead. I bounced on the edge of the mattress and sighed. It was stuffed with grass. I'd miss our down-filled mattress back in Kansas. Two small windows on either side of the bed broke the monotony of the whitewashed walls. At the foot of the bed, a wooden rocker sat beside a handmade set of shelves.

"Come see my room! Come on." Jamie grabbed my hand and dragged me into the room next to ours. His room was much the same as ours, except smaller. Without a word, I went back out to the living room and climbed the ladder. Mice had taken over the loft. Scrambling down as quickly as possible, I announced, "We need a cat right away!"

"Hey! A cat?" Jamie jumped up and down. "Rags likes cats; I know he does."

James stood by the table, his face sober. "I'm sorry I can't provide better for you, Chloe."

I whirled about in the center of the room. "What are you talking about? I feel like a little girl getting to play house. I already have so many ideas for brightening the place."

He walked up behind me and slipped his arms about my waist. "Hey, don't get carried away. If all goes well, we'll be here only for a month, at the most."

But I wasn't listening. I was running down the list of

household things I'd packed in one of the trunks. I had so much to do.

"Sheriff Jones's wife has a braid rug she'll let us use for the bedroom. And the former owners left their pots and pans and a few other kitchen utensils in the basket over there. When she cleaned, she threw out a bunch of stuff behind the cabin."

"What kind of stuff?"

"Oh, a few apple crates, some old baskets. I don't know. Why?"

"Baskets? Crates?" I could see the baskets dangling from the open beams and the crates converted into bedside stands and storage bins.

During the next few days, James spent long hours at the mine going over the books and inspecting the entire operation. Jamie started attending the seven-student, one-room school in the back of Walsh's Mercantile, and I settled the cabin to my liking. Mrs. Jones brought over two large braided rugs for us to use, as well as a multicolored afghan, which I placed over the stains on the back of the couch. I felt a wave of pride when James returned home and complimented me on the new pillows I'd made for the couch and the curtains I'd sewn for the windows.

Mrs. VanArsdale dropped by the next morning with a dozen eggs as a thank-you and a calico kitten named Sunshine. "Mrs. Bovee told me you were lookin' for a cat. She heard it from Granny Shepherd who heard it from Sadie Jones."

I laughed and thanked the woman. Obviously the mountain telegraph worked as efficiently as did Western Union. She turned to leave. "Since we have no church here in Columbine, a group of us meet together at the jail every Sunday evening to study the Bible and sing. You're invited to come, if you like."

Church held in the jail? I hoped my reaction didn't register on my face. "How nice. Thank you. I'm not sure James would feel comfortable with that, but I'll ask." When she left, I promptly forgot about the invitation.

A week after moving into the cabin, we told Jamie about the baby. His reaction was a shrug and "that's nice." When I mentioned Jamie's less-than-enthusiastic response, James consoled, "He's getting used to his new school. A baby brother or sister is the farthest thing from a young boy's mind. As the birth gets closer, he'll take an interest."

With Jamie in school most of the day, my life fell into a comfortable routine. Throughout the day, when I was washing dishes at the sink, making beds, or darning stockings, I found myself spinning dreams for the child developing within me. Purchasing an empty journal at the tiny mercantile in town, I began writing down my feelings. I also bought five yards of white flannel to begin preparing the baby's layette and several skeins of yarn for booties and for mittens for Jamie.

One afternoon as I sat on the sofa knitting a blanket for the baby with Sunshine curled up beside me and Rags by my feet, a shadow passed the kitchen window. Rags growled, and the cat scooted into the bedroom to hide. Thinking it was James coming home early from the mine, I hopped up and ran to the door to meet him.

When I opened the door, Rags lunged out of the house, barking and growling. No one was in sight, but I could immediately tell that the footprints in the snow didn't belong to James. Rags reluctantly returned to my call before I closed the door behind me and gazed at the rifle James had hung over the fireplace. *I suppose I should learn to use that thing someday.* Even as I thought it, I knew I'd never take the time.

While my days were relatively calm and stress free, life for James had become a giant mystery. At the mine, he discovered a disturbing number of irregularities suggesting that Otis Roy was guilty of both fraud and negligence, but James didn't want to reveal his suspicions until he'd examined and compiled all the evidence. He had to make frequent trips to our lawyer in Hahn's Peak and to the assay office and county courthouse in Steamboat Springs.

The morning after the first big snowstorm, we reluctantly admitted to ourselves that we would be staying in Columbine longer than originally planned. There seemed to be nothing to do but make ourselves at home for a long, hard winter.

Room for Fear,
Room for Faith

A cozy fire crackled in the fireplace. Outside a west wind howled, causing the glass windowpanes on that side of the house to hum. Standing in front of the sink, I sliced the last carrot and tossed it into the boiling water, then cut up and added an extra onion for good measure. Already I could taste the delicious vegetable stew I'd serve for supper. Rags nibbled on a chunk of potato I'd dropped while I disposed of the scraps. Sunshine purred at my ankles, coaxing me to sit a spell and pet her.

"Not now, precious. You'll have to wait your turn. First, I need to write a note to Hattie, then patch the knees of Jamie's school pants." I walked to the desk and removed my writing supplies. Making myself comfortable at the table, I began my letter home. I'd barely written the salutation when Rags barked and trotted over to the door. When the visitor knocked, Rags growled and pawed at the door to be let out.

"Go lie down." Thinking it must be Mrs. VanArsdale dropping by for a visit, I hurried to the door and swung it open. "The minute I heard . . ."

I stared in surprise at the tallest Indian I'd ever seen, an Indian with vibrant blue eyes. Dressed in work boots, canvas pants, and a heavy buckskin jacket, the dark-skinned man tipped his narrow-brimmed hat. "Ma'am, I have a packet of mail for you. Mr. McCall asked me to deliver it to you because he had to return directly to the mine."

"Uh, oh, uh, yes, uh, won't you please come in out of the cold?" I stepped back to make room for the broad-chested man to fit through the doorway. A skittering of snowflakes drifted across the floor before I could close the door. Rags growled from behind the far end of the sofa.

The man removed his hat and slapped it against his trouser leg. Taking off his gloves, he reached inside his jacket, pulled out a packet of letters, and handed them to me. He blew on his hands while I shuffled through the envelopes. I recognized my mother's writing as well as Joe's and Mr. Putnam's.

"This one should have gone to the mine." I held out Mr. Putnam's letter to him. "You might want to take it to the office with you."

The man shook his head, still warming his fingertips with his breath. "No, Mr. McCall meant for that letter to be delivered here."

I shrugged. "Would you like a hot cup of tea? I have the teakettle on the stove right now."

He eyed me suspiciously for a moment. "That would be nice, thank you. Then I need to go."

"Well, make yourself comfortable, Mr.— I'm sorry, I didn't catch your name."

"Indian Pete. Everyone calls me Indian Pete."

He strode over to the table and sat down as directed. Rags followed, sniffing the man's trousers and boots. I bustled about the kitchen preparing his tea. "What is your tribe?" I'd grown up near the Allegheny Indian Reservation across the border in New York State.

"My mother was a Rogue; my father, a trapper."

I set the cup and saucer down on the table in front of him and another on the opposite side of the table. "Ah, that's where you got your blue eyes, from your father."

He folded his hands around the cup, absorbing the warmth of the tea through the porcelain. "Yes."

"Cream? Sugar?"

He shook his head.

I sipped the hot liquid gently. "You work at the mine?"

He nodded, averting his eyes from mine. "Yes, sometimes."

"Sometimes?" Rags came over to my side and begged to be petted.

"Sometimes." The stranger gulped down the tea and stood.

"Do you and your family live near here?" Without a word, he picked up his hat, strode to the door, and opened it.

"Thank you for the tea, ma'am. If I were you, I'd keep this door barred when you're here alone." His blue eyes snapped with censure. "Gold brings out the worst in men."

Taken aback by his harsh tones, I stammered, "Uh, yes, uh, you're right. Thanks for reminding me." He nodded, ducked to keep from banging his head on the lintel, and stepped out into the winter morning.

That evening at the dinner table, both Jamie and I listened with rapt attention as James told us about the man called Indian Pete. "Pete was born and raised in southern Oregon and was sent to study law in San Francisco by Methodist missionaries. After years of trying to fit into the white man's world, he set out on his own. Some of the men at the mine say he killed a man and is on the run, but I doubt it after getting to know him."

"Killed a man?" Jamie's eyes widened.

"Son, never judge a man by rumor. Sheriff Jones has no record on Pete." James continued, "On my second visit to the mine, Pete warned me to be careful, to be on my guard at all times. When I learned about his legal training, I brought him into the office to help me. I've found him to be a reliable friend and knowledgeable assistant."

I seconded my husband's assessment. "He was a gentleman while he was here. Rags took to him almost immediately." Upon hearing his name, Rags got up from the hearth and waddled over to me for attention. Idly I scratched the dog's head.

"Daddy, can we invite Indian Pete for Thanksgiving dinner like the Pilgrims did in Massachusetts?" Jamie looked from his father, to me, then back again.

Interpreting my smile to mean yes, James nodded his approval. "If we invite Indian Pete to eat with us, it will be because he is a friend, not because he is an Indian. However, it will all depend on how Chloe feels."

"Mama?"

The idea of entertaining guests triggered my enthusiasm. "You know, it might be a good idea to invite your manager, Otis Roy, also." I'd never met the man James was investigating. "And maybe the VanArsdales. Perhaps Mr. Avery—"

"Hold on there, Chloe girl. Aren't you getting carried away?"

I smiled coyly. "We can talk about it later. Why don't you find a text to read tonight?"

Soon after we arrived in Columbine, we had begun reading the Bible and praying together after our evening meal. I suspect that the news of the baby prompted James's decision, but I liked the change. As a result, we seemed to bond even closer as a family.

At breakfast a few days later, James announced that he needed to travel to Steamboat Springs to consult the county assay records.

Jamie looked up from his bowl of oatmeal. "May I go too, Dad?"

"No, son, you have school today."

James placed his dishes in the sink and peered out the kitchen window. "I don't like the looks of the sky. If a storm blows in, I might have to stay overnight. I'll have Indian Pete stop by to be sure you two are all right."

I poured a portion of the leftover milk into Sunshine's dish, then poured the rest into the milk can. "I'm sure we'll be fine, dear."

Jamie carried his dishes to the sink and disappeared to his room to get ready for school.

"Nevertheless, I'll feel better knowing he's looking out for you," James responded. "And please, keep the door barred when I'm not here."

"Indian Pete has been telling tales out of school, huh?" Scraping the leftover oatmeal into Rag's dish, I carried the pan to the sink to be washed. "I know I should. But when I come in from the outhouse, I forget to bar the door behind me. By the way, did you ask him about Thanksgiving?"

"Yep. Could you choose a shirt, a change of under-clothes, and socks for me while I get the valise down from the loft?" We used the loft to store our trunks and smaller luggage as well as my supply of herbs. James headed toward the ladder.

I stood with my hands on my hips. "And he said?"

"Huh? Oh, he said thank you. But," James held up one finger, "let's limit the guest list to him."

"Fine," I mumbled as I hurried into our bedroom and over to the shelves where we stored most of our clothing. "Was that so hard to say? I never would have known if I hadn't asked."

From out in the other room, James called, "Did you say something, honey?"

I snatched a blue-striped wool shirt from the shelf along with a pair of long johns and wool socks. "I said—oh, never mind." I realized my irritability was unfair. "I just hate being left behind while you go traipsing—"

James stood in the doorway, laughing. "I know. A trip to Steamboat Springs ranks right up there with Paris and Rome."

"You're incorrigible!" I whipped about and threw his clothing at him. He caught and hurled them back at me. The socks fluttered harmlessly to the bed, but the long johns landed dead center on my head. And like a giant octopus, the four appendages draped down around my shoulders, causing James to dissolve into a fresh bout of laughter.

"Laugh, will you!" I jerked the garment off my head, twisted it into a rope, and snapped it at James's legs.

"You wanna play rough, huh? Looks like it's time for a counter charge." He leaped across the bed. I shrieked and ran around the foot of the bed, but James cut off my escape before I reached the door. Wrapping his arms about me, he pinned my arms to my side. "Say uncle."

I wriggled and squirmed while he laughed. Realizing I couldn't overpower him with strength, I used cunning. As I quieted, James relaxed his hold long enough for me to inch my hands up and tickle his stomach. He doubled over, and I scurried to the other side of the bed.

"Why, you little . . ." He stopped and sniffed the air. "I smell smoke."

"Of course you do. There's a fire in the fireplace. Did you really think I'd fall for—" I sniffed the air.

"No, it's different. That's sulfur—matches." He ran out of our bedroom and into Jamie's. "Son! What are you doing? Chloe, get a pan of water, quick."

I rushed to the sink, grabbed the basin of water, and dashed across the living room. Jamie stood horrified, watching his father stomp out flames in the middle of the floor. "What were you trying to do?" James shouted.

Before Jamie could answer, I dumped the basin of

water on the flaming paper. James stared down into his son's terrified face. "Talk, boy!"

"I-I-I was trying to burn the edges on a treasure map I made for my history assignment so it would look old. Now I have to make the map all over again," he wailed.

"Better you remake the map than for us to have to rebuild the cabin!" James growled. "Of all the harebrained things to do, set a fire in the middle of your bedroom floor! Do you know how long it would take for your bedding to catch fire and the whole room to be engulfed in flames?" He snapped his fingers. "Like that!"

"I'm sorry, sir. I won't do it again."

"You'd very well better not!" James stormed from the room.

I ran to the kitchen, calling, "I'll get a mop to clean up the water."

"No, you won't." James grabbed my arm as I ran past. "The boy will clean up his own mess!"

I shrugged and looked at the forlorn child. His chin resting on his chest, Jamie took the mop into his room. James stomped into our bedroom and returned with the valise. "I have to be going." He kissed me goodbye.

I glanced over my shoulder at Jamie's closed door. "Don't you think you'd better kiss Jamie too?"

James glared. "I'm still upset at him."

"That doesn't have anything to do with loving him," I whispered.

He frowned, handed me the case, strode into his son's room, and kissed him goodbye.

The first snowflakes fell around nine in the morning. By noon, the boardwalk to the outhouse was covered with several inches of snow. The empty water buckets stacked next to the door looked like a whitened sentinel. Five minutes after begging to go out, Rags and Sunshine whimpered outside the cabin door. This time I remembered to bar the door after letting them in.

Feeling a draft through the house, I checked the bedroom windows in our room, then Jamie's. I found his window open a crack. As I shut it, my eyes rested on a box of matches hidden behind the curtain. I considered taking them after the morning's scare, but changed my mind. *I'll ask him about them tonight.*

I'd just returned to my knitting when Mrs. VanArsdale came by with a dozen eggs. Rags lifted his head once, then went back to sleep by the fire. After removing her coat, the woman made herself comfortable in the armchair near the fireplace. "I wanted you to know how much we appreciated the recipe for the poultice. It stinks to high heavens, but it works. The minute Noah feels pain, I take out the salve we keep mixed up and rub it on his joints."

"I'm so glad." I fixed us each a cup of hot chocolate, then seated myself on the couch and picked up my knitting needles.

"I told Ma Duncan about it. She said she was going to come by to see if you had a remedy for sore gums. So when's the young-un due?"

"Actually, I do. It's made with black currants and honey." I paused. Her last question suddenly registered in my brain. I dropped a stitch. "Excuse me?"

The old woman grinned and gestured toward my stomach. "I said, when's the young-un due?"

"How did you know? We haven't told anyone, and it's not due till June."

She chuckled. "Shucks, every woman in town knows."

"Does it show?" I ran my hand across my flat abdomen.

"No." She laughed again. "But children talk."

Jamie? He hadn't said a word about the baby at home.

Thinking about Jamie, I mentioned his little bonfire that morning.

A warning frown distorted her usually cheerful demeanor. "A child and matches can spell trouble. Every mining town I know has, at least one time or another, burned down. That's why Noah and I chose to build our place a mile away."

I thanked her for the advice and vowed to put the box of matches "out of the way of temptation," as my mother called it.

We talked for an hour or so; then Ula rose to her feet. "Well, I've got to be headin' home before the snow gets too deep." I helped her into her coat. "You know, we'd still love to have you attend our little worship service sometime. It's a good way to get acquainted with everyone."

"I forgot about that." I walked her to the door and lifted the bar. "I'll talk with James when he gets back from Steamboat Springs tomorrow."

"Good, 'cause we'd love to have you." She wrapped a tattered woolen scarf about her head and neck. "See you soon. Take care." The woman waved and forged into the storm.

I don't know how much time had passed when Rags again barked and ran to the door. This time the wiry hairs on his back stood up as he growled and pawed at the door. I glanced up from the mittens I was knitting for Jamie. "Rags, go lie down." Sunshine bristled and disappeared under our bed in the next room.

After a few more barks and snarls to let me know he was in control, the dog obeyed. He stretched out in front of the hearth, his lower jaw pressed against the wide-planked floor. At the sound of a crash, we both leaped to our feet and ran to the door. Before lifting the bar, I called out. No one outside could have heard me for all of Rags's barking. I considered grabbing the rifle from the wall. *Don't be ridiculous! James and Indian Pete are making you skittish.*

I opened the door a crack. Rags pushed past me, leaping and snarling, and he disappeared around the corner of the cabin. I peeked out of the door and discovered that the water buckets had been toppled. Bending down to restack them, I saw a man's footprints near the kitchen window and around the spot where the buckets stood. A shiver of fear coursed my spine. Calling Rags inside, I closed the door and barred it immediately. Rags lay on the rug in front of the door and refused to move.

I tried to concentrate on my knitting, but couldn't. It seemed silly to get upset over footprints in the snow and a few overturned buckets, so I picked up my Bible for assurance. Rags glanced over his shoulder at the sound of my voice.

"It's time I begin supper. Jamie will be home soon. Let's see, johnnycake would sure taste good tonight." I placed my knitting and the Bible down on the sofa and stood up.

Whistling a lively rendition of "Clementine," I stoked the fire in the oven. After whipping up a batch of corn bread, I poured the batter into a square baking tin. "When Jamie gets home, I'll have him bring in some milk from the cold cellar."

As I put the pan into the oven, I remembered the rifle over the fireplace. *It's gonna be a hot day in Antarctica before I let some good-for-nothing transient steal from us.* I removed the rifle and studied the firing mechanism; I had no idea how to load the gun or how to shoot it. *Oh, well, they don't know that.* I leaned the rifle next to the sink and washed my cooking dishes.

As I placed my mixing bowl on the shelf, I heard voices. Rags barked and lunged at the door when someone knocked. Through the window I could see the sheriff and a group of men carrying a body wrapped in a blanket. I lifted the bar and opened the door.

I watched in horror as the men trooped into the house and placed their burden on my kitchen table. Sheriff Jones removed his hat. "Miz McCall, rumor has it that you know something about doctorin'."

I eyed the still form beneath the bloodied blanket. "This guy's a horse thief. We chased him up the gully toward the Rainbow Mine. Downed 'im too." The sheriff glanced around at his men proudly. "With one bullet in the shoulder. Now, he's gonna die before we can get him to Judge Ames in Steamboat Springs. So we's hopin' you could patch him up so the judge can string 'im up."

I blinked and shook my head. "If the poor guy's going to die anyway, why go to all the trouble?"

The sheriff shrugged. "Seems like the Christian thing to do. So will you help us? My men'll hold him down while you remove the bullet."

I took a deep breath before lifting the blanket from the man's face. The ashen color accentuated the fact that he was barely old enough to shave. Sliding the blanket down his body, I saw the hole oozing blood down his arm and shoulder. *You've never passed out yet at the sight of blood. You aren't going to start now!*

"Sheriff, I need your help. I need a kettle of water boiled. I need someone to go up to the loft and bring me a clean white sheet from the metal trunk. And while you're up there, bring down the strips of cotton rolled up in the right-hand corner of the camelback trunk." I ran to my sewing basket beside the sofa and found my scissors. "Could one of you get the bottle of rubbing alcohol from under the sink?"

The sheriff's eyes lighted up. "Alky, ma'am?"

I laughed and snipped away at my patient's shirt. "You wouldn't want to drink this stuff, sheriff."

The sheriff chortled. "Can't be any worse than the rotgut old Hendricks serves at his bar in Hahn's Peak."

The men laughed.

My patient groaned and stirred. "Quick, I need three of you to hold him still." The men jumped to do my bidding.

As I lifted the pieces of the flannel shirt from the wound, blood spurted from where the wound had dried to the fabric. I staggered when the wave of nausea swept through me.

"You all right, ma'am?" one of the men asked.

"Fine, fine. Just hold him still." As I inspected the wound, I could see the bullet imbedded in the man's collarbone. An inch closer to the neck, and he would have died right away.

"Hold him fast, gentlemen . . ." I moistened a cotton strip with the alcohol. Gently, I dabbed the injury. The patient groaned. *Oh, dear God, please keep this kid unconscious until I finish.*

I glanced toward the sheriff. "Hand me one of my paring knives, please."

"Yes, ma'am." He returned with my favorite peeler. I wondered if I'd ever be able to use the knife again without remembering the horror of this moment. "Pour boiling water into a cup and bring it here."

The sheriff stared in disbelief.

"Sheriff, do it now!"

Reluctantly, the man carried out my order. The sheriff heaved a sigh of relief when I dipped the knife and my scissors in the alcohol, then in the scalding liquid. "What did you think I was gonna do, dump boiling water on the wound?"

The sheriff reddened. "Well ma'am, to be honest, I didn't rightly know."

"Sheriff, go wash your hands, then come help me here. I can't see what I'm doing for all the blood. I need you to use the cotton strips to keep the area clear of blood while I work."

The sheriff's face paled.

"Sheriff?" I ground my teeth as I dug around the bullet to loosen it. My patient groaned and struggled. I had to keep his mind off the gore. "Keep him still! Sheriff, how old is this kid anyway?"

A strange gurgle erupted from the lawman's throat. "Fifteen, I s'pose."

"Fifteen? You shot a fifteen-year-old?" Blood filled the wound. "Remove that blood, Sheriff!"

"Yes, ma'am." Out of the corner of my eye I saw the sheriff stagger back, then slump to the floor. "One of you men, you!" I pointed to the full-bearded deputy holding my patient's feet. "Wash your hands and take over for the sheriff."

The man's face blanched, but he did as I ordered. As I probed the shoulder, I felt the bullet move. "Great! I think we almost have it."

Soon the bullet was out, the injury cleaned and bandaged with the cotton strips. "There, I think that takes care of everything but the sheriff."

"While you two carry our patient onto my bed, I'll bring your boss around." I waved a bottle of smelling salts under the sheriff's nose.

The sudden banging at the door brought the two deputies racing back into the room, their guns drawn. The sheriff staggered to his feet and unholstered his sidearm. I flattened myself against the kitchen wall.

The kitchen door flew open, and in burst Indian Pete, his rifle leveled at his side, his eyes blazing. "What's going on here? Are you all right, Mrs. McCall?"

Jamie broke free from behind Indian Pete and ran into my arms. "Are you all right, Mama? We thought someone had hurt you when we saw blood in the snow outside."

I wrapped my arms about the boy. One glance at the bloodied sheets on the table and the discarded cotton strips, and I could only imagine what Indian Pete must have thought as he charged into the cabin.

"All right, everyone, put your weapons down. I don't

want a massacre in my parlor. Besides, I don't have enough bandages for all of you." Slowly the lawmen lowered their handguns.

"Pete, everything is fine here. I just did surgery on an injured prisoner. That's where the blood came from." Wary, Indian Pete eyed the sheriff's posse, uncocked his rifle, and lowered it to his side.

The odor of burning corn bread sent me scurrying to the oven. I carried the charred johnnycake to the door and tossed both pan and bread into a snowbank. I stepped back inside and closed the door. "Anyone for buttermilk pancakes?"

Indian Pete hung around until I gave the lawmen permission to move my patient. The three of us watched the sheriff and his men hoist the young man onto their shoulders and walk away. "If that kid lives to hang, it will be a miracle." I turned toward Indian Pete. "I was serious about the pancakes. You will stay for supper, won't you?"

He shook his ebony mane of hair. "No, I just wanted to make sure the boy got home safely in the storm. Now I must go."

I pleaded with him to stay a while longer, but he continued to refuse. Finally there was nothing to do but wish him well.

After Indian Pete left, we barred the door and I returned the rifle to its place on the wall. Rags paced and whined all evening; Sunshine didn't come out of hiding until morning.

Indian Pete dropped by the next morning to walk Jamie to school. I thanked him for his concern for the boy's safety. "But it's really not necessary," I added.

He tipped his hat and smiled. "Ma'am, Mr. McCall trusted me with his most prized possessions. I'd feel mighty low if anything happened to them."

James arrived home by midafternoon. While I fixed him

a hot lunch, I told him all that had happened during his absence. James glowered into his soup. "I don't know if I want the sheriff bringing dangerous criminals around here."

"There was nothing dangerous about this poor boy. Besides, I couldn't turn away anyone who was in pain."

"No, I suppose not. Makes me feel good to know Indian Pete is around." He leaned back from the table. "Oh, by the way, I ran into Mrs. VanArsdale in Hahn's Peak today, and she invited us to a worship session at the jail each Sunday evening. She said she had mentioned it to you."

I smiled wryly. "Persistent little lady, isn't she? I didn't think you'd be interested."

"Well, the other night I read where it says believers should worship together. It might not hurt."

We attended the meeting the following week. When we asked why they held the meeting on Sunday night, Sheriff Jones quipped, "It gives the drunken miners time to sober up from their Saturday-night binge and be released before the meeting starts." The sheriff thanked me again for doctoring his prisoner. "The boy's in the Steamboat Springs County Jail awaiting trial."

The program was simple. Noah VanArsdale called us to order, and Ula offered prayer. The man thanked his wife, then welcomed us to the group. "At this time, we're reading the Gospels. Seemed appropriate with the holidays coming and all." He smiled at James. "You may want to catch up during this next week so you won't miss nothin'."

While the wind howled and shook the town's wooden structures, we each took turns reading from the seventh chapter of Matthew. Beth Walsh read verse 7. "Ask, and it shall be given you; seek, and ye shall find . . ." She stopped reading at the end of verse 11.

I tapped my foot in frustration.

Noah noticed my irritation. "Any questions? Mrs. McCall?"

I smiled and shrugged. I wasn't sure I was ready to open up to a roomful of strangers.

Mrs. Jones's hand flew into the air. "Well, I sure do! There've been many times I've prayed for things that didn't happen. So this asking and seeking and opening doesn't always work, does it?"

Mr. VanArsdale smiled. "Theologians have been debating this issue for centuries. And if you took verses seven and eight by themselves, it would seem God isn't a God of His word. That's why it's necessary to include verses nine, ten, and eleven."

James shook his head. "I don't understand."

The old man looked at James. "Read verses nine and ten once more."

James obliged. Mr. VanArsdale stroked his jaw before speaking. "You're a father, Mr. McCall. Would you try to feed your son a stone when he was hungry for bread or a snake when he asked for a fish? Of course not, and neither would God."

I couldn't contain myself any longer. It seemed we were getting nowhere. "Sir, what do stones and snakes have to do with answered prayer?"

"Nothing and everything." He grinned at me. "What the Saviour is saying here is that God is a loving Father, like you, Mr. McCall. He would never give us something that would be harmful to us, in the long run. This is where faith begins."

"What do you mean 'in the long run'?" Mrs. Jones frowned. "Losing my mother to influenza when I was only eleven couldn't have been good for me."

"I wish I could tell you why things happen as they do, but if I could, I'd be God. What He is saying here is, 'I'm your Father, and I give you, my child, only good gifts. I know what's best for you.' "

The old man leaned forward, his eyes intense with compassion. "The entire Bible is a story about people learning to trust the Creator. That's why we're here tonight, to learn more about Him so we can know that He is trustworthy."

"But is He?" I asked.

"Each of us must decide that for him or herself, Mrs. McCall. As for me, God has done incredible things in my life. He's been with me every step of the way. So I haven't a doubt in the world as to my Saviour's dependability." The assured smile on the man's face caused me to blush with embarrassment.

A parade of faces marched through my memory—Pa, Bertha Schnetzler, Zerelda Paget, Mary Elizabeth, and now, Noah VanArsdale, faces of people confident in their faith in God. Each one had supplied a piece of a gigantic puzzle that had become what I believed about God. Yet, the center piece of the puzzle was still missing. Would I ever find that vital piece to the puzzle?

Mr. VanArsdale's voice interrupted my musings. "May I give you an assignment this week?"

I nodded.

"Read the book of Job. As you read, think of it as a play, a drama being performed for the universe."

Throughout the reading of the rest of Matthew 7, I thought about Mr. VanArsdale's words. "Not a doubt in the world." *If only I could have a faith like that.*

Terror by Night

I read the book of Job as I had promised. *This man was applauded for his patience? He doesn't sound very patient to me. The patient One in the story is God.* However, one verse stuck with me. Job 13:15. "Though he slay me, yet will I trust in him."

The next week, when I told Noah about my conclusions regarding Job, he laughed. "You like to read, Chloe? Tell me what would happen to the story of Job if you considered God the main character instead of Job? Think about it."

I did, often. I couldn't shake the thought from my mind, so I reread the story. *Of course, God is trying to help Job see that there's a bigger plan than just one man and his troubles. Yet the Creator of all living things cares enough to reason with that one man.*

The thought haunted me. Like a spoiled child, I'd always prayed for solutions to my own problems without regard to the world around me. Now I found myself praying differently.When I looked at a snowflake or watched a deer nibble at slender blades of grass peeking through the snow, I thought of the greatness of God, the Father, instead of myself.

November passed in a flurry of snowstorms.On Thanksgiving Day Indian Pete came to dinner. Before we ate,

James read Psalm 139. Chin in hand, I leaned on the table and watched the flames in the fireplace. I felt a comforting warmth knowing God saw me, isolated among the sweep of giant, snow-covered peaks. *Ascend up into heaven or make my bed in hell.* I gazed lovingly at my husband. I hated the thought of his going down into the mine, hundreds of feet below the earth's surface. While I couldn't protect him, God promised to be there with him.

When he read about "wings of the morning," my imagination carried me over the mountains to Denver and our balloon flights. The words of verses 13 and 14 took possession of my thoughts. *Possessed my reins—in control, covered me in my mother's womb.* Unconsciously, I leaned back and caressed my own abdomen. *The God of the universe knows and sees my unborn child. Fearfully and wonderfully made.* I'd never thought much about the workings of my body, except as a curse right from the Garden of Eden. But now, with the miracle growing inside me, the words "fearfully and wonderfully made" took on new dimensions. I closed my eyes and smiled to myself.

James continued reading. "How precious also are thy thoughts unto me, O God! how great is the sum of them! If I should count them, they are more in number than the sand: when I awake, I am still with thee."

I glanced about the table at each face, praying, *Thank You, Father, for thinking about and caring for us even here in the wilds of Colorado.*

Later, Indian Pete kept us spellbound by telling stories about life as the son of a trapper.

"Did you ever see a real live bear?" Jamie asked. "There was a bear skin on the wall when we moved in, but Mama made Daddy take it down."

Indian Pete laughed. "I don't blame her. I don't much like to see beautiful animals slaughtered just so they can decorate some hunting lodge or a rich man's den."

"So did you? Did you see a bear?" Jamie persisted.

"Many times. In the woods of southern Oregon, grizzly bears are common."

"Did ya run or shoot 'em?" Jamie's eyes glistened with excitement.

"Neither. I either stood still until the bear backed off or slowly backed away myself. Bears don't usually bother people if they are left alone."

"O-o-o." The boy's eyes widened farther. "What about mountain lions?"

Indian Pete glanced over at James, then back at the child. "In my experience, a cat will attack only if it's trapped or starving."

I smiled as I watched my husband's face display the same excitement as his son's. I wondered if either would be able to sleep that night.

The weekly attendance at the jail fluctuated with the weather. We read through the book of Matthew and started the book of Mark. I tabled my doubts for a while and enjoyed discovering the similarities and differences between the two accounts.

James didn't talk much about the problems at the mine, but the worry lines deepened on his forehead. One evening after preparing a cup of wintergreen tea to soothe another of James's headaches, I sat down across from him at the table. Jamie had already retired for the night.

"You used to talk with me about what was bothering you, but you don't anymore."

He ran his fingers through his hair and massaged the back of his neck. "Every day I find more discrepancies in the books. It looks like I'm going to have to bring the law into it. So you see, it's better you don't know."

I folded my hands on the table. "I don't understand."

"What you don't know can't hurt you."

"Yes, it can," I argued. "Today Ula VanArsdale stopped

by and told me that your manager, Otis Roy, was drinking at one of the bars in Hahn's Peak and making threats toward you and Jamie and me."

James snapped his head up. "What kind of threats?"

"He said something about how accidents happen around mining camps. Then later he said, 'You know how women and children make dangerous mistakes.'"

James reached across the table and took my hands in his. "That's why I have Indian Pete keeping a close eye over you two, especially when I'm out of town. Maybe it's time you learn to use the rifle."

I pulled my hands free and stood up. "No, I don't think so. Besides, Rags is a great protector."

My mind was relieved to know it had been Indian Pete's footprints in the snow outside the cabin. It had been Indian Pete's fingerprints on the windowsill. It had been Indian Pete who knocked over the stack of buckets by the front door.

A week went by, then two. The pure white snow and the crisp mountain air made me eager for Christmas. It was time to do some Christmas shopping. One morning, after Jamie left for school, James and I drove the wagon to Hahn's Peak, then boarded the train for Steamboat Springs. While the shopping couldn't compare with Denver's, it felt like big time to me after two months in Columbine. As I looked over the wide assortment of items, I spied a pair of ivory combs. Catching my reflection in a wall mirror near the display of ladies' hats, I held the combs up to my hair.

Hmm, I thought. *Nice. Hey, you're not here to buy gifts for yourself.* I returned the combs to their velvet-lined box and continued my search for Christmas gifts. I had a delightful time buying trinkets for my family. When James returned from a business appointment, I encouraged him to do the same for his family.

He groaned and shook his head. "What could I possibly buy them in Steamboat Springs that they couldn't find at a better price and of better quality in Boston?"

"Do you think my folks need this stuff I'm buying?" I held up a Mexican lace shawl I'd chosen for my mother. "It isn't the gift that counts; it's that you care, that you took the time to do something nice for those you love."

Reluctantly, he bought a locally made quilt embroidered with Rocky Mountain wildflowers.

I admired the delicate stitching on our town flower, the columbine. "Your mother is going to love this. You have to admit that it's something she couldn't get in Boston." I turned to the next display and held up a blue-and-white wool afghan. "Don't you think Drucilla and Ian would appreciate this for the baby?"

The thought of Drucilla's baby made my throat tighten. I wondered how she'd been feeling. I ran my hand across my own stomach and smiled. I felt lucky to have experienced only a few days of morning sickness. And instead of the pregnancy sapping my strength, I'd never felt so invigorated.

After buying presents for Jamie and for one another, we packaged and mailed the family gifts, then dashed to the station for the train home. Patches of mist drifted down the slopes toward the river. Snowflakes drifted down around us as our train wound its way through the evergreen corridor toward Hahn's Peak. Once at Hahn's Peak, we hurried to the blacksmith shop, where we'd stabled our horse and wagon.

The snow intensified the silence of the woods during the ride home. As excited as I'd been to go to Steamboat Springs that morning, it did not equal the excitement I felt at seeing the light shining through my own kitchen window. When Jamie and Indian Pete greeted us at the cabin door, I made Jamie close his eyes so James could hide the Christmas packages under our bed.

After supper, as Pete prepared to leave, I stopped him at the door. "You will be with us on Christmas Day, won't you, Pete?"

"I'm afraid not, Mrs. McCall. I have responsibilities in Utah."

"Well, stop by before you leave. James and I bought a little thank-you gift for you. We appreciate your kindness, both with Jamie and keeping an eye on things when I'm here alone."

The man looked at me questioningly. "That's very nice of you, but there's no need."

I grinned at him. "That's what makes it Christmas, isn't it?"

I'd taken to calling him Pete after the incident with the sheriff. It's not that I wanted to overlook his Indian heritage; it just wasn't important to our friendship. When I suggested he call me by my first name, he shook his head.

"No, Mrs. McCall. I don't mind your calling me Pete, but I cannot call you by your first name. It wouldn't be proper." Being his boss's wife, I understood his reluctance.

A week after our trip to Steamboat Springs, James received a telegram from Phineas Putnam in Denver. "Dear James, Have important news on Renegade. Stop. Need to see you immediately. Stop. Bring wife and son. Stop."

My husband studied the yellow piece of paper for some time. The thought of staying at the Putnams' guest house with its indoor plumbing and electricity sounded like the best Christmas gift ever. *We could stay throughout the holidays and celebrate the arrival of the new century to the fireworks of Denver.*

I glanced at James. He'd read my mind. By the look in his eye, I knew I'd been building pipe dreams, as Pa called them. "Sorry, honey, it will have to be a quick trip there, one night, two at the most. Things are getting complicated between me and Otis at the mine. I don't dare be gone for a week, let alone two."

I sighed. "It would have been a shame if Jamie had to miss his program at school. He's been practicing 'The Night Before Christmas' for weeks." I chuckled at the suspicious grin on his face.

"Didn't he learn that last year?"

I shrugged. "I guess he failed to tell Mrs. Walsh that."

After supper, James took his son into his lap and told him about the quick trip he had to make to Denver and that he would miss the school Christmas program. The child's face lengthened into a pout. "Why?"

"To tell the truth, son, I'm not sure why. Mr. Putnam just said it was urgent."

"So is my program." Jamie folded his arms and stuck out his lower lip.

"I know. And if there were any way I could avoid making this trip, I would." He looked to me for help. My knitting needles clicked out my frustration. I shrugged and glanced down at the ball of yarn by my side.

The next morning we had a special breakfast together. Before we ate, James read Genesis 31:49, "The Lord watch between me and thee, when we are absent one from another." We joined hands around the table as James prayed for each of us and for our friend Indian Pete.

I puttered about the house throughout the day. After lunch, when Rags barked and ran to the door, I smiled to myself, knowing that Indian Pete must have come by to check on me. *How ridiculous, coming by without saying hello. How can he know I'm all right?*

I swung the bar free and flung open the door. Rags bounded out into the snow, yapping as he ran toward a man walking away from the cabin toward town. "Pete!" I called. "The teakettle is on."

When the man heard my call, he glanced over his shoulder, then broke into a run, with Rags barking and lunging at his heels. *It's not Indian Pete!* Racing back into the cabin, I grabbed the rifle. I rushed back in time to see the stranger trying to shake himself free, but Rags relentlessly hung on to one pant leg.

"Call off your dog, Red, or I'll shoot him," the stranger shouted, aiming his Colt .45 at Rags. I didn't know what made me angrier, his threat to kill the dog or his reference to the color of my hair.

"You shoot that dog, and you're a dead man, mister!" My hands shook as I leveled the gun at him. While I knew the weapon wasn't loaded, he didn't. "Now, slowly return your gun to your holster. Slowly, I said!"

Undiluted hate replaced fear in the man's eyes as he carried out my order.

"Raise your hands high above your head." He lifted his hands into the air.

"Rags, come here. Rags! Come here!" Reluctantly the mongrel released the man's pant leg and slunk to my side.

Squinting into the rifle sights, I shouted, "Get off my land and don't come back, you hear?"

Before disappearing into the woods, the man shouted over his shoulder, "You might have won this one, Red." He emphasized the nickname. "But accidents do happen to dogs and little boys, you know."

I staggered back into the cabin, second thoughts bombarding my mind. *Maybe he was just passing by, maybe he needed help, maybe . . .* My eyes rested on the boot print under the window. *Someone passing by wouldn't be peeking in windows. If he needed help, he would have knocked on the door.* I stepped outside to study the print. It was the same print I'd seen previously. No wonder Pete looked at me so strangely when I thanked him for dropping by so often. An icy chill skittered up my spine. *Then who is the stranger? What is he looking for?*

I hurried back inside and barred the door. That evening as Jamie and I prepared to leave for the Christmas program, Pete knocked at the door. "I'm here to attend your program, Jamie."

"Really?" Jamie's face broke into a grin for the first time since he learned of his father's unexpected business trip to Denver.

Jamie took Pete's hand and mine. The three of us tromped through the snow to the mercantile, where the children performed to an appreciative audience. During Jamie's flawless performance, I wished his father could have been there. Mrs. Walsh ended the evening by having her students sing "Silent Night."

As we reached the cabin, I turned to Jamie. "Son, please go to your room and get ready for bed. I need to talk with Indian Pete before he leaves."

"All right, Mama." Jamie extended his hand toward Pete. "Thank you for coming with us tonight to the program."

Pete shook the boy's hand. "Thank you for inviting me."

After Jamie disappeared into his bedroom, I said softly to Pete, "Something happened this afternoon. I wouldn't say anything except, well, with James gone . . ."

Pete's intense stare unnerved me.

"It's probably nothing." I caught myself. "No, it's definitely something. A stranger came snooping around the cabin this afternoon. He threatened to shoot Rags when Rags grabbed his pant leg. And I threatened to shoot him." I paused to compose myself. Pete waited impassively.

"I can't blame him for being frightened. The dog went berserk. But before the man left, he threatened both the dog and Jamie." I rubbed my arms to bring back warmth to my suddenly cold body. "How did he know about Jamie? Jamie wasn't here."

In an even tone, Pete asked, "Can you describe the man? Have you ever seen him before?"

"Let me see. He's shorter than you by maybe five inches. He was wearing a dark plaid jacket, and his hat was pulled low over his forehead." Panic rose inside me as I forced myself to remember. "His face was scarred, like he had smallpox as a child. And no, I've never seen him before, but he's been here before."

Pete's eyebrow arched questioningly.

"Remember when I thanked you for checking up on us so often when James was gone? Well, it was this man's boot prints I found at the window instead of yours."

Pete's expression remained impassive. "From now on you must keep the door barred. Don't remove the bar unless you know who is outside."

After Pete left, I scooped up Sunshine in one hand, the lantern in the other, and headed for Jamie's bedroom to say good night. Once in my bedroom, I picked up my Bible, wrapped a quilt about me, and spread out on top of the bedding.

I opened the Bible to Psalm 23. Reading through the familiar words, my fears dissipated. Then I read Mary's favorite chapter, Psalm 91.

"Dear Father," I prayed aloud, "thank You for the promise of Your protection. Be with James tonight, wherever he may be. Help him to solve the problems at the mine so we can go back home to Kansas soon. Amen."

Too tired to read any longer, I crawled off the bed and changed into my flannel nightgown. Unbraiding my hair, I forced myself to brush it the required one hundred times. When I turned out the light and climbed into bed, Sunshine snuggled down next to my back, and Rags curled up at my feet.

My head had barely dented the pillow when wild, frightening dreams spiraled through my brain. I found myself running across the prairie, the odor of a grass fire accosting my nostrils. Flames danced and swirled across the prairie as I tried to escape. I heard Jamie calling me back, back to the flames. I stopped and turned.

"Chloe! Help!" I leapt from sleep to consciousness in an instant. My room was filled with smoke.

"Chloe! Help! The cabin is on fire!" Rags yipped as I threw the covers back, then jumped out of bed. Forgetting slippers and dressing gown, I bounded from my bedroom to Jamie's, pushed open the door, and grabbed Jamie into my arms. Flames engulfed us as we ran to the kitchen door. I struggled to lift the bar, but finally the door opened, and I rushed out of the cabin toward the nearest snowbank. I could feel the fire gobbling up my nightgown.

"Rags? Where's Rags? Where's Sunshine?" Jamie shouted, trying to wriggle free.

From nowhere, a soggy blanket descended over us, plunging us into total darkness. I felt hands rolling me over and over again. Then as quickly as the blanket fell, it lifted, leaving me gasping for breath.

Hands lifted me to my feet. Other hands held Jamie. "Rags!" I lunged toward the burning cabin. "I've got to go find Rags."

The same hands that helped me up held me back. Screaming, I fought to break free. "Rags is in there! So is Sunshine! Please, please, please . . ."

I awakened to searing pain in my feet and a totally different pain in my abdomen. I moaned. "Jamie . . ." My mouth felt dry, my lips parched. A cool, moist cloth rested on my forehead.

"It's all right," a voice comforted. "You're safe, and so is your son." I opened my eyes. Ula VanArsdale smiled down at me.

"Where am I?" I struggled to sit up, but she pushed my

shoulders back against the mattress.

"Where's Jamie?"

"He went to school this morning. And you're in my cabin. I have a poultice of bicarbonate of soda and water on your feet for the burns."

The horror of the night returned. My eyes widened at the sudden cramp in my abdomen. *My baby!* "My baby! Is my baby all right?"

Ula nodded. "So far."

"So far," I cried. "What do you mean, 'so far'?"

"Just that. You came close to losing it during the first twenty-four hours, but the contractions are farther apart now."

"First twenty-four hours? How long have I been lying here?"

"Three days. Would you like to see your husband?"

I nodded and rolled my head to one side. The pain in my feet brought tears to my eyes. I lifted my covers, trying to see the condition they were in, but both feet had been bandaged.

James rushed into the room, his face distorted with anguish. He sat on the edge of my bed and kissed my forehead. "Oh, sweetheart, I'm so glad you are awake. I was so worried."

"Tell me the truth. How's Jamie?"

James took my hands in his. "He's fine. His eyebrows and hair were singed. He has a minor burn on his right hand, probably from trying to open the door to his room. Other than that, he's fine."

"And Rags?" My lower lip quivered.

He avoided my eyes by caressing my fingers. "He's all right too. But Sunshine, well . . ."

"No, not my Sunshine," I whimpered.

"Darling, it's a miracle you and Jamie escaped without serious injury. If Indian Pete hadn't been close by, I hate to think of what might have happened." He placed his hand tenderly on my stomach. "And for now, we still have our precious baby."

James wiped away my tears with his fingers. "When I got back the next morning, Pete met me at the station and drove me here."

"And the cabin?"

He shook his head. "Gone."

"I'm thirsty. May I have a drink?" I tried to sit up.

James held a glass to my lips and supported my back enough so I could sip the water without spilling it. It wasn't until my head returned to the pillow that I sensed something was different.

My hand flew to my forehead. I could feel a fringe of irregular bangs. James tried to draw my hand away, but I persisted. I felt of the side of my head. The same short fringe around my ears. I ran my fingers along the side of my head to the back. *Gone! My hair is gone!*

James grabbed my hand away from my head, gently kissing the palm. Sobbing, I pulled away and turned my face to the wall.

"It will grow back, darling. It will grow back." James tried to comfort me.

I heard his voice, but my mind refused to hear his words. How could I explain the devastation I felt? My hair had always been my pride. It made me feel unique, even beautiful. It sounded trivial after everything else that had happened, yet no matter how hard I tried to be reasonable, I couldn't escape the truth. Now I was a homely woman with freckles. *How can James love me now?*

As he stroked my shoulder and arm, repeating over and over again that my hair would grow back, I remembered how he would lift the mass of curls off my back, then let it filter through his fingers, whispering his love for me.

"I-I-I'm tired, James. I need to sleep."

"Of course, darling. I should have thought of that. I'll come back after you take a little nap." He kissed my forehead and slipped out of the room.

Another contraction forced the loss of my waist-length mane of hair from my mind. Ula bustled into the room and placed her hand on my abdomen, then smiled. "They don't seem to be as strong as before. I think we've passed the danger mark."

I tried to return her smile. "When can I get out of this bed?"

Ula's face clouded. "Not until the contractions have stopped for at least twenty-four hours, I would guess. But then, who am I to tell you?" She lifted the sheet to check the bandages on my feet. "I'm sure it doesn't feel like it, but the burns on your feet and ankles are not serious. The poultice seems to be healing them nicely. Now I'll let you rest for a while."

I must have slept, for when Ula brought me a supper tray, Noah carried a lantern for her. I didn't realize how hungry I was until I inhaled the delicious aromas of baked beans and freshly made bread. Not until she stuffed a second pillow beneath my head and shoulders did I remember my hair. "There, that should make you comfortable."

"Has Jamie come home from school yet?" I asked.

Ula glanced at Noah, then back at me.

Fear filled my chest and throat. "What's wrong?"

"I shouldn't be the one to tell you this, but when Jamie didn't arrive home on time, your husband went down to the mercantile, and Mrs. Walsh said Jamie didn't show up at school today."

"What?" I sat up and swung my legs off the side of the bed. Sudden pain coursed through my feet and legs, and I groaned as Ula and Noah helped me back under the covers. "Then where is James?"

Noah took a deep breath. "Out looking for him."

I glanced toward Ula. "And Indian Pete?"

Deep furrows formed in her forehead. "Looking also, along with half the town. Wherever Jamie went, Rags followed."

I closed my eyes. *What next? Why would he want to run away?*

Around nine in the evening, I heard Sheriff Jones's voice in the kitchen. Ula showed him into the room.

"Mrs. McCall? I came to let you know that we're doing all we can to find your son. And," he reached inside his heavy woolen coat and held a spitting ball of golden fury toward me, "look what showed up in your outhouse this afternoon."

"Oh," I gasped, grabbing the animal before she could run and hide. "Sunshine." I held her up where I could see her. "You're all right. You're all right. Wait until Jamie sees you." I closed my eyes and whispered, "Thank you."

Sheriff Jones cleared his throat. "T'wern't nothin', ma'am. I just happened to stumble across her . . ."

I cuddled the kitten and crooned, "Poor kitty, you must have been terrified. You're fine now." Sunshine began to purr.

"Don't worry about the boy. Half the county's out lookin' for 'im." The sheriff wished me well and excused himself.

I slept fitfully that night. Whenever I awakened, my hand drifted to Sunshine. And at the foot of my bed, Ula sat crocheting in a rocker, the lantern flame turned low.

The next morning, I heard a knock at the outside door and then James talking with Noah. Ula rushed out to the parlor. "Any luck?"

James brushed past her and over to my side. His day-old beard emphasized the strain evident on his face and in his eyes—I didn't have to ask if they'd located Jamie. He knelt beside the bed and buried his face in my shoulder.

Silently, I caressed his neck and the back of his head. Over and over, he sobbed the words, "My son, my son!"

"He's going to be all right. I know he's going to be all right."

"He's been gone almost twenty-four hours. What are the chances a seven-year-old boy could survive last night's temperatures?" James lifted his head. The pain in his eyes ripped at my heart. He dropped his head onto my shoulder once more. "Oh, Jamie, why did you run away?"

Father, How much more grief can one man carry? Please, dear God, I know You love James even more than I. Help me to help him through this nightmare. Suddenly, I knew what I had to do. I couldn't let him give up, no matter how bleak everything seemed.

I grabbed his shoulders and pushed him away. "James, you are giving up without a fight. I know you're exhausted, but you've got to get hold of yourself." I steeled myself against the shock and hurt I read in his eyes. "No matter how cold it was last night, Jamie is a strong little boy. And Rags is a fierce protector. Now take a short nap and eat some breakfast; then get out there and find our boy!"

The sorrow in my husband's face made me feel lower than a potato slug. *Who am I to talk, lying here being cozied and coddled? No, that's not true. I'm fighting for the life of our second child while he fights for that of our first.*

Counting Blessings

Hours later the pale light coming through the north window of my room reminded me that darkness was coming soon. Frantic tears surfaced as I thought of Jamie wandering in the woods with only a small dog for protection. I remembered the look in James's eyes when I had placed my hands on both sides of his face and prayed. I'd never known such a moving experience as, staring into his pain-ridden dark eyes, I prayed for him and for our son. And I could tell by the changing expressions on his face that he had experienced the same phenomenon.

Right before my eyes I had seen peace replace his turmoil and a revitalized determination course through him. It was as if strength had flowed through my hands to him. However, I knew better. The strength came from a higher Power.

James had placed his hands over mine, leaned forward, and whispered, "Thank you, precious one. I'll never forget this moment, regardless of the outcome." He kissed me, then kissed the palms of my hands. Standing to his feet, he glanced out the window, then back at me. "I have a job to do before another night falls." Then he strode from the room.

Now I watched the gathering shadows, hardly noticing as Ula bustled in and out of the room, checking on my comfort. Not wanting to talk, I closed my eyes and allowed myself to drift somewhere between sleep and conscious-ness until the sound of excited voices startled me awake. I sat up. "Who's there? Ula? Who's out there?"

My bedroom door opened, and the silhouette of a man filled the doorway. Sunshine, who'd been sleeping beside me, bristled, then relaxed. Silently, he closed the door and walked to the foot of my bed. I tried to read the expression on his face, but, as usual, Indian Pete's face remained impassive.

"Mrs. McCall, we found Jamie."

I sat up on the bed. Terror swept through me. "Where is he? Where's my son?"

He walked around to the side of my bed. "He's all right, a little cold, a little dirty, but all right."

"Bring him here. Bring him to me," I demanded.

"Wait! You and I need to talk before you see him."

"Why? You said he wasn't hurt."

Pete pulled up the straight-back chair and sat down. "No, I said he's all right. But he is hurting, inside, not out."

"I don't understand."

Pete leaned forward, his elbows on his knees. "For some reason he's blaming himself for the fire."

"How can it be his fault?" I shook my head. Then I remembered the matchbox on his windowsill. I'd forgotten to confiscate it as I'd planned. *No, certainly he'd been asleep when the fire started. It probably started from a green log exploding in the fireplace or something.*

"Mrs. McCall? Mrs. McCall!" I heard Pete calling my name. "Please, listen to me. For some reason, I can't get Jamie to say anything else. So I don't know why he thinks he's at fault."

I groaned and fell back against the pillow. *No, Lord, don't let the child regress to where he was when I first met him. He's come so far. Open up his mind and his heart.*

Please, please! Open up his heart.

I propped myself up on one elbow. "Pete, I've got to see him. Please, bring him to me." The man stood and walked to the door. "And thank you, dear friend," I gulped back my tears, "for bringing him home to me."

Pete nodded. A gaggle of voices spilled into the room as he opened the door and stepped into the brightly lighted kitchen. Seconds later, Noah brought Jamie to me.

"Oh, Jamie." I held out my arms to him, expecting him to run into them. Instead, he walked stiffly to me and allowed me to hug his rigid body. Rags had no such reserve. He bounded into the room, barking and running in circles of happiness. Sunshine aroused herself from my pillow and rubbed noses with the excited dog. Satisfied with his welcome, Rags laid down by the foot of the bed; Sunshine curled up beside him.

"Sorry." Noah tried to order the dog from the room.

"That's all right, Mr. VanArsdale. Rags is no bother. I'm so glad to see them both alive and unhurt." When our host left, Jamie straightened and stared at the wall behind the bed. Thinking about my scorched hair, I asked Jamie to turn down the flame. He obeyed.

"What happened? Why did you leave? Your dad has been worried sick." His body jerked at the mention of his father. *I'm going at it all wrong. Please, Lord, help me not to mess this up. I need Your wisdom, not mine.*

"The important thing is that you're back, safe and sound. I'm sure your dad has already heard the news and is on his way home to us right now." Jamie stared at me, his eyes emotionless. It was the same look he had had on the train when his mother was giving birth to his sister, Agatha. "Please, Jamie, don't shut yourself off from me. I love you so much. That's what matters."

I saw his eyes flicker to my stomach, then back to my face.

"The baby? He is going to be fine." I took the child's reluctant hand and placed it on my stomach. "See? He's settling right down in his cozy cradle for another six months or so. You can't feel him moving yet, but you will."

Feeling the tension ease in his body, I coaxed him to sit on the edge of my bed. "That was pretty scary the other night, wasn't it? Accidents like that happen sometimes." Tears swam before my eyes. I stroked his hand, lovingly touching his fingers until I could speak again without crying. "But we have a loving God. Look." I pointed to the animals sleeping at the foot of my bed. "Even Sunshine made it out safely."

Jamie nodded, the curtain lifting from his eyes. "Honey, you could never do anything so bad that your daddy and I would stop loving you." I placed my hand on my stomach. "This baby won't change things between us either. You're my number-one son, cowboy. I need you." I fought another round of tears and won. "Remember when I told you about my family, about Riley and Myrtle and Hattie and Ori and . . ."

He nodded.

"Do you know that my Ma and Pa had more than enough love to go around? And I'm sure if God gives them ten more babies, they'll not love me any less. That's the way God made us—with bunches and bunches of love." I tickled Jamie's tummy, and he squirmed and tried not to smile. When I drew him into my arms, this time he didn't resist. A sob erupted from his chest, followed by a second and a third. I rubbed his back and cried along with him.

His words came in an avalanche of pain. "They said the baby was going to die. They said it was my fault. They said you might die too."

Stunned, I finally found my voice. "Who? Who said all this?"

"Mrs. Jones and the other ladies. I heard them talking

at the mercantile."

I lifted his head with my two hands and stared into his eyes, like I had into his father's a few hours previously. "Jamie, let me ask you one question; then we'll never talk about it again. Were you playing with matches the night of the fire?"

His eyes widened with surprise. "No, no, Mama. I was sound asleep."

"Had you been playing with them before you went to bed?"

His head wagged from side to side. "No, I didn't touch them after Daddy got so mad at me."

I heaved a sigh of relief and squeezed the boy again. Fighting against the urge to shout for joy, I looked him straight in the eye. "Son, let's get one thing straight. You are not to blame for the accident. If anything had happened to me or to Sunshine or to the baby, it wouldn't have been your fault."

His rigid little body melted against me, and I held him in my arms for some time. When he straightened, his smile faded. It was as if he were looking at me for the first time. "Mama, your hair. It's all gone."

I gulped back the pain. "Yes, I'm afraid so."

"Even your eyebrows!"

I felt my forehead. He was right, even my eyebrows were gone.

A hopeful smiled formed at the edges of his mouth. He touched my cheek with his hand. "But aren't you glad the fire didn't burn your freckles?"

Out of the mouths of babes. Laughing through my tears, I gave him another hug. "Oh, Jamie I love you so much."

This time when he squirmed free of my grasp, I knew it was different. He was only a normal little boy resisting my "smothering," as James called it.

"Don't you like being hugged?" I teased.

He grinned. "Yeah, I guess."

"Oh, Jamie!" I laughed and hauled him back into my arms. "You are so precious."

Rags barked and pranced to the window. An instant later, the bedroom door flew open, and my husband burst into the room. "James Edward McCall! Where have you been?" He swept the boy into his arms. Jamie's feet dangled helplessly in the air. "Your mother and I have been worried sick. Don't you ever, ever pull a crazy stunt like this again!"

I'd never seen such a violent reaction from James. Jamie's face was ashen; his eyes bulged with fear. I tried to get up, to rush to Jamie's rescue, but the pain in my feet reminded me I wouldn't get too far. Slowly James released his hold on the child.

"Oh, son, I was so scared I'd lost you forever. And it would have been my own fault. I left you two here alone."

"No, Daddy." The solemn-faced Jamie shook his head from side to side. "It wasn't your fault. Mama says it wasn't anybody's fault. It just happened."

James shot me a surprised look, then placed his hands on the boy's shoulders. "I guess you're right, son."

Jamie's stomach growled. We laughed.

"Why don't you go rustle up a bowl of chili from Mrs. VanArsdale while I talk with your mother for a while."

Needing no second invitation, the child bolted for the door, Rags close behind. Ever the parent, James threw in a parting word. "It wouldn't hurt to wash up first. You smell like a grizzly bear."

We talked for some time. He told me how Pete had followed the tracks toward Steamboat Springs. He found the boy and the dog curled up in a hollow log, shivering against the wind. His tone changed. "I went back to the cabin . . ."

I held my breath. "And?"

"Everything's gone . . ." His voice trailed off into melancholy.

I bit my lip. "We're still here. As you said before, everything that's really important—"

He placed a finger on my lips. "I know. I know, and you're right, my love. You're right." Kneeling beside the bed, James kissed me tenderly, first on the lips, then the forehead, then each eye, both my cheeks, and my chin. I tried to push the memory of my singed hair and eyebrows from my mind.

"How did I ever get so lucky? You are so beautiful." He breathed the words onto my neck.

A tear slipped down the side of my face. James raised up and looked at me. "Why are you crying?"

"I'm not beautiful anymore. My hair," I sobbed out the words. "It's gone. I don't know how you can stand to look at me."

He drew back and grinned sardonically. "What? The invincible Chloe Mae Spencer McCall wallowing in self-pity? I don't believe it."

"James, I'm serious. I'm ugly!"

He snorted. "I'm serious too. I've never known you to act so shallow. After all that's happened, you're worried about losing a few locks of hair?"

I turned my face to the wall. "You don't understand."

He took me by the shoulders and gave me a gentle shake. "I understand very well. All your life you've believed that your beauty and self-worth lie in your gorgeous red hair. It doesn't. It's what's inside that counts, not what you look like or even what you do. It's insulting to me to have you think my love for you is as shallow as the length of your hair!"

When I started to protest, he shushed me with a kiss. "I love you for who you are—the kind, compassionate, impetuous woman who never gives up, who never backs down in an argument. That's the woman I love."

I ran my fingers through the uneven strands of hair at the base of my neck. I didn't try to fight my tears this time. "I'm sorry. You're right. It will grow back; it will grow back . . ."

He gathered me into his arms. Like a summer storm drenching the dry, parched prairie, my pain and anguish of the last few days poured out, making room for healing.

At Ula's gentle knock, James dried my tears, then opened the door. The woman smiled uncertainly at James. "The sheriff wants to talk with you for a few minutes. And Chloe does need her rest."

James threw me a kiss and left. Ula turned down the flame on the lamp, patted my arm, and closed the door gently behind her.

Lying there in the darkness, I felt overwhelmed with gratitude. The baby's layette, the half-finished afghan, the Christmas presents we'd purchased in Steamboat Springs, the Bible Aunt Bea had given me were gone, but I didn't care. They were only things, and things could be replaced. All that was truly important to me was unharmed. Overwhelming joy filled my soul—I wanted to sing and dance and run barefoot in the snow. I wiggled my sore toes. *Well, maybe not barefoot in the snow.* I fell asleep with that thought.

Though James and Jamie visited me several times a day and the VanArsdales were nearby all the time, I was surprised during the next four days at how few of my friends dropped by. I was feeling better, itchy, in fact, to escape my confinement. I tried to reason with myself. *The excitement is over. People have their own lives to live, even here in Columbine.*

The next morning, James arrived carrying my breakfast tray. That was a surprise because he and Jamie were staying with the Walshes.

"Good news! Ula thinks it's safe for you to get up today."
He gestured toward the window. "It's a beautiful day for a
drive, and the Walshes have lent us their sleigh."

No news could have sounded better to my ears or to my
aching back. Lying in bed for so long gave me aches in
places I didn't know existed. "Great!" I threw back the
covers. "Let's go." Sunshine glared, leapt from the bed,
and scooted behind the oak dresser.

James shook his head. "Not before you eat your eggs
and toast. Your body needs to replace the strength you
lost."

I scowled, then complied.

In record time, I was dressed in one of Mrs. Walsh's
linsey-woolsey dresses and in new undergarments James
had ordered from the Hahn's Peak general store. My new
boots stung my toes, but I didn't complain. James beamed
as he held out a pair of matching ivory combs. I blanched.
My hands flew to my hair.

"Oh, I'm sorry. I wasn't thinking." The horror filling his
face touched my heart. I smiled and examined the deli-
cately carved combs.

"It will grow, darling, it will grow. By next summer,
you'll see . . ."

I picked up the gray woolen bonnet Ula had found in her
trunk and put it on my head. My smile faded as I caught
sight of my reflection in the dresser mirror. James stepped
up behind me, reached around my shoulders, and tied the
ribbon. Turning me slowly to face him, he whispered, "You
are so beautiful. Never forget that."

When I walked out into the kitchen, Ula fussed over me
like a mother bear with her only cub. She draped her best
shawl over the coat someone had donated for me to wear.
"Now, take care. Don't overdo."

She shook her finger in James's face. "Don't let her
overdo!"

Rags barked at our feet as we climbed into the sleigh. "Come on, Rags," James called. "Hop on." The dog responded instantly and settled down by my feet. As James flicked the reins, I asked him about Jamie.

"He's spending the day with Indian Pete." The horse trotted down the almost deserted main street of town. "If you're up to it, I thought we'd drive to the mining camp and see if there's any hope for that abandoned manager's cabin. While there's only one bedroom, there is a loft Jamie could use. Of course if you'd rather not, you could spend the rest of the winter with the Putnams, in—"

"I'm sure the cabin will be fine. Remember, when we first saw it, you didn't think much of our last one either." I dreaded starting over again. I felt tired, too tired to face what lay ahead. Brushing the thoughts from my mind, I let the sunlight flooding down on my shoulders warm my spirits.

"But you haven't seen this one." He shook his head in disgust. "I never thought I'd take a bride of mine to live in such squalor!" I slipped my arm into his and snuggled close.

"We're almost there," James announced after a while. "It's just around the next corner."

I closed my eyes for a moment. *Dear Lord, help me to be gracious. Help me not to disappoint James. Help me to remember that this is harder for him to face than for me.*

The evergreen trees parted into a clearing. On one side of the clearing sat an unpainted shed I presumed was used for storage. James pointed to a larger building beside it. "That's the mining office." He raised his hand toward the hill. "Up there's the mine."

I was still gazing at the hole in the side of the mountain when the horse stopped before a small log cabin. Though the cabin certainly was not impressive, I could tell that the area around it had recently been cleared, but I wondered why newspapers covered the windows. James waited for my reaction.

I squeezed his arm. "We'll be cozy this winter, won't we? So are you going to sit there all day, or are you going to help me down from this sleigh?"

His face remained impassive as he hopped down and placed his hands about my waist. Once my feet landed securely on the ground, I took his arm and started toward the front door. As he opened the door, I held my breath, expecting to see spiders and mice scurrying for cover. Instead, a sparkling clean wooden floor greeted me. Cautiously I stepped into the darkened room. At that moment, pandemonium broke loose, and laughing, shouting people came at me from every side. Someone ripped the newspapers off the windows so sunlight could flood into the room.

"What? What's going on here?" I turned to look at James. He grinned and shrugged as the women of the town surrounded me.

Mrs. Jones took charge. "Come on, let me show you around your new home."

Dumbstruck, I gazed about the kitchen and small seating area in front of the fireplace. The multicolored afghan on the love seat and the red calico pillows on the seats of the two hand-made wooden chairs added spice and hominess to the room. A kerosene lantern sat in the middle of a square wooden table. Four unmatched chairs surrounded it.

"I don't believe this. It's, it's perfect. James, you said—"

"I said," he reminded, "that the cabin hadn't been used in a long time."

"And he was right, dear!" Beth Walsh laughed and led me to the kitchen sink. "The pump works." She swept the flour-sack curtains aside under the counter. "We all cleaned out our kitchens in order to stock yours. We've been working for days to get this place in livable condition. You should have seen the mice droppings!"

I shuddered. The woman continued. "The men repaired the roof and cleaned the well and the outhouse while we women took care of the inside. Didn't you wonder why no one came by to see how you were doing?"

I nodded slowly, my eyes welling with tears.

Mrs. Jones laughed. "Well, don't think we didn't keep track of you. James brought us daily reports on your progress." She pointed toward the loft. "See? Jamie's all set, with a bed, a mattress, bedding, and well . . ." Her eyes filled with apology, "we didn't have an extra dresser, but Noah nailed some apple crates together for storage. They should do until you can get something better."

I tried to speak, but words failed me. The women ushered me into the bedroom. White muslin curtains hung on loops from stripped aspen branches above the two glass-paned windows. "We had a sewing bee the other night and finished the curtains and two rag rugs, the one by the front door and the one here by the bed." A red-and-blue crazy quilt covered the giant hand-hewn wooden bed that filled most of the room. A chair, a lamp stand, and a camelback trunk completed the room.

Beth lifted the trunk lid. "Here are a few nightgowns that will get you through the next few weeks until you can get to Steamboat Springs. And remember, when you're ready to sew your baby's layette, let us know. We'd love to help."

I took a deep breath. "It's beautiful. Everything is just beautiful. Why did you do this for us? We're virtually strangers."

Mrs. Jones wrapped her arms around me. "No one is a stranger for long in these mountains, dear. We need one another to survive. As much as you needed us in your crisis, there'll come a time, sooner or later, when you'll be able to return the favor—that's how it works here."

I thought of Minna's and Aunt Bea's words after the grasshopper infestation. I remembered the shipments of grain and hay that farmers in other areas of the state gave to Hays to help the animals survive. I could see James's face over the heads of the women. The tears in his eyes prompted mine. The ladies of Columbine drew him into the circle and wrapped their arms about our shoulders and about our hearts.

Pete arrived with Jamie after our neighbors left for home. The excited child scampered up the ladder to the loft. "This is my room, really?"

James laughed and grinned. To Pete, he said, "I can't thank you enough, my friend, for saving Chloe's and my son's life, for finding Jamie, and for everything else you've done. There's not enough money in the world to repay you, but I'd sure like to try."

Pete's face darkened. "No. Money means nothing to me."

Sensing the man was insulted, James hastened to explain. "I'm sorry. I guess I'm so used to thinking that money is the answer to everything. I forget that the important things of life, like friendship, are priceless." James held out his hand to Pete. "Please forgive me."

Pete didn't hesitate to take hold of my husband's hand. Then the men embraced, pounding each other on their backs, as men do. "Well, I got to be heading home. See you tomorrow, James, Mrs. McCall." He waved toward the loft. "Good night, Jamie."

Jamie peeked over the edge of the loft. "Good night, Indian Pete." The child disappeared back into his exciting new world. I strolled across the room to inspect my new kitchen. The dishes were chipped, some were cracked, but each spoke of love, a kind of love I hoped one day to understand.

"Look." James stood by the hearth, holding a book in his hand. Inscribed in gold on the cover were the words *The Holy Bible*. He opened it and read, "To James and Chloe, your friends in Christ, Noah and Ula VanArsdale."

With the Bible in one hand and his other hand about my waist, we walked outside the cabin to gaze at our new world. A bank of clouds now obscured the tops of the mountains behind us, and a biting wind whistled through the pine needles. I shivered.

"I'd better get you inside before you catch cold, little mommy." James tucked the Bible under his arm and pointed toward the mountain. "Looks like a storm building to the north."

I glanced for a moment at the clouds, then turned my face decidedly toward the clear southern sky. One star twinkled above the treetops. Behind me I heard my husband's warm baritone voice. "Star light; star bright . . ."